What She Saw . . .

'*What She Saw* could not be a more different book
about romantic awakening. If you are bright, grew up
in an American suburb – and don't know which you hate
more, other people or yourself – Lucinda Rosenfeld has, with
this clever, superlatively entertaining novel, written
your autobiography.'
Observer

'[Rosenfeld's] deft prose and remarkable insight allow her
to make a smart point about the ease with which many of us
define ourselves through others rather than searching
for our own identity'
Face

'A collection of deceptively snappy dispatches from the
darker outposts of the dating game. Its reportage is slick
yet deadly accurate, its characters damningly hilarious.'
Los Angeles Times

'Engaging, nostal
Publishers

'Rosenfeld knows how to blend sadness with wit. If it is true that her narrator collects a rogues' galley of heartbreaking stinkers, it is even truer that her voice remains deliciously fresh, even at times memorable.'
Washington Post

'It's all familiar – from life, however, not literature, to its great credit – and it is as spectacularly honest as it is entertaining'
Observer

'Intelligent chicklit with balls'
Big Issue

LUCINDA ROSENFELD was born in New York City on the last day of the 1960s. She grew up in New Jersey and attended Cornell University. She has written for the *New York Times Magazine*, *Harper's Bazaar*, *Elle*, *Word* and *Talk*. She was a nightlife columnist for the *New York Post* from 1996 to 1998. She lives in Brooklyn.

LUCINDA ROSENFELD

PICADOR

WHAT SHE SAW

---

in

Roger Mancuso,

Günter Hopstock,

Jason Barry Gold,

Spitty Clark,

Jack Geezo,

Humphrey Fung,

Claude Duvet,

Bruce Bledstone,

Kevin McFeeley,

Arnold Allen,

Pablo Miles,

Anonymous 1–4,

Nobody 5–8,

Neil Schmertz,

and Bo Pierce

A NOVEL

First published 2000 by Random House, Inc., New York

First published in Great Britain 2001 by Picador

This edition published 2002 by Picador
an imprint of Pan Macmillan Ltd
Pan Macmillan, 20 New Wharf Road, London N1 9RR
Basingstoke and Oxford
Associated companies throughout the world
www.panmacmillan.com

ISBN 0 330 48653 5

1 3 5 7 9 8 6 4 2

A CIP catalogue record for this book is available from
the British Library.

Printed and bound in Great Britain by
Mackays of Chatham plc, Chatham, Kent

for suzy, sam, monkey, l.b., b.b., b.d., and bernard—

this is good-bye

Well, let it pass, he thought;

April is over, April is over.

There are all kinds of love in the world,

but never the same love twice.

—F. Scott Fitzgerald,
"The Sensible Thing," 1924

CONTENTS

What She Saw . . .

1. Roger Mancuso

or *"The Stink Bomb King of Fifth Grade"*

ON THE TUESDAY before Easter, a substitute teacher appeared behind Mrs. Kosciouwicz's metal desk. His face looked like a dented Yukon potato. His jazz shoes were the color of cement. He was tall and thin except for a pillow-sized potbelly that spilled helplessly over his plaid pants. "I'm Mr. Spumato," he announced to the assembled fifth-graders. "And I'll be your sub until further notice."

Euphoria swept through the classroom at the thought of Mrs. Kosciouwicz never coming back.

She was always lecturing them about the importance of sitting up straight. She made them read the dictionary and watch boring filmstrips on the origins of math. She was highly intolerant of lateness and (despite her own abysmal record) deranged on the matter of absenteeism. Over the educational-games shelf, she'd hung a poster of a beak-nosed owl reading PROCRASTINATION IS THE THIEF OF TIME. On the back of the door, she'd tacked another one asserting SILENCE IS GOLDEN. The only time she baked them cupcakes was when Reagan beat Carter. The only time she let them leave school early was when Reagan got shot. Her pull-on pants were the color of dog shit. Her bosom hung down to her waist. Her bifocals hung from a necklace. She was probably only sixty.

She seemed about as old as ancient Mesopotamia.

Roger Mancuso's hand shot up—not before he'd blurted out, "Did Mrs. K. croak—or what?"

"What is your name, young man?" snarled Mr. Spumato.

"Mick," he answered. "Mick Jagger."

"Well, Mr. Jagger," said Spumato, trying to drown out the tsunami of laughter that rose from the back row. "If you'd like to take your question to the principal, I'd be happy to accompany you to his office."

"OOOoooohhhhh," crooned the class in unison.

"I just wanted to know if the old lady was alive," countered Roger.

"You'll know what I tell you!" cried Spumato.

"I'll know what I want," said Roger. "And I want to know what happened to my friggin' homeroom teacher."

Now the class cheered. Poor Spumato. He must have known he was losing control. He couldn't have been happy about it. He pointed a single, trembling finger at his nemesis. "One more peep, Mr. Jagger, and you're outta here for good!" Then he cranked his thumb backward over his shoulder in the direction of the principal's office, in case anyone thought he was kidding. (No one did.) The class fell silent—even Roger, who went back to his guitar magazine. The rest of them fixated on Mr. Spumato's flaccid backside jiggling like a half-cooked egg yolk as he began to script grammatical terminology on the board.

He about-faced several minutes later. "Who can tell me the difference between a pronoun and a noun?" he wanted to know, his tobacco-stained moustache twitching ever so slightly. But not a single hand rose. "None of you little punks knows the difference between a pronoun and a normal noun," he tried again. And then again: "I SAID WHO THE CRAP KNOWS THE DIFFERENCE BETWEEN A NOUN AND A PRONOUN?"

Now the class shrieked in ecstasy. *Crap* was the kind of word Mrs. K. deemed grounds for suspension, and here was the substitute teacher making unrepentant use of it.

"Spumato! Spumato! Spumato!" Roger started to chant, palms pounding rhythmically on his ink-stained desktop, and the rest of the class quickly joined in. "Spumato! Spumato! Spumato! Spumato!"

It was when Spumato started to shake that they finally shut up. They were suddenly mortified for their sub—for his failure to control them, for his irrational fear of their harmless delirium. They stared at their hands. They prayed for the bell. They didn't really want to see him fall apart.

They were rescued by the introduction of a terrible odor.

It wafted through the classroom, inflicting punishment on all possessed of a sense of smell. It wasn't long before the situation became insufferable. Their throats threatening to close, they ran for the door gasping. The smart ones pinched their noses. "Come back here, you little punks!" roared Mr. Spumato.

But then he, too, succumbed to the stench—and followed the stampede into the hall.

That was the last anyone saw of Plaid Pants.

As for Roger Mancuso, after confessing to the stink bomb, he was suspended for three days and threatened with expulsion. He was only too happy to have the time off to listen to his favorite Rolling Stones album, *Some Girls,* another hundred times. And upon his arrival back at Whitehead Middle (a.k.a. Blackhead Middle and/or Shit-Head Middle) the following week, he was awarded a hero's welcome, complete with chanting, backslapping, synchronized farting, and a new nickname: "Stinky."

———————

HE WAS ALSO presented with a change of seats. Seemingly back from the dead, Mrs. K. moved the so-anointed Stink Bomb King to the front row, one seat to the left of Phoebe Fine, who couldn't believe her luck. Not that she was expecting Stinky to feel the same way. When he slipped a note under her elbow, she didn't even think it was for her. Then she saw her name printed on the outside. She waited until Mrs. K. turned her back to write the word *volunteerism* on the board. Then she pushed the note into her lap.

Waiting for her was the following declaration: "YOU LOOK FINE!"

Her face turned red; her hands began to tremble like Mr. Spumato's. Was this Stinky's idea of a joke? Was he passing the note on someone else's behalf? Was he mocking her last name? Was she merely a convenient target? Had he heard from someone, who'd heard from someone else, who'd heard from her best friend, Brenda Cuddihy, that she had a huge crush on him—and was this his way of telling her that he already knew?

Or might he have meant exactly what he'd written?

The latter possibility seemed unlikely, especially considering the only extracurricular contact she'd had with Stinky in the past year consisted of a single, recent occasion during which he'd circled her with his BMX bike on her way to her violin lesson, sung her excerpts from *Fiddler on the Roof,* and demanded that she play him "The Devil Went Down to Georgia." (She kept telling him she didn't know how. He eventually performed a wheelie and disappeared.) In short, it didn't seem like Stinky Mancuso was madly in love with her. If anything, it seemed like he thought it was pretty weird that she played the violin.

But what if he liked her for the reason that she was unique among her peers? Which is to say that he'd never encountered anyone quite as "gifted and talented" as Phoebe, with the encouragement of her parents and teachers, imagined herself to be?

Reluctant to make eye contact until she had more information, Phoebe stared straight ahead for the rest of the class period. And when the bell rang, she jumped out of her chair and bolted for the door.

In the girls' room some time later, she caught up with Brenda Cuddihy. "Did you tell Stinky I liked him?" she challenged her Born Again best friend.

"I swear on the Bible I didn't tell anyone!" her Born Again best friend held fast.

"Well, look at this," said Phoebe, pulling Stinky's note out of the patch pocket of her tie-dyed apron dress and handing it to Brenda, who read it out loud before she gasped, "Oh my God, Stinky likes you!"

"How do you know he's not just joking around?" said Phoebe.

"Well, he didn't send *me* a note," said Brenda.

"Well, you don't sit next to him in homeroom."

"So?"

"So there."

"So nothing—I bet Stinky wants to go out with you."

"Well, I don't want to go out with him."

"But I thought you had a crush on him!"

"I did," Phoebe told her. "But I don't anymore."

But she was lying; she was just scared—scared of boys in general and what they might require of her, but perhaps even more terrified of finding herself attracted to the very thing her daffy, well-meaning, culturally contemptuous parents had worked so hard to protect her from—namely, the world out there in all its crudest, crassest, most inglorious expressions of animal need.

It wasn't merely that Stinky Mancuso was a huge fan of the bat-eating heavy metal musician Ozzy Osbourne. His favorite expression was "Ya mental"; his second-favorite expression was "Ya gay." As early as fourth grade, he'd been spotted palling around with Whitehead's hearse-driving drug-dealer-in-residence, Rupert Slim. He was notorious for having talked some special-ed kids into taking down their pants in the middle of the playing field. A cheap tin arrowhead pendant dangled from the gold-toned chain he wore around his scrawny neck. He kept a red plastic comb with an aerodynamic handle in the back pocket of his Lee jeans—even though he had buzz-cut hair.

He wore a different rock concert T-shirt every day of the week.

———

THE ONLY CONCERT T-shirt Phoebe owned was emblazoned with the logo of the Lincoln Center summer series "Mostly Mozart." Her father, Leonard, was a professional oboist who moonlighted on the English horn and the oboe d'amore. Her mother, Roberta, was a semiprofessional violist. Her older sister, Emily, was a dedicated if singularly untalented student of the cello. Phoebe herself had been started on the violin (Suzuki method) at the age of five. More than a vocation, however, classical music was the air the Fine family breathed, the religion they practiced, the shelter under which they sought refuge from the technological excesses of the current century. It blared from the family "Victrola" all day every day, if it wasn't already being played live in their music room.

On Saturday nights, while Phoebe's classmates sat zombie-style in front of the television humming along to candy-bar commercials, the Fine family—who owned a black-and-white TV the size of a toaster oven—rehearsed Mozart's Oboe Quartet in F Major. Roberta and Leonard's idea of a fun party was inviting over a few friends to wolf down stale coffee cake between movements of Schubert's *Trout* Quintet. Nor was Phoebe entirely convinced that the murder of John Lennon, the news of which had spread like wildfire through Whitehead Middle band practice the previous December, wasn't the first either one of her parents had heard of the Beatles.

And on long car trips in summer—the Fine Four were always parading across the heartland en route to yet another obscure chamber music festival in which Leonard felt financially obliged to participate despite the obscenely low weekly rate—they invariably wound up playing "Name a Classical Composer for Every Letter of the Alphabet." It would be Leonard and Roberta in the front seat and Phoebe and Emily counting license plates behind them until they'd counted all fifty states and their itsy-bitsy rear ends had become branded with the diamond pattern of the vinyl upholstery and Emily had willfully extended her legs past the imaginary line that divided the backseat into two distinct fiefdoms, prompting Phoebe to moan "Mmmoooooooooomm!" and Emily to mutter, "Worship them, wart face!"

That's when Roberta would interject, "I have an idea. Let's try to name a classical composer for every letter of the alphabet!"

Phoebe and Emily would groan. But it was always clear to Phoebe that Emily was merely making a show of her discontent. It was clear by the way she always volunteered to start.

She always started with "Tomaso Albinoni."

Leonard would continue with "Berlioz." Roberta would chip in with "Chopin." Phoebe would do her part with "Debussy." So the game would go: "Elgar, Fauré, Grieg, Haydn, Ives, Janáček, Kabalevsky, Liszt, Mussorgsky, Nielsen, Offenbach, Puccini, Quantz, Rachmaninoff, Schubert . . ." Until it was Phoebe's turn again.

"Tarantella," she'd stammered the previous summer, rather than take the chance that Tchaikovsky's name started with a *c*, as it should have.

"Tarantella's our congressman, you moron!" Emily had squawked gleefully.

"Emily," Roberta had scolded her older daughter, "don't be obnoxious to Bebe."

So the game had ended, with Phoebe falling asleep—the best defense, she soon learned, in the face of adversity. When you were asleep the only people who could get to you were the people in your dreams, from which you always eventually woke to find out they were no more than that: people in your dreams. Conversely, there was no way to wake up from real life except to go back to sleep.

Thus began Phoebe Fine's love affair with the bedroom.

———

NOT THAT SHE had an unhappy childhood. Leonard and Roberta were endlessly doting parents. Despite constant bickering, she and Emily were dedicated playmates. There was always enough food on the table (London broil, frozen spinach bricks, Mueller's shells floating in two inches of water; cultural snobs didn't necessarily make for culinary snobs). And as suburban towns go, Whitehead, New Jersey, population 7,963, site of Phoebe's formative years, boring as it may have been, was a pretty okay one to grow up in. Nestled between the twin behemoths of the Department of Motor Vehicles in Lodi and the

Paramus tenplex, it was both a hop, skip, and jump away from several major interstates and a manageable forty-five minute drive to midtown Manhattan. And there were no strip malls cutting a garish swath through the center of town—no tattoo parlors, record stores, movie theaters, fast-food chains, topless bars, or car dealerships either.

What Whitehead did have were, in no particular order: two supermarkets, one dry cleaner, two liquor stores, one TV-repair shop, one jeweler, two dress shops (one for hefty women, one for regular-sized), three convenience stores (one twenty-four-hour, two not), one pharmacy, two banks (one drive-through, one walk-in), six outdoor tennis courts, one indoor racquet club featuring squash but no racquetball, one public park, one Veterans' Memorial, one Lions Club, one reform synagogue, four churches (one Catholic, one Episcopalian, one Methodist, and one Baptist), one pet store featuring gerbils but no hamsters, one bagel store (later expanded into a frozen-yogurt and bagel emporium), one recreation center, one Chinese takeout joint, two pizzerias (Sal's, which doubled as a video arcade complete with Pac-Man and Asteroids, and which served up pizza so greasy that it was common custom to tilt your slice into Sal's garbage can before you ate; and Leo's, a family place complete with Golden Oldies on the stereo and waiter service), one diner (Al's, which later became Betty's, after Al lost all his money in Atlantic City), one candy store, one designated bomb shelter, one historic landmark (a Civil War–era drill hall), one actors' guild, one barbershop, two beauty salons (one featuring man-on-the-moon style bubble hairdryers from the 1960s, ladies of a certain age, and a fake French name; the other, a strictly blow-dry affair called Hair's Looking at You), one chocolate shop, two ambulances, one judo studio, three fire trucks, fifteen policemen, one shelter for abused women, one middle school, one elementary school, one high school, one amateur chamber orchestra, one family-planning clinic, one oral surgeon's office, two baseball fields, one gift shop, one bridal shop, one chamber of commerce, and one Halloween/costume shop, which sold fake blood.

It was a diverse town, to boot. Which is to say that about a third of the kids in Phoebe's fifth-grade class had Italian last names (Mancuso, Manzotti, Sportiello), another third Irish (O'this, O'that), and the last third German Jewish (Glickman, Perlmutter, Blumberg). To say nothing of the one-of-a-kinds like Alice Nguyen, the painfully shy Vietnamese refugee whose family had been sponsored by the local Methodist church and who still had trouble pronouncing her *r*'s; or Tony Brown, the only black fifth-grader, whose father, it was rumored, had gone to jail for assaulting his wife with a crowbar, and whose populous clan lived in a two-family house down by the drill hall.

And there were as many college professors and psychotherapists living in Whitehead as there were mechanics and landscape gardeners, their "respectable" salaries differentiating them from the five households in town known to receive federal assistance. Of the latter, the Cuddihys were perhaps the highest-profile, thanks to their large numbers (six girls, two boys); their hair color (a shocking shade of strawberry blond); and the athletic achievements of the second-eldest daughter, Maureen, who was single-handedly responsible for Whitehead's countywide reputation as a basketball stronghold. The Cuddihys were so poor—Mr. Cuddihy was housebound with metal legs, while his wife (a.k.a. Culottes Cuddihy) served sloppy joes in the middle-school cafeteria—that Maureen's gym teachers were reduced to purchasing her high-tops out of their own pocket change. Everyone said Maureen would get a free ride through college if only she could pass math. Unfortunately, she couldn't, thanks to a crippling case of dyslexia that incited her classmates to nickname her "Neeraum." (Phoebe was the only one who ever called Brenda "Adnerb.")

And the residential blocks of Whitehead were long and shaded by mature maples whose leaves turned into abstract expressionist canvases in mid-October and were subsequently raked into humongous, crepitating leaf mountains into which Phoebe and her friends would jump from the hoods of their parents' parked station wagons in the dusky hours before dinner. And the houses were a nice size. Most of them were set back from the street. Some came with half-acre plots. There were split-levels with circular driveways and white-gravel front yards, three-story Victorian "dollhouses" with stained-glass windows and fairy-castle turrets, and Depression-era bungalows with screened-in front porches and ivy creeping up their stucco siding. It was to this latter category that the Fines' purple house— Phoebe never entirely recovered from that embarrassment— belonged. Though in all fairness, it was pretty cozy inside. And it had a bigger-than-average backyard, where Leonard grew his prize tomatoes and Phoebe built obstacle courses out of old tires and sawhorses and tried to beat her own record for time.

And Phoebe was grateful to have her own bedroom—plenty of her friends had to share with a sibling, and some, like Brenda, with multiple siblings—even while she always resented its minuscule size. Having been born three years before her, Emily had been awarded the "real" bedroom. Not that Phoebe had asked to be born second. Not that she'd asked to be born! But since she had been, she tried to make the best of it—occupying herself with a host of before- and after-school electives (band, chorus, bell choir, Spanish Club, yearbook); classes (pottery, gymnastics, tennis); lessons (violin, piano, and, briefly, flute); independent projects (joke books, journals, found-object models of national landmarks); contests (poster, poetry, essay, coloring); collections (rocks, minerals, marbles, stamps, postcards, playbills, matchbooks, foreign currency, foreign newspapers, shirt cardboard, puffy stickers, baby teeth, dried boogers, foot skin); and hobbies (beading, chemistry, shortwave radio, biking, reading, calligraphy, origami, watercolors). All of which didn't leave much time for boys. For example, she still hadn't gotten around to writing back to her East German pen pal, Günter Hopstock.

She always found time to daydream about Stinky Mancuso.

AT NIGHT PHOEBE lay awake beneath her pink and orange poly-cotton elephant-motif sheets, asking favors of the Almighty, whom she didn't necessarily imagine to be a white bearded fellow in keeping with the Judeo-Christian tradition but on whom she nevertheless projected such avuncular qualities as having a soft spot for overachieving ten-year-olds like herself. "Oh, please, God, whoever you are," she'd whisper into the cold. "Just let Stinky be in homeroom tomorrow. I swear I'll clean my room and practice third position really hard. Oh, please!"

Though if God wasn't coming through with the results she wanted, she was just as happy to put her faith in out-and-out superstitions. For example, if she could make it to school both without having stepped on a single crack in the sidewalk *and* without having had to wait for a single light to turn green, she'd feel she had every reason to expect to find Stinky Mancuso standing at attention at seven forty-five in the morning, his hand over his heart, reinterpreting the Pledge of Allegiance— "for which it stands" became "for Richard Stans"—a Founding

Father?—along with the rest of Mrs. K.'s class. In fact, Phoebe's superstitions proved about as effective as her prayers and even complete silence, since Stinky was just as often out of school as he was in.

Answers to the ongoing mystery of his whereabouts were occasionally provided by his classmates.

There was the morning Patrick McPatrick, Jr., son of Patrick McPatrick, Sr., of McPatrick Landscape Gardening, startled everyone by rising from his beveled seat and informing Mrs. K., "Roger has asked me to tell you that he's not feeling himself this morning."

Of course, this made the class fall off their seats and clutch their stomachs for air. It also made Mrs. K. trumpet, in her signature postmenopausal baritone, "Shut your mouths, or you'll all go to the principal!"

In truth, almost no one was ever sent to Whitehead Middle's diminutive Greek principal—no one, that is, except for Stinky Mancuso, who considered himself, if not a close personal friend of Mr. G., as he was known—his last name was even harder to pronounce than Mrs. K.'s was—then certainly a partner in crime. According to Stinky, Mr. G. hadn't merely hobnobbed with the Hells Angels at Altamont; he'd been on the front lines of Woodstock, close enough to Jimi Hendrix to see the liquid acid seeping off his terrycloth headband and into his brain. And he still liked the "good weed" every now and then. In fact, he kept a little Baggie in the top drawer of his desk for when he was in the mood, which was all the time. And when he was high as a kite, he liked to "get it on" with Mrs. Carter, the art teacher with the long middle-parted hair and the drawstring peasant blouses that barely obscured her heaving, braless milk bags. And she never said no. She always said yes. She couldn't get enough of Mr. G. That's what Stinky said.

Stinky said Mr. G. was a pal for letting him skip school as often as he did.

AS FATE WOULD have it, however, Stinky was very much present in homeroom the day after Patrick McPatrick's announcement (this despite the fact that, on her way there, Phoebe had had to wait for nearly every light to turn green). And that afternoon, during a filmstrip on the invention of the abacus—Mrs. K.'s audiovisually inclined retiree husband, Mr. K., ran the projector—Stinky sat down next to her on the activities rug, then proceeded to sprinkle spiral-notebook confetti in her hair. It was then that Phoebe began to wonder if Stinky's interest in tormenting her was more than a matter of convenience.

She became even more convinced his note was no joke when, the following day in gym, he laid his mat down next to hers, then offered to spot her for the sit-up test.

"I don't care," she told him, which was her way of saying, "Please do." Then she rolled onto her back, linked her hands behind her head, and waited for Stinky to spring into action. A wide grin encompassed his peanut-shaped face as he dug his hands into the toes of her no-name sneakers—so hard that she screamed, "Ow!"

"Oh, sorry," he said.

"Quiet back there," barked Mr. Bender.

"What?" asked Stinky with an auspicious snap.

"Mr. Mancuso, is that gum you're chewing?"

"Tobacco," Stinky corrected their ex-marine gym teacher.

"WHATEVER IT IS I WANT IT OUT NOW!" bellowed Bender.

Then he launched into his usual tirade about all the kids he'd watched choke to death on chewing gum during competitive athletics. He was just getting to the part about Billy So-and-So's mother and how hard she was crying at Billy's funeral when Stinky returned from garbage duty and assumed his earlier position at Phoebe's feet. By then, she'd begun to drift. But even with her lids down, she could feel Stinky's bug eyes peering inquisitively at her body. And why shouldn't he have stared? She was wearing her best zip-up sweatshirt (navy blue acrylic with red piping) and elastic-waist chinos that tapered to the ankle. (Fifth-graders didn't change for gym; they were supposed to be too young to sweat.) And thanks to the low humidity, her winged hair was feathering nicely.

Being the sole athletic member of the Fine family, however—Emily had asthma, and Roberta and Leonard were both tea-drinker types who hadn't broken a sweat since 1955—Phoebe was also someone who cared deeply about her physical-fitness test scores. And so, to the tune of "Ready, set, go," she touched her elbows to her knees, then her head to the mat, back and forth, back and forth, until, five minutes later, she'd set a new Whitehead Middle record. Needless to say, Mr. Bender was impressed—as was Stinky. "Shit," he said. "You're really good at sit-ups—especially for a girl."

"We have to do sixty of them every week in gymnastics," she told him by way of explanation.

"Like Nadia Comaneci?"

"I wish." (It just so happened that Nadia Comaneci was her current idol.)

"Can you do a back handspring?"

"Only with a spotter. I'm better at the uneven bars."

"What's wrong with the even bars?"

"They're for boys."

"What's wrong with boys?" Stinky was smiling when he said that—as if he were trying to get at something else.

Phoebe didn't help him out. "There's nothing wrong with boys," she said, grimacing. "I just happen not to be one of them."

"Prove it," Stinky hissed.

"I SAID QUIET BACK THERE!" Bender broke in, to Phoebe's enormous relief.

Then he launched into a diatribe about all the kids he knew who'd died making too much noise—so much noise they hadn't heard the alarm that would have alerted them to the fire that eventually engulfed them.

Mr. Bender was married to the other gym teacher, Mrs. Bender, who doubled as the sex-ed teacher. It was she who'd warned the boys that if their jeans were too tight their "sperm factories" could overheat, causing permanent damage to their reproductive capabilities. After that all the boys started wearing sweatpants to school—all the boys except for Stinky. For whatever reason, he was willing to take the risk.

———

"IT'S FOR YOU, crumpet," warbled Leonard, surprising Phoebe in the kitchen after school a few days later.

It was independent-project time in social studies, and she was measuring out flour for a papier-mâché model of the Short Hills Mall. She hadn't even heard the doorbell ring. She went to the porch with chalky hands. She thought it might be Brenda seeing if she wanted to play with the Cuddihys' new mutt, Michelle.

She wasn't expecting to find Stinky Mancuso standing there.

"Hello, crumpet," he said, mimicking Leonard's pseudo-British intonation.

"Shut up," said Phoebe, knowing full well Stinky would say anything he felt like saying.

"Are you gonna let me in?" That's what he felt like saying next.

It took Phoebe by surprise.

She had somehow forgotten that they were separated by a screen door. Or maybe she was secretly hoping Stinky would leave before she had the chance to open it. But he didn't. So she unlatched the hook. At which point Stinky walked right in and then right past her, into the Fines' Victorian-eclectic music room, where Roberta sat in a straight-backed chair practicing her viola. "Well, hello there," said Roberta, laying down her bow on the rusted ledge of her music stand.

"Hey," said Stinky. "I'm Roger."

"Well, hello there, Roger," said Roberta. "I'm Mrs. Fine."

"What are you playing on that big violin?"

"It's actually a viola," snapped Phoebe's mother, still the defensive former violinist who'd turned to the viola because her mastery of the violin's upper registers was never what it should have been—and because the competition was slightly less stiff. "And I'm rehearsing the orchestral score to a famous operatic work by a seventeenth-century English composer named Henry Purcell. It's called *Dido and Aeneas*."

"Dude," muttered Stinky, nose wrinkled with the glorious impossibility of it all. "Your mother's playing *Dildo and Anus*." Then he let out a great firecracker of laughter. He was the only one. Phoebe stared at her feet in shame. She wasn't entirely sure what a dildo was, but she knew exactly what an anus was. More important, she knew it didn't make for pleasant conversation in front of her famously prudish mother.

But then, Roberta Fine was someone who heard exactly what she wanted to hear. Which is more or less what she heard that afternoon. "Here, would you like to try?" she smiled cordially, her instrument extended toward Stinky's tiny, jutting chin.

But he backed away. "That's okay," he said on his way out of the music room.

Mortified for her mother—or was it for herself?—Phoebe followed Stinky out the back door and into the yard, where they pushed each other around in a wheelbarrow. When that got boring, they tortured some slugs—cut them in half with Stinky's Swiss Army knife just to see if they would live like they were supposed to be able to, with only half a body. (They didn't.) Then they lay feet to head in the hammock and talked about school. "Mrs. K. makes bad farts, huh?" said Stinky.

"Whoever smelt it, dealt it," Phoebe reminded him.

"Yeah, well, whoever denied it, supplied it," rejoined Stinky. Then he poked her stomach with a long gnarled stick he'd found over by Leonard's tomato plants, causing Phoebe to jerk backward and the hammock to rock from side to side, until it settled back into inertia—just like them. "Hey, Fine," said Stinky after calm had been restored. "Where'd you get a name like Fine?"

"I don't know—I just did," she told him. "Where'd you get a name like Mancuso?"

"Beats the fuck out of me. Never met no one named Mancuso."

"What about your father? Isn't he Mr. Mancuso?"

"Never met no one named Mr. Mancuso," he told her.

Then he hurled his stick, boomerang-style, into the yard.

But Phoebe wasn't ready to leave it alone. (That was before she knew to leave some things alone.) "Well, what about your mom?" she pressed on. "Isn't she Mrs. Mancuso?"

"Never met no Mrs. Mancuso."

"Well, who do you live with, then?"

"I live alone."

"You live alone?"

"I got a grandma that stops by—when I let her. She's a nice lady but she gets on my nerves."

"Is her last name Mancuso?"

"She's just Grandma."

"So where'd you get the name Mancuso?"

"It's just a name." Stinky unwrapped a piece of Bazooka and popped it in his mouth. "I could change it if I wanted to."

"Change your name!" To Phoebe the concept was inconceivable. Never mind the fact that her own Grandpa Solomon had changed theirs from the ethnically charged Feingold to the comparatively mellow Fine some fifty years before her birth. "To what?"

Stinky chewed for a few seconds, began a bubble, then changed his mind and let it snap across his lips. "To Keith," he said, sucking the wad back into his mouth. "When I grow up, I just might be Keith Richards. . . . Hey, you got anything to eat?"

But he didn't wait for an answer; he was already headed back inside.

"There might be some granola bars," said Phoebe, following him into the kitchen, where he circled her mall-in-progress. "What the hell is this?" he wanted to know.

"It's for social studies," she told him. "Aren't you doing one?"

But Stinky had more important things on his mind. "Where'd you say those Twix bars were?"

"I didn't say Twix bars, I said granola bars," she said, pulling the box off the shelf, and handing it to him.

He devoured his first bar in ten seconds flat.

"These suck," he scoffed halfway through his second one.

"So how come you're eating them?" she asked him.

" 'Cause I'm hungry," he answered.

"Don't you have to eat dinner soon?"

"I don't *have* to do anything," he said on his way back into the music room.

Roberta had disappeared, but her viola lay supine on her chair. Before Phoebe had the chance to object, Stinky had positioned the instrument at the height of his crotch and was pretending to wail on it, his head bobbing up and down to an imaginary beat, his buckteeth biting down on his lower lip. Phoebe thought it was pretty funny, but she rolled her eyes rather than give Stinky the satisfaction of hearing her laugh.

"How do you play this thing, anyway?" he asked her, having tired of air guitar.

"Here, I'll show you," she said, steering his chin to the chin rest, then his left hand to the scroll. (She was thrilled to find her expertise, for once, in demand.)

Her hand over his, she guided the bow along the highest string. Whereupon a spine-chilling moan reverberated throughout the Fines' purple house. "The big violin fuckin' rocks!" decreed a red-faced Stinky after silence had been restored.

"Please watch your language," an invisible Roberta called out from the den, but she didn't sound all that mad. She was probably secretly delighted to have found a fan of her frequently maligned and forever neglected instrument. Indeed, but one playable piece in the entire classical repertoire—namely, Berlioz's *Harold in Italy*—had been written to showcase the viola. And while Leonard always claimed *Harold* was his all-time favorite piece, Phoebe always suspected that her father was merely trying to make her mother feel better.

It wasn't clear she ever did.

At least she'd never learned to laugh along with the viola

jokes that were common sport in her and Leonard's social circle. (*There's a sixteen-wheeler coming straight at your car. If you swerve left, you kill the conductor. If you swerve right, you kill the violist. Which way do you swerve? Right: business before pleasure.*) Nor had it escaped Phoebe's notice that she'd been started on the very instrument that had eluded her mother. In short, she was slated to become the violin success story Roberta Fine couldn't tell herself.

"I hate to interrupt your fun, kids, but it's getting awfully late," said Roberta, appearing at Stinky's side to repossess her instrument. "Roger, your mother's probably starting to wonder where you are!"

"Thanks for the wheat germ," was all he said.

Phoebe heard the screen door slam behind him.

———

HE WASN'T IN school the next day.

Or the day after that.

But the next afternoon, art class having just ended—Mrs. Carter had everyone silk-screening unicorns on T-shirts again—Phoebe was standing in line for the water fountain outside Mrs. K.'s class when Stinky appeared out of nowhere, then cut to the front, without comment from his permanently cowed classmates. "Hey, Fine—you going uptown Friday night?" he said before he bent down for a drink.

"I don't know—maybe," she told him.

Then she started to back away from a potentially dangerous situation—namely, Stinky's water-filled cheeks. But it was only a false alarm. The Stink Bomb King gulped down the contents of his mouth and let out an exaggerated "Aaaaahhhhhhh" before he asked her, "What's the matter—the maestros won't let you?"

"The maestros don't care," she lied.

In fact, she had no reason to believe that Leonard and Roberta would ever let her hang out on the hoods of parked cars in the immediate vicinity of Whitehead's only twenty-four-hour convenience store free of parental supervision between the hours of seven and midnight—the unofficial definition of "going uptown."

On the other hand, the nature of Friday nights uptown had changed dramatically since the Whitehead Recreation Center (a.k.a. "the recacenter") began hosting a weekly roller-disco party on its all-purpose athletic court. All the kids in school were talking about how cool it was—even those kids who, like Stinky, were adamant in their belief that "disco sucked." What's more, admission was free.

"Be there or ya gay." Stinky disappeared around the bend.

"IT'S BRENDA'S BIRTHDAY and Mrs. Cuddihy is taking everyone roller-skating at the recacenter on Friday night," Phoebe falsely informed Roberta later that evening. In fact, Phoebe and Brenda intended to go roller-skating on their own, and Brenda's birthday wasn't for two weeks.

"Now, if that woman tries to convert you, I want you to tell her that your mother would like to speak to her," said Roberta. "Do you understand?"

"I understand," Phoebe assured her mother, who, though lacking any religious convictions of her own—it wasn't as if they belonged to Whitehead's Reform synagogue, and when they had to go to White Plains for Phoebe's cousin Jonathan's bar mitzvah, Roberta had acted as if it were a huge imposition—had been extremely unhappy to learn that Mrs. Cuddihy had asked Brenda to ask Phoebe if she was interested in joining a youth-oriented Bible-study class on Thursday afternoons. (She wasn't; she always hated studying.) But Phoebe's apathetic relationship to her schoolwork wasn't the point. The point was that Phoebe felt guilty about lying to her mother, but not that guilty. She'd heard about white lies. She figured maybe this qualified as one. She didn't want Roberta to worry the way she had last Halloween when she and Brenda had stayed out trick-or-treating until well past dark, even though they were supposed to be home before. But at the very last minute they'd heard about a "really good house" on the other side of town rumored to be handing out silver dollars as if they were M&M's, and they'd been unable to resist.

As it turned out, that "really good house" had been handing out chocolate coins, which were tasty but not worth getting into trouble for, which is exactly what Phoebe and Brenda got in. Roberta hid the very candy Phoebe had worked so hard to obtain. Brenda wasn't allowed to watch TV for a week—a major blow considering the Cuddihy kids, despite their religious background, usually had unrestricted access to network television, whereas Phoebe and Emily were limited to one hour per day. (They could see all the public-television programming they wanted—as if they wanted it. At least, Phoebe didn't.)

Indeed, it was only under duress that she subjected herself to those British period dramas that made Leonard hallucinate with pleasure. The *Masterpiece Theatre* theme music was catchy, sure. As for the plots—all those pasty English people getting worked up about who got to sit where in the barouche—Phoebe was less than riveted. Her favorite evening drama was *The Dukes of Hazzard.* There were guaranteed to be at least two good car chases per episode. And the Duke brothers—unlike Emily—always treated their kid sister, Daisy, with the utmost respect. The only problem was that the show ran a full hour. So watching it meant forgoing her otherwise daily *Brady Bunch* and *I Love Lucy* rerun fix. That's where Brenda came in. Phoebe could always count on her best friend for detailed plot descriptions of the previous night's shows.

When that got boring, they'd talk about religion. Tears brimming in her lugubrious brown eyes, Brenda would implore Phoebe—herself of the gray-blue-eyed persuasion—to convert from her heretic faith. "How can I walk to school with you every morning knowing you're going straight to hell?" was Brenda's preferred line of reasoning.

"But I told you, we celebrate Christmas!" Phoebe would seek to reassure her. "And I swear I've only been to synagogue once in my entire life!"

Never to any avail.

———————

BUT THAT FRIDAY night, as Phoebe and Brenda made their way "uptown," they hardly spoke at all, such was their abject fear of their immediate surroundings. No matter that they knew every shrub along the way by heart—every mailbox, streetlight, telephone pole, and patch of grass with four-leaf clover potential, too. In fact, they walked the same six blocks to and from Whitehead Middle every weekday morning and afternoon of their school-year lives. At the advanced hour of 7:30 P.M., however, so very foreboding seemed the landmarks of their school route that they might as well have been negotiating the slums of Rio de Janeiro. The rosebushes seemed eager to prick their fingers, the telephone poles intent on crushing their skulls. There was no doubt in either girl's mind that famed serial murderer Son of Sam, though reported to be incarcerated, was lying in wait inside the bright blue mailbox on the corner of Catalpa and Main.

The little stone house on the corner of Briarcliff was another kind of horror story—the real kind. A year earlier, a veteran of the Vietnam War had sweet-talked his way into the basement, where he'd strangled to death a Whitehead ninth-grader in her own rec room. Brenda and Phoebe had stumbled upon the crime scene on their way to fourth grade. It had rained the night before. There were felled branches all over the street, and colored leaves blowing everywhere, and two Whitehead cop cars parked at right angles on the front lawn. And standing behind the yellow tape contemplating the silence of that little stone house on the morning after the storm, they'd known something was terribly wrong. The curtains were drawn, and they'd correctly associated drawn curtains with hearses and funeral homes. At the time, however, they were more excited than they were frightened by the idea of untimely death. It didn't seem to have anything to do with them. Then they grew up a little and realized it did.

Then they were terrified every time they walked by that house, that real-life haunted house, and never more so than they were that evening, alone after dark en route to their very first roller-disco party.

––––––––

BUT THEIR TERROR only grew realer when they pushed open the Recreation Center's steel door. Milling about the trophy-lined corridor were a collection of Whitehead High students who appeared closer in age to the girls' parents than to Phoebe and Brenda. Not that they appeared to have much else in common with their Bible-and-Berlioz-obsessed elders. They were wearing sleeveless mesh football jerseys and faded blue jeans with frayed bottoms. And they were chewing on toothpicks and shoving one another and laughing about the "back entrance." (As far as Phoebe knew, the recacenter didn't have one.) But it was too late to turn back, so Phoebe and Brenda got in line to rent skates, a task they accomplished with the week's accumulated milk money. Ten minutes later, their fingers damp with nervous excitement, they laced them up and rolled out onto the all-purpose athletic court.

A strobe light had been attached to the ceiling, and the floor was flickering blue, red, and green. And the music was so loud they had to yell, "What?" at each other over and over again. And everywhere they looked there were feet flying, and heads bobbing, and girls wiping out, only to be scooped up off the shiny blond-wood floor by their pale, pimply, vaguely sinister-looking boyfriends. Under the scoreboard, a guy in a Tom Petty T-shirt was French-kissing a pretty blonde in designer jeans and a turquoise velour V-neck sweater. It was a good while before Phoebe and Brenda spotted Stinky. He was standing by the sidelines trying to trip passing skaters. He didn't even have skates on. He was wearing black-and-white Adidas soccer cleats and a Stones T-shirt depicting a giant red tongue. Phoebe and Brenda skated right by him before coming to a grinding halt at the corner of the bleachers.

He took his time ambling over to where they stood. "You girls dancing or what?" That was his opening line.

And it was a pretty stupid one, Phoebe thought. So she said, "Do we look like we're dancing?"

Brenda giggled.

Stinky announced to no one in particular, "I'm gettin' a soda."

"What kind are you getting me?" asked Phoebe.

"I'm not going back out there," said Brenda, shaking her head.

"I'll be right back," Phoebe assured her best friend, but it wasn't her best friend she was thinking about just then.

At Stinky's lead, she rolled off the court and back down the trophy-lined corridor. The burnouts were still there, but they'd mostly relocated to the windowsills. "Check it out," slurred one gangly figure overhead, his long legs swinging beneath him like Tarzan's vines, his face reduced to two nostrils in the tightened hood of his gray sweatshirt. "It's Stinky Fuckin' Mancuso."

"Dude," said Stinky. "It's so fuckin' hot in there."

Then he reached inside the soda machine and scored himself a Coke and Phoebe a Tab.

"Thanks," she mouthed in disbelief. That he knew how to get free sodas.

That he knew these quasi adults!

"Let's go outside," said Stinky.

Phoebe thought of Brenda, waiting for her on the court. Then she thought of Leonard and Roberta, waiting for her at home. It wasn't precisely guilt she felt; it had more to do with fear-tinged fascination. "Okay, but not for very long," she told him, amazed to find herself so effortlessly removed from everything she knew and trusted.

Then she followed Stinky back out through the Recreation Center's steel door and around the side of the building, through the parking lot, to the wooded entrance of Nutley Park.

———

OVER THE YEARS, the Veterans' Memorial statue had turned a putrid shade of green. But in the glow of the street lamps that night, it looked even more sickly. Stinky and Phoebe climbed up its base, and sat down on the narrow ledge that separated the dedication stone from the soldier. A hundred feet away the suburban traffic seemed to trickle by in slow motion. "Want one?" said Phoebe, reaching into her jacket pocket and pulling out a fresh box of candy cigarettes. She thought her choice of sweets would make her seem knowing. She thought a guy like Stinky would appreciate the symbolism of a candy cigarette.

But he only laughed, reached into his own jacket pocket, pulled out a real box of Kool menthols, and offered one to Phoebe, who declined.

It wasn't just that Leonard would be horror-struck if he ever smelled cigarettes on her breath. (To a double-reed instrument player, tobacco was akin to suicide.) But she didn't know how to smoke, and she certainly wasn't going to try to figure it out in front of Stinky Mancuso. So she just sat there while he puffed away. She was thinking about how some of the kids in school were saying he might have to stay back a year if he didn't start doing his homework. She was thinking she could help him do it, when he asked her, "Your mother still playing *Dildo and Anus*?"

"Is your mother still wearing army boots?" she asked him back.

"My mother's wearin' shit," he said, downing the last sip of his Coke.

"Your mother's a nudist?" Phoebe thought she was being funny.

But Stinky didn't laugh. He didn't answer either. He stood his empty Coke can on its end. Then he raised himself to his feet and proceeded to stomp the thing flat. He sent it flying in the direction of a nearby sandpit, and tossed his cigarette in the same direction. Then he lowered himself back onto the ledge and grumbled, "I'm gettin' out of this shit hole, and soon."

Phoebe's stomach lurched. She didn't want Stinky to move away. "You're moving?" she squeaked.

"Depends whether I feel like it," he shot back.

"But where would you go?"

"Anywhere I like."

"What about your grandmother?"

"What about her?"

"Would she move too?"

"She's not going anywhere."

"Why not?"

"She can't even get out of bed—not unless I pull her."

That's when he grabbed Phoebe by the jacket collar and brought her to his mouth. His lips tasted like cigarettes. Startled, she pulled away. "What's the matter?" he said, elbowing her in the ribs. "You scared or something?"

Phoebe pulled her jacket tight around her heart-motif T-shirt and stared into his eyes—eyes as big and black and insistent as the eyes of the raccoons that terrorized the Fines' attic every spring. "Brenda's going to be really mad if I don't go back soon," she told him.

But Stinky didn't seem all that worried about it. He reached down and untied one of her skate laces. "Now you can't go anywhere," he said. And for a second or two she believed him—believed she was a prisoner of Stinky Mancuso. And the thought of it left her speechless and flashing back to the day last year when her mother had abandoned her at pottery class. Okay, Roberta was only five minutes late to pick her up. But Phoebe was the last one there. Even the pottery teacher had gone home. "You like the Stones?" asked Stinky, interrupting her nightmare.

"They're okay," said Phoebe, swallowing hard. In fact, she'd never heard a single one of their songs. "I like Ozzy better." (She hadn't heard any of Ozzy's songs either.)

"Well you're *some* girl," he said.

"Shut up," she said, but only because she couldn't think what else to say.

"No, *you* shut up," he told her.

Then he tried to kiss her again. But he only got her cheek. So she turned her cheek so he got her lips. And they must have stayed like that, glued together, wet olive to wet olive, for at least ten seconds, during which time Phoebe again found herself flashing back—this time, to a certain traumatic moment in second grade, when Karen Meyers, during a filmstrip about the Egyptian pharaohs and how they buried their servants alive, passed around a note that read, "Phoebe loves all the boys," prompting the boys to direct a stream of decidedly hostile kissing noises in Phoebe's direction, thereby compelling Phoebe to return the favor with actual kisses, loaded with cooties and conferred on the prepubescent lips of nearly every male subject in the class. To think that, for several years afterward, she'd worried that the incident might be used against her in some future game of Truth or Dare!

Now she relished the opportunity to spread word of this new indiscretion. In fact, the expected pleasure of "telling all" to Brenda Cuddihy far exceeded the immediate pleasure of the kiss, which was, in all honesty, slightly gross.

"So you wanna go out?" That's what Stinky Mancuso said when he came up for air.

Phoebe's heart was beating in her throat. "I'll tell you on Monday," she told him.

Because she thought a proposition like that required careful consideration.

———

BUT ON MONDAY there was no Stinky to tell. There was no Stinky on Tuesday either. And on Wednesday, when he finally did appear in homeroom, he wouldn't make eye contact with Phoebe or anyone else. He was sitting so far down in his seat she thought he might slip off. He was bouncing the eraser tip of his pencil against his three-ring binder, the blue cloth covering of which he'd defamed with ballpoint pen to read, "Rock is my religion and Judas is my priest." "It's your breath going up your nose," he growled at Patrick McPatrick after Patrick McPatrick asked him if he didn't "smell something funny." He wouldn't even answer "Present" when Mrs. K. took attendance—in her usual, punctilious fashion, like an army drill sergeant, by last name first. It was pretty clear he was in a bad mood.

Phoebe was thinking she could help him snap out of it.

"Dear Stinky," began the note she slipped under his elbow while Mrs. K. rambled on about the English settlers and how generous they were to have shared their corn with the Lenni Lenape—according to Mrs. K., a band of extremely friendly Indians who once made their home in and around Whitehead and who could be found farming, fishing, and hunting when they weren't shaving their heads and faces with sharpened mussel shells, slicking down their hair with bear grease, repelling mosquitoes with eagle fat, applying raccoon grease as sunscreen, foraging for edible plants, locating their animal spirits, communicating with sticks and symbols, or brawling with settlers while under the influence of "fire water." "The answer is yes. Love, Phoebe."

She watched him slip the note into his back pocket.

She never found out if he unfolded it.

———

SHE SAW STINKY for the last time that night—out the side window of her parents' station wagon. Phoebe, Leonard, and Emily were on their way to the Methodist church, where Roberta was playing an all-Bach program with the Whitehead Symphonia. Stinky was standing by himself in the traffic island across the street from the Recreation Center, his hands buried in the pockets of his gray vinyl Members Only windbreaker, a single soccer cleat grinding a cigarette butt into the blackened pavement below. It was already dark—dark enough that Phoebe doubted he could see her sitting there in the backseat with her nose pressed to the glass. At least, she hoped he couldn't, because if he could, he should have waved, and he didn't. He just stood there staring straight ahead as if he didn't see anyone or anything. And maybe he didn't.

Even so, you'd think he could have said good-bye.

But he didn't; he didn't even say where he was going. He disappeared without a trace. Just like the Lenni Lenape. None of the kids in school knew why. And Mrs. K. wasn't talking. She crossed "Mancuso, Roger" off the class list without comment. She never uttered his name again. It was as if he never existed. Or maybe Phoebe was the one who never existed. In the end, it seemed, she was just "some girl" Stinky once knew, *didn't anymore.*

She was a lot more than that to Roberta and Leonard.

In her double stops they heard traces of Paganini. In her slow movements they found reason to recall Milstein. They said she was a natural. They said she had the makings of a soloist. It didn't matter that her talent was questionable. Or that she planned to become a newscaster or a chemist. It was enough that she trekked over to Mildred Street every Wednesday at four for her private lesson with Mrs. Bernstein, developed indestructible calluses on four of the five fingertips of her left hand, suffered the embarrassment of having the semipermanent abrasion under her chin mistaken for a hickey. It was enough that she pretended to like their music. That's how easy it was maintaining the affection of her parents—a whole lot easier than it was maintaining the affection of boys like Stinky Mancuso, boys who didn't seem to care if you pretended to like the Stones or not, boys who asked questions to which they didn't apparently want the answers.

Boys who were kissing you one minute and were gone the next.

———————

SHE CAME ACROSS the obituary a few weeks later. She was sliding rubber bands over rolled-up copies of the *Whitehead Ledger*—she'd taken on a paper route to supplement her skimpy allowance—when one rolled open. It was the last name that caught her eye. "Eugenia Mancuso Dead at 74," read the headline. "Beloved Mother and Grandmother Active in Community Affairs. . . . Her only son, Vincent, and daughter-in-law, Mary, died in an automobile accident in 1976. . . . Survived by a nephew, Boz Mancuso, of New Rochelle, N.Y., and a grandson, Roger Mancuso, formerly of Whitehead, now also of New Rochelle. . . ."

That was the last Phoebe heard of Stinky, though not the last she thought of him or of the stink bomb for which he was named. For in that terrible smell, she somehow perceived that the antiseptic odors of suburbia—of newly cut grass and lemon-fresh furniture polish and brand-new basketballs—were not the only odors there were, that there were other smells she might one day sniff, some that merely stunk, but others that spoke of a larger drama than the one being played out in the not-quite-hallowed halls of Whitehead Middle.

Besides, school had been a lot more fun when Stinky was there. After he left town, the weekdays dragged on like classical-music concerts. The intermissions were never long enough.

2. Günter Hopstock

OR "The East German Pen Pal"

Dear Phoebe Fine,

I am pleased to meet you. I come from the GDR. My name is Günter Hopstock. I am 13 years old. I was born on the 22.05.67. I learn in the 8 class. I have brother and a sister. My brother is 14 years old, and my sister is 12 years old. My mother is 36 years old. She is a teacher. My father is 37 years old. He is an engineer. Do you speak German? From 4.7.1981 to 31.8.1981 we have school holidays (finish school). What's your age? When were you born? We built a new house with many rooms. We have: 3 nursery, 1 bedroom for my parents, and 2 sitting rooms (1 with new furniture and 1 with old furniture). We also have a swimming pool that is 5 meters long and 1.5 meters wide. I have a rock collection. I would like to be a geologist. Please write back.

Sincerely,
Günter Hopstock

WHITEHEAD, NEW JERSEY, MARCH 30, 1983

Dear Günter Hopstock,

*You wrote me a pen pal letter two years ago. Sorry it took me so long
to write back. I was really busy. You know—friends, school, tennis,
shopping, skinning squirrels, taking apart and putting back together
computers, that kind of thing. Do you still have a swimming pool that
is 5 meters long and 1.5 meters wide? Also, do you wear Speedos or
trunks? I have a mother and a father, too. I can't remember how old
they are, but there's a good chance they're older than I am. (I'm 12
now.) I have a sister, too. She's 15 and really conceited. You must be
around 15 now yourself. Please send a picture so I can tell if you're
cute. I already have a huge crush on Matt Dillon, C. Thomas
Howell, and our Russian piano tuner with the crooked teeth, Igor.*

*Last summer I was in Switzerland, fairly near Germany. It was
really nice there—if you like cheese. I hate cheese. I only like sweet
foods. My favorite foods are sugar, corn syrup, and dextrose. What
kind of music do you like? I like Flock of Seagulls and Schubert,
especially his unfinished symphony. I have a rock collection, too.
Maybe someday we can compare mica. I also have a stamp collection.
Your country has such beautiful stamps! My favorite stamps are from
Nazi-occupied Estonia. I also really like the John and Jackie series
from Sierra Leone. Have you heard of Valley Girls in Germany? I'm
like, "totally" one "for sure." By the way, I don't speak a word of
German so nanananananananananana.*

*Are you a good student? I get straight A's. My school is really
easy. Last year, they started letting in kids from a town nearby that
doesn't have its own junior high. They're very "low class" (my
mother's favorite word) and obnoxious. All they do is sit around and
smoke, and if you turn your homework in on time they call you a*

"dexter." So next year I'm going to private school with a bunch of snobs. I guess you don't have snobs in the GDR because it's Communist. Speaking of which, are you a Communist? I'm not very political, but I think Ronald Reagan is a dope and should go back to acting in chimp movies. My parents voted for Jimmy Carter. I would have too because I don't have any of my own opinions.

Do you have any suicidal classmates? I do. Also, have you seen E.T.? I've seen it twice, but I hated it. I saw it because it was the cool thing to do. You know, peer pressure. When I'm bored, I think about dying. I think the worst way to die would be in a plane crash, followed by drowning, gunshot, knife wound, avalanche, strangulation, fire, car crash, riptide, Chinese water torture, and getting run over by a bus. Do you have London broil in the GDR? You're lucky if you don't. Also, do your parents save twisty-ties? My parents have a whole drawer full of them. When I grow up, I would like to be an astronaut, a clown, or a tortured artist. By the way, my favorite song is "Every Sperm Is Sacred" by the Monty Python gang.

Well, I'm off to a wild party now. So I guess I'll sign off, you hunk. What base have you gone to? I'm in between second and third (don't ask me how).

Write back soon.
Love always and forever,
Phoebe Fine

P.S. Do you ever just ask yourself "why"?

3. Jason Barry Gold

OR *"The Varsity Lacrosse Stud"*

RATHER THAN GET naked in full view of Jennifer Weinfelt, who liked to prance about the girls' locker room in her 32D purple mesh bra making nasty comments about other girls' flat chests and fat asses, Phoebe and her current best friend, Rachel Plotz, changed into their party dresses in the handicapped bathroom over by the nurse's office. Then they piled into Rachel's stepmother's champagne-colored Mercedes coupe, with Rachel in the driver's seat and Cat Stevens on the stereo singing "Wild World." And wasn't that the case? "I, like, cannot believe we're going to Aimee Aaron's Sweet Sixteen," said Rachel on the ride over.

"Well, it's not like we're *not* friends with her," said Phoebe.

But she knew Rachel was right. Despite the lengths they'd gone to to befriend the most popular girl in school—bleaching all ten pairs of her Guess jeans was just the beginning of it—it had still come as something of a shock to find invitations to the big event (forty-fives of the Kool and the Gang single "Celebration" with the labels rewritten to commemorate the particular celebratory moment of Aimee's sixteenth) waiting for them on their respective beds.

They arrived at Parthenon West at ten past eight.

Floodlights cast a rubicund shadow across the parking lot, with its glistening array of new-model Audis and Jaguars. With the help of a valet parker dressed up as a birthday candle, it soon included Rachel's stepmother's Mercedes. By then, Phoebe and Rachel had disappeared through a red-roofed portico supported by two oversized Corinthian columns and into a cavernous ballroom where two rows of crescent-shaped booths upholstered in pink-and-gold vinyl flanked a black marble dance floor, and several hundred Mylar balloons inscribed with the birthday girl's name nearly obscured a neo-rococo ceiling.

A buffet dinner consisting of chicken Florentine and rigatoni with sun-dried tomatoes had been laid out in silver-plated chafing dishes over Sterno candles on a silver-spangled cloth. Hired help included a fortune-teller, a mime, a pastel artist, and a guy dressed up as a funky chicken. Phoebe and Rachel had to wait their turn to congratulate Aimee Aaron, dressed impeccably in a black velvet off-the-shoulder cocktail dress and matching black velvet beret cocked coyly on her long, brown hair. "You look so beautiful," they said, air-kissing their host hello.

"Thank you, and thanks so much for coming!" Aimee smiled fraudulently before she turned away to real-kiss her real friend Stephanie Cohen.

At which point Phoebe and Rachel found an out-of-the-way table in close proximity to the ladies' room—Rachel was experiencing heavy flow—and sat down.

Across the dance floor, a collection of more and less embarrassing relatives, some in floral mumus, others in sleek white pants suits cinched at the waist with stretchy gold belts, chattered among themselves. Three tables away, Aimee—surrounded by twenty-five of her adoring best friends—seemed equally oblivious to Phoebe's and Rachel's presence. "Well, this is fun," snipped Rachel an hour into their unspeakable disappointment.

"Well, don't get mad at me about it," Phoebe snapped back.

But she knew it was too late. She knew Rachel already was.

The feeling was mutual.

Each other's only close friend, Phoebe and Rachel had long resented the isolation the other one represented, even while possessiveness prevented them from branching out. That said, both girls had somehow envisioned that Aimee Aaron's Sweet Sixteen would transport them to another level of social acceptance. Only here they were as alone as they'd ever been, with no evident recourse to integration. (It wasn't as if they could just go sit down at Aimee's table.)

And then, suddenly, they weren't alone at all. To their immediate left, albeit with his back to them, sat the captain of the varsity lacrosse team; the on-again, off-again boyfriend of Aimee Aaron; the driver of a navy-blue BMW convertible whose vanity license plates bore the three initials of his tri-part name. He didn't seem to notice that there were other people sitting at the booth. He proceeded to untie one suede buck, remove it from his sock foot, and shake it violently over the floor, whereupon a microscopic piece of gravel went skipping beneath an adjacent table.

"Usually, when a gentleman sits down at a table with ladies, he says, 'Hello ladies,' " began Rachel in a bitchy voice.

Phoebe wished she hadn't. She hated scenes. And she didn't see how antagonizing the most popular guy in the twelfth grade—she and Rachel had just begun eleventh—stood to enhance either one of their social lives.

But to her shock and bewilderment, Jason Barry Gold turned around and smiled convivially, like a feudal lord bestowing the privilege of his company on his serfs. "Well, hello, ladies," he said. "And how are we tonight?"

Rachel didn't answer.

Phoebe mumbled, "Fine," her excitement matching her suspicion as he slid himself into the booth next to her.

Though they'd been in mock trial together the previous year, Jason Barry Gold had never spoken to her directly.

Now he wanted to know, "What are you girls hiding in the corner for?"

Then he let loose a loud burp.

Rachel rolled her eyes.

Phoebe muttered, "Gross."

"Come on, it's biology," said Jason, reaching a long arm around Phoebe's black lace shift, a vintage purchase from a recent weekend excursion to Eighth Street in Greenwich Village with Emily. "People burp."

Phoebe thought she'd die. What would Aimee Aaron think? And what were Jason's intentions? And was she about to become the butt of some obscene joke that would be retold in a loud whisper during Monday-morning assembly, eliciting throaty guffaws from the whole lacrosse team? For Phoebe, adolescence had produced such a paucity of male admirers that she had trouble imagining the attention she did occasionally receive was motivated by anything short of sadism.

And yet, despite her better judgment, she found herself electrified by Jason's proximity, and fluttering her lashes accordingly. She thought of Stinky. She had always been attracted to men who showed no shame when it came to bodily functions. Maybe because they deflated the shame she felt about her own bodily functions. She found menstruation unseemly. She failed to see the point of pubic hair.

"People control themselves, too," she said, attempting wit in the face of her fear.

"Yeah, well, in my personal opinion, control is overrated,"

replied Jason, his free hand gripping the frosted exterior of her non-alcoholic strawberry daiquiri. "Don'tcha think?"

As he lifted the glass to his lips, Phoebe shot Rachel a look intended to communicate her deep distrust of their surprise visitor. She knew Rachel would never let her forget it if she thought that Phoebe thought she had even the slightest chance with Jason Barry Gold. (She could already hear Rachel teasing her: "Things going well with Jason?")

But Rachel wasn't interested. She gazed blankly at the dance floor, her eyes as glassy and depthless as two little skating rinks. Then she stood up and announced, "I have to use the rest room."

"Hope you get some rest," said Jason.

"Duh," said Rachel, frothing at the mouth.

"I'll watch your bag if you want." Phoebe tried to protect her best friend from hurt, even while her best friend seized upon the smallest opportunity to uncover Phoebe as an unmitigated dork. That was the arrangement. That was the injustice of it.

She was taking her bag with her.

Together, Jason and Phoebe watched Rachel Plotz waddle away, her jaw clenched defensively, her fringe purse jitterbugging against her polka-dotted peplum. Then they were alone. Then Phoebe turned to face him, thinking she'd never really looked at him before—or, at least, not at this close range. And what she saw had the simultaneous effect of inspiring awe and making him that much realer. His layered hair was styled backward into a point. His nose was long and broad and not unhandsome. His olive complexion helped create the illusion of a more chiseled face than he actually had. He was wearing a white oxford shirt and pleated beige trousers that tapered to the ankle.

That Phoebe was willing to overlook the whitehead that decorated his left cheek was just another testament to his social clout.

"So what do you think of the party?" she asked him.

"I've been to better," he answered with a yawn. "So how's the tennis team?"

That he knew she was on the tennis team! Phoebe readjusted her neck and shoulders beneath Jason's dead weight and told him, "It's okay, but I really only like playing with my father."

She couldn't believe she'd said that. No sooner had the sentence exited her mouth than she was contemplating suicide, hating herself for not thinking before she spoke.

"I'm sure you do," smiled Jason, his eyebrows leaping like pogo sticks.

"You know what I mean," squeaked Phoebe.

But it was too late for explanations. Jason shook free his arm and rose to his feet. "Tennis," he said then. "A fine game, if I do say so myself."

Using a plastic spoon, he gave his best imitation of a topspin forehand.

"You should come see us play on Monday after school," suggested Phoebe, knowing full well he never would. "It's the first round of the Counties, and they're at Pringle this year."

"Very cool," said Jason, finishing off her juice concoction like a stiff shot of whiskey.

"Hey, that was my drink!" she protested.

"I'll get you another one," he promised.

But she had her doubts. His attention seemed suddenly caught up by another scenario being played out several tables away. What it was she couldn't say for sure, but it seemed to consume him. "Listen," he said, laying a careless hand on her bare shoulder. "I'm gonna go check on the guys. I'll catch you later."

"Later," she said.

But it wasn't the guys he apparently felt compelled to check on. With a sinking feeling in her stomach, Phoebe watched Jason Barry Gold glide over to the birthday girl, take her in his arms, and dance a few steps with her, his lips barely moving inside her diamond-studded ear. What was he saying? Were they on again or off again? And who was Phoebe Fine to think it had any bearing on her pathetic life?

SHE SPENT MOST Friday nights at the Paramus tenplex watching John Hughes movies with Rachel. *Sixteen Candles, Pretty in Pink, The Breakfast Club:* she'd seen them all twice, three times. Thursday nights were a different matter. She spent those rehearsing Brahms's Second Symphony with the All-County Youth Orchestra in the basement of an Episcopalian church in Mahwah. Years later, she grew attached to that very symphony—would lie awake with all the lights off, swooning to its overwrought themes. At the time, however, its raw emotion struck her as pompous. Nor did it seem to bear even the slightest relation to any of the pressing issues in her life—namely, not being embarrassing, getting decent scores on the S.A.T.s, losing her virginity in a timely fashion, and getting her revenge on Jennifer Weinfelt. That said, Brahms was the least of her complaints with the ACYO.

The conductor, Walter Major, made disturbingly sexual facial expressions during all the slow movements and took out his career frustrations—obviously he would have preferred to be conducting the Berlin Philharmonic—on the second violins, of which Phoebe was one. Even worse, she had to share a stand with a righteous pimple-face named Kwan who was always correcting her bowings—her fingerings, too. Not that it ever occurred to her to quit. Despite her acid-tongued letters to Iron Curtain pen pals, she didn't have a rebellious bone in her body.

She still considered family to be destiny. Which is not to say she wasn't increasingly resentful of the hand she imagined destiny to have dealt her—the hand that had denied her the leather couches, Central American cleaning woman, three-car garage, and color TV with remote control that all the other kids at Pringle Prep had.

Phoebe had matriculated in the ninth grade. Pringle Prep wasn't like Whitehead Middle at all. It wasn't even in Whitehead. It was in the next town over, a town whose abandoned railroad tracks literally divided rich from poor, and black from white and predominantly Jewish, with the exception of one or two over-the-hill R&B stars who lived in gated Italianate mansions up on the hill, over by Pringle's playing fields. It was Roberta who'd insisted that Phoebe transfer there, because, for one thing, Phoebe had begun speaking "Jersey-ese." (She'd say, "I'm goin' a scouull," instead of "I'm going to school.") For another, it was Roberta's contention that with a diploma from Pringle Prep, Phoebe would have a better chance of getting into a good university or music conservatory—the kind whose clear plastic bumper sticker would look impressive affixed to the back window of the family station wagon for all the neighbors to see. There was already a clear plastic Yale University sticker affixed in this very manner. Emily had gotten in early admission.

It wasn't exactly a surprise.

By her junior year, Emily had won all the academic prizes the school had to offer, so the school invented more prizes on her behalf. In addition to editing the school newspaper, she sat on an independent council of faculty, administrators, and alumni who met bimonthly to brainstorm on the topic of pedagogical theory. As for her S.A.T. scores, they were a near-perfect 1,580. Still, Emily Fine was perhaps best known as the only student in the history of Pringle Prep to have researched a history term paper at the Library of Congress, where she ploughed through more than two thousand primary documents issued by the Freedman's Bureau. ("White Lies: Race, Politics, and Dialectical Materialism in Reconstruction Georgia" was the name of the resulting screed.)

Phoebe didn't begrudge Emily the success so much as she did Leonard's and Roberta's excessive pride in it. Never mind the Yale sticker. To Phoebe, it seemed as if her parents looked to their children to succeed where they had only ever survived, their love of classical music grossly outweighing their drive to climb its arcane but increasingly cutthroat hierarchy. Indeed, every month another orchestra folded; every year Henry Purcell crept further into obscurity. And the classical-music audience was shrinking, graying, shriveling up like an old peach. And there weren't enough jobs for all the fresh-faced musicians Juilliard dumped on the city streets each June. Not to mention the fact that there were only two oboists in every orchestra, compared with nearly three dozen violins. Never mind the paltry number of violas. This is the kind of talk Phoebe heard at home, at dinner, and in the car to Grandma Lettie's house in Tarrytown.

She heard another kind of talk from the top of the stairs, where she sat obscured from view trying to eavesdrop on the purportedly private conversations Leonard and Roberta conducted late at night in the kitchen in hushed tones, and sometimes, if they were being extra paranoid, in broken French. They spoke of Leonard changing careers—of him becoming a real estate or travel agent like Mr. Grossblatt, who used to play the bass clarinet but now booked flights to Aruba because the music money wasn't coming in the way it should have been. If only Leonard had been a little more like Rachel's father, Mr. Plotz, who wore

Italian suits and made pots of money doing things no one understood at a company called Technotron Incorporated. But he wasn't like Mr. Plotz at all; he was a freelance oboist. Which meant that Phoebe was a freelance oboist's daughter. Which meant she didn't stand a chance at real popularity, built as it was not just on cup size and charisma but on the ability to afford ski vacations in Park City, Utah.

At Whitehead Middle, Phoebe had been safely middle-class; at Pringle, where she was one of the so-called financial aid students, she found herself well below the poverty line—a point of fact made clear on her first day of school, for which she made the mistake of arriving not just by car pool but in a zip-up sweatshirt and white painter pants. In their elaborately patterned Benetton sweaters and snakeskin cowboy boots, her new classmates showed their contempt through their colored contact lenses. That's why Phoebe started shopping at Suburban Sophisticates, a designer-seconds emporium in shouting distance of Teterboro Airport, just off Route 46. The place reeked of overbuttered popcorn and ammonia-rich floor cleaner. Every other garment seemed to feature a fuchsia lipstick stain. The carpet that lined the ladies' changing room never seemed hygienic enough for bare feet. There was an abandoned day-rate motel (MIDNIGHT SPECIAL $27!) at the edge of the parking lot. But Roberta told Phoebe that if she wanted the same things rich kids had, this was the only way she was going to get them— with pulled threads, mangled insignias, and two different-length sleeves no one was supposed to notice.

Except they did—especially Jennifer Weinfelt, who would fix her eyes on Phoebe's paraplegic polo players and ask, "Is there something, like, wrong with your shirt?"

Another time Jennifer pointed at the plastic flower ring on Phoebe's middle finger, and asked her, "Is that, like, a flower?"

"By the way, Jennifer, in case you haven't noticed, your skin's falling off," Phoebe was tempted to say, was going to say, because Jennifer's acne-blemished skin had turned red and flaky on account of her Retin-A prescription. But she never would have. She didn't have the nerve for scenes. She was still thinking she could make people like her. She hadn't yet learned that it's a waste of time to try—that they either do or they don't, and usually they don't. But even if they do, they still say nasty things about you—just not to your face. So she answered, "It's just, like, a ring," because it *was* a ring—just not one of the silver and gold Tiffany's bands that Jennifer sported on her short, tan fingers.

"Oh—right," Jennifer responded, as if Phoebe had just shown off her termite collection.

———

RACHEL RETURNED FROM the rest room with a new coat of Silver City Pink anchored to her thin, downturned lips. "Like, what was *that* about?" she demanded to know.

"I have no idea," Phoebe told her.

"Well, you sure weren't acting like you didn't know . . ."

"Didn't know what?"

"Didn't know what Jason was, like, doing here."

"Did *I* invite him to sit down?"

Rachel lifted one overplucked eyebrow to the heavens. "I don't know who invited who, but you certainly weren't acting like you minded sitting next to him."

"You were the one who started talking to him!"

"I was just trying to make a point, whereas *you*," she said, pausing for effect, "were flirting your ass off."

Phoebe grimaced and turned away. At times like this, she really hated her best friend—even if she was only trying to protect her. Rachel would claim so much if Phoebe challenged her motives. She'd say, "You should be glad someone cares!" (That's what Rachel always said when Phoebe challenged her motives.) "Look," said Phoebe, turning back to Rachel. "If you have a better idea of who to hang out with at this party, then go ahead."

"Fine," said Rachel, rising from the table, but not before she'd helped herself to another palmful of nuts. (Phoebe wanted to tell her to stop—Rachel was gaining weight at an astounding speed—but understood it wasn't her job.) "Are you coming or not?"

"Fine," said Phoebe, following her best friend onto the dance floor, where fifty or so of their classmates were jumping up and down to the kinetic beat of "Twist and Shout."

The two girls staked out a remote corner near the mime— well, maybe it wasn't *that* remote. In truth, it was no accident that Phoebe positioned herself a mere two feet from where Jason Barry Gold was busy hamming it up for the party photographers. And still, upon discovering (two minutes into her own half-hearted shuffling) that the elbow nudging her spine belonged to Jason, she was startled enough to find her knees buckling beneath her.

"Whoa, baby, careful," said Jason, grabbing her around the waist as she fell toward him, into him. "Don't want you lying down—yet."

"Uhhhhhhhhh," growled Phoebe, her eyes narrowed with evident disgust even as she made no effort to free herself from his grip. That must have been obvious to Rachel. Out of the corner of her eye, Phoebe watched her best friend stomp off in the direction of the buffet table. In that moment, however, antagonizing Rachel Plotz seemed like a risk worth taking. Indeed, experience suggested that tomorrow they would go to the mall, Phoebe would help Rachel spend her father's money, and they would make up. In the meantime, "Twist and Shout" was winding down. Phoebe lifted her arms into the air for the last time, then shimmied her body down into a crouching position. The space between the songs seemed interminable. Her body frozen on the floor, she prayed that deejay Johnny Jamtastic was on her side.

It turned out he was. The next song up was the midtempo pop ballad "No One Is to Blame." A collective groan reverberated throughout the plasterboard walls of Parthenon West. Phoebe's new dance partner had no part in it. Unique among his peers, Jason Barry Gold could exhibit enthusiasm for slow dancing without being taken for a wuss. That's how cool he was. Rumor had it he'd slept with ten girls in the eleventh grade alone. "I love this song," he told Phoebe, who told him, "Me, too," before he opened his arms to her and she fell in between them, linked her own arms around his sweat-soaked neck and surveyed the scene for future recounting.

Rachel had disappeared, but Jennifer Weinfelt was skulking back to Aimee's table. She wasn't the only one. Within seconds, the dance floor stood empty except for a handful of established couples, not including Jason and Phoebe, whose immediate concern was that Aimee, dancing with her endodontic-surgeon father not four feet away from where she and Jason swayed to the music, would object to the sight of someone dancing with her on-again, off-again boyfriend—at her own birthday party, no less!

After Aimee offered her a perfunctory smile on her way around a fatherly spin, however, Phoebe concentrated her efforts on making sure that Jennifer Weinfelt saw her in her moment of glory. As she and Jason moved across the dance floor in slow, rocking circles, she tried in vain to catch her archenemy's perpetually bloodshot eye. It was only after Jason pulled her closer—so close that she could see the individual pores on his face, and many were clogged—that Phoebe settled her score with Pringle's most notorious bitch. Their eyes met for no more than a second.

It was a second that Phoebe would replay for months to come.

And it was a second that inspired Phoebe to succumb to the sensation of Jason Barry Gold himself—to press her stunted hips into his pleated pants and close her eyes. That way, she could enjoy the friction between them without having to think about its origin. She was squeamish about sex, but she wasn't not interested.

———————

THE NIGHT PROGRESSED. The ranks of more and less embarrassing relatives began to thin. The buffet table was cleared and filled again—this time with two enormous chocolate tarts, one in the shape of a 1, and the other in the shape of a 6. Whereupon deejay Johnny Jamtastic interrupted the musical proceedings to wish the birthday girl "a really good one," prompting Aimee Aaron's twenty-five best friends to break into song— "Happy Birthday," in particular. At which point, sweaty and exhausted, Phoebe and Jason parted ways—Jason in the direction of the cake, Phoebe in the direction of Rachel Plotz. But where had she gone? And could she have been mad enough to leave without Phoebe? And what was Phoebe supposed to do now— now that it was twenty to twelve?

If he didn't hear otherwise, Leonard had promised to swing the Electra around at midnight. So Phoebe would have to call home now if she was driving back with Rachel, who lived in Franklin Lakes, a good twenty-five minute drive from Whitehead. Which is why Phoebe always made backup arrangements to get home, even if Rachel always ended up driving her there. But if she called to cancel Leonard, and Rachel really *had* left, then how would she ever get back to Whitehead?

Phoebe circled the ballroom a final time, pausing here and there to inquire as to her erstwhile best friend's whereabouts— all to no avail. ("Rachel Plotz was here?" was the common refrain.) Eventually resigned to the idea that Rachel had left without her, she decided to pay a quick visit to the fortune-teller. For a Carmen, she looked pretty Anglo-Saxon. She had a small, turned-up nose, a pale blond bun, and a freckly forehead. She reached for Phoebe's hand with her long, gem-laden fingers. "Your life line is long," she purred. "What else can I tell you?"

Phoebe kept her voice low. "How old will I be when I lose my virginity?"

Carmen ran her index finger down the length of Phoebe's thumb, then diagonally across her palm in the direction of her wrist. Then she came to an abrupt halt, gazed up and into Phoebe's eyes with her own watery blue ones, and whispered, "You'll be nineteen."

"Nineteen?" Phoebe croaked in frustration.

"You'll appreciate it more at that age," clucked Carmen.

"I'm sure I will," grumbled Phoebe.

Then she made her way over to the coat check.

"Thanks so much for having me," she told Aimee Aaron on her way out.

"Thanks so much for coming!" said Aimee.

Phoebe might have said good night to Jason Barry Gold as well. But he was currently huddled with his lacrosse-team buddies, and the prospect seemed daunting. Instead, like a suburban Cinderella, she scurried out the side entrance and into her father's waiting car. "Hi, Dad," she said, relieved to find none of her classmates watching. (It was bad enough getting picked up by your father; getting picked up in a barge with a taped headlight was unspeakable.)

The two of them vanished into the maze of malls, car dealerships, plastic-surgery offices, and discount bedding outlets that passed for "the way home."

"Did you have a good time?" Leonard asked her somewhere between Bloomingdale's and Bennigan's.

"It was okay," she told him.

He didn't ask any more questions. She didn't volunteer any more information. She was lost in Jason Barry Gold. She was replaying their slow dance—step by step, turn by turn. It wasn't easy after Leonard cranked up the volume on the radio and cheeped, "Oh, I love this piece"—just like he always did when the *Symphony Fantastique* came on. But this time she kept her annoyance to herself. Right then, right there, she understood that *no one was to blame*—not even her father.

SURE ENOUGH, RACHEL wasn't talking to Phoebe the next morning. But that afternoon they had it out. Rachel didn't mention Jason Barry Gold's name even once. Instead, she made the case that Phoebe had abandoned her at the party—*even though Rachel was the one who drove off without telling Phoebe she was driving off.* At least, that's how it seemed to Phoebe. She said, "I thought you left. I looked all over for you."

"Obviously you didn't look all over," said Rachel. "Because I was in the bathroom. Okay?"

"For forty-five minutes?"

"I had my period?"

"Well, I thought you'd gone home."

"Well, you thought incorrectly."

"Well, sorry."

"Whatever."

Then they drove to the upscale mall at the intersection of Route This and Route That, where they bought Rachel some long-sleeved rugby shirts at the Ralph Lauren store, a peach sleeveless turtleneck at Ann Taylor, and a pair of Guess overalls at Saks Fifth Avenue (by way of Hackensack). By the time they pulled out of the parking lot, they were best friends again. Though Phoebe sometimes wondered why. In truth, Rachel Plotz wasn't so much nicer to her than Jennifer Weinfelt was. But then, niceness had never been the glue that kept the two girls best friends. Rather, it was loyalty that bound them— loyalty that allowed Phoebe to keep excusing away Rachel's chronic bitchiness. To know that she had someone to sit with in the cafeteria at lunch, someone to gossip with on the phone at night, someone to drive to the occasional party with on the weekends—someone whose mere existence in her life and phone book served to assuage the persistent fear that she was a complete and total retard—for Phoebe, that was, if not enough, then at least something to hold on to in the sleepless hours of the night.

———

THE NAME CALLING had begun in seventh grade. In addition to being termed a retard, Phoebe had been labeled a dexter, a dufus, and a dorkmeister. It wasn't entirely her fault. There was her bowl haircut, her goofy grin, her good grades, her visible violin case, her no-name sneakers (derided as "skips"), and her body's stubborn refusal to develop secondary sexual characteristics in keeping with her age group—sure. And yes, thanks to a sudden vertical growth spurt, she occasionally walked into walls, hit her head on hanging plants, that kind of thing. But it was also in seventh grade that Whitehead Middle opened its doors to the school-poor "toughs" of neighboring Riverbank, a dilapidated old fishing and dredging village that cut a two-mile tapeworm beneath the undulating cliffs of the Hudson.

Several years into the future, Riverbank would be overrun by cash-rich Korean car-company executives, who would bulldoze the old paper-cup factory on the hill to make room for condominiums built in the style of English manor homes. Many would be equipped with sunken Jacuzzis. Almost all would feature exquisite views of the Manhattan skyline. A certain percentage would house obedient tots whose first instruction on the viola would come courtesy of Roberta Fine. (A lesser percentage would seek out Leonard for instruction on the oboe.) Back in Phoebe's time, however, go-go bars and head shops were still the biggest business in Riverbank, while the two-family houses that lined the town's elevated main thoroughfare had yet to be vacated by the offspring of the river workers—truck drivers and cocktail waitresses, the children of whom seemingly aspired to little more than ridiculing those members of Whitehead Middle (Phoebe included) who showed enthusiasm for activities other than getting high, building bonfires, attending rock concerts, purchasing beverages at Beverage Barn, and sitting around doing nothing.

Moreover, as the Whitehead kids began to follow the lead of the so-called Riverskank, Phoebe found herself ostracized by her oldest friends, with her no-show at the Tom Petty concert at the Brendan Byrne Arena marking the beginning of her fall from social grace. Why didn't she attend? 1) She had no particular affection for Tom Petty, never mind the Heartbreakers; 2) She'd just as soon have been home rewallpapering her dollhouse; 3) She imagined herself getting lost in a crowd of jostling teens only to wind up keeping disappeared Mafioso Jimmy Hoffa company in one of the Meadowlands' infamous egg-carton and Dorito-bag alps; 4) She couldn't imagine Roberta and Leonard ever allowing her to attend a rock concert. But she could have asked. She didn't bother. That must have been obvious to her friends. Not a week later, at the Whitehead High Talent Show, while a heavyset girl named Naomi sang "The Body Electric," Brenda Cuddihy, her lashes caked with electric-blue mascara, made it all too clear that she was embarrassed to be seen sitting next to Phoebe on the bleachers. She placed her matching blue ski parka between them. When Phoebe tried to move it aside, Brenda instructed her to "keep your dirty paws off."

Shortly thereafter, Phoebe was voted "Weirdest Dresser in the Eighth Grade" for purposes of the Middle School yearbook—was made to pose in a Miss America–style sash reading "Weirdest Dresser in the Eighth Grade, Phoebe Fine," so the yearbook photographer could immortalize the insult, and all, presumably, because she'd once donned an embroidered smock top Leonard had brought her back from Guatemala City, site of the Trenton Philharmonic's Christmas '83 tour. Here she'd thought its decorative needlework would call attention away from the lack of development underneath. Instead, her classmates taunted her with cries of "peasant" and "hippie." Her only comfort was the thought that it could have been worse; she could have been the new girl, Veronica Dunleavy, who eventually gave up protesting and starting answering to the competing nicknames "V.D." and "Dog."

Even worse, she could have been Dolores Rodriguez, a certain oversized Riverskank who favored a certain brand of scoop-neck black leotard top that made it all too easy for Patrick McPatrick, Jr., to reach down her back and unhook her bra, time after time. Dolores's protests were loud and impassioned. Once she even slapped her assailant across the face. But it was pretty clear she liked the attention. It was the opinion of her classmates that she liked the attention a little too much. They called her a slut and a whore. They made her cry on the bus back to Riverbank. Not long afterward, she surprised them all by overdosing on her mother's sleeping pills a week after her mother went after her father with a carving knife implicated in the sudden death of a certain rooster living in their backyard—or so it was said.

It was also said that Dolores Rodriguez had had her stomach pumped—Phoebe imagined an oil-rig-sized contraption siphoning the liquid content of Dolores's stomach into an Alaska-bound pipeline—while Dolores's mother had been sent to a loony bin. Needless to say, Dolores's suicide attempt was an exciting thing to contemplate. Far more exciting, for example, than the anorexia nervosa that landed little Deirdre Sherman in the hospital attached to an I.V. dripping pink gunk into her arm while she slept. And upon her return to Whitehead Middle, Dolores was greeted with newfound respect. People started saving seats for her on the bus and in the cafeteria. Patrick McPatrick stopped reaching down her back—and started reaching down Phoebe's with a fistful of yellow snow on her way out of school "as punishment," he was kind enough to explain, *"for being so friggin' frigid."*

———

THE FOLLOWING SUNDAY, in preparation for the first day back to school since Aimee Aaron's Sweet Sixteen, Phoebe tried on seven different outfits:

1) beige Et Vous khakis with narrowed ankles (hand-me-downs from Phoebe's second cousin, Sasha), paired with a white-and-purple-striped cotton Gap sweater,

purchased at the downscale Bergen Mall and accursed with a not terribly noticeable torn thread on the back shoulder;

2) olive-green Liz Claiborne corduroy jeans with narrowed ankles (hand-me-downs from Lenore Greenbaum, the borderline anorexic wife of Travis Greenbaum, principal oboist for the New York Philharmonic), and a long-sleeved black ballerina-neck T-shirt of Emily's;

3) khakis (see above) and a pale pink Ralph Lauren polo shirt with a mysterious bleach stain beneath the left armhole, courtesy of Suburban Sophisticates;

4) button-fly Guess jeans (Phoebe's prize possession) bleached and bejeweled with hand-sewn calico knee patches, plus Roberta's Indian cotton blouse with the drawstring collar, a relic of the 1970s;

5) Guess jeans (see above) and a white Hanes T-shirt (men's size extra-large) with Leonard's forest green Shetland sweater tied around the shoulders;

6) light-blue long-underwear bottoms of unknown provenance (i.e., found in the attic, at the bottom of a cardboard box filled with ceramic spoons, lace handkerchiefs, and early recordings of Schubert lieder), with one of Leonard's white concert shirts hanging out on top;

7) floor-length raspberry-hued cotton-flannel Putamayo-style drop-waist jumper hand-sewn by Leonard's essentially deaf mother, Phoebe's Grandma Edith.

In the end Phoebe chose the drop-waist jumper, reasoning that Jason Barry Gold had probably been attracted to her for the very reason that she wasn't immediately and overtly attractive. Which is to say that her beauty was subtle if it was anything. Maybe it was nothing. But she wasn't ugly—she knew that much. She may have had chubby cheeks, rabbit teeth, a flat chest, and eyes more gray than blue. But she had long legs, a clear complexion, and a bump-free nose. And her shoulder-length hair could have been worse. While a bit on the stringy side, it was still shiny and a nice shade of light brown.

Oh, but who was she kidding? So often when Phoebe looked in the mirror she didn't even know who she was looking at. That's how ugly she was—ugly by virtue of the fact that she was unmemorable, a slab of alabaster awaiting a sculptor who never arrived, a "nothing burger" if there ever was one. Take her nose: it just kind of ended. Just as her forehead just kind of began—kind of like the weeks in a year and the years in a life. It was the same with her waist and her hips, and her neck and her shoulders. There was nothing definitive about her. She was just this blob of human flesh—just this girl running laps behind the gym until she thought her legs would snap, her heart explode.

Of course, as it happened, despite her better efforts, Phoebe didn't see Jason once the whole schoolday—not in the halls, the cafeteria, the gym, or the library. But after school, while she traded topspin lobs with a stub-nosed string bean from Elizabeth Academy who muttered "bitch" under her breath every time they changed sides, she caught sight of him leaned up against the fence. She couldn't believe he'd remembered the Counties! Or maybe he'd merely stumbled upon them on his way to lacrosse practice. He was dressed to play, complete with helmet, shoulder guards, and gloves. Either way, it was his show of support that inspired her to take the offensive in what had so far been a lackluster match, with she and Stub Nose tied at 4 all and each of them holding serve.

At the very next lob that came her way, Phoebe pounced, driving the ball hard and fast down the line. Stub Nose must not have been expecting it. In her zeal to get her racquet on the ball, she tripped over her own feet and fell onto her ass, while her return (if you could call it that) sailed sideways into Court 2, where Pringle Prep's second doubles team was busy double-faulting an entire game. It was an unpleasant confluence of events for Elizabeth Academy's second seed. And still, by screaming "FUCK ME!" at the top of her lungs, it wasn't entirely clear whom she intended to address.

Jason Barry Gold took the exhortation personally. "I'd rather not," he informed Phoebe's opponent, who returned the favor with her middle finger. But the provocation rolled right off him. "Beautiful shot," he said, turning his attention back to Phoebe, who shot him her best smile and offered up a simple "Thanks," further infuriating Stub Nose, who thundered, "I WANT THAT DICKWEED OUT OF HERE NOW," her oversized Prince racquet pointed at the fence like a sawed-off shotgun.

But "that dickweed" was already gone—though not in spirit. Her heart full with the memory of Jason's endorsement, Phoebe took the first set 6–4, then the second set 6–love, thereby advancing to the quarterfinals in what was widely regarded as a major upset for Pringle Prep. After the match her teammates crowded 'round to offer their congratulations. Even Bradley Clay, varsity tennis's notoriously withholding coach, had these laudatory words to offer: "Way to hustle, Phoebe." Moreover, so elated was she by the events of the afternoon that she barely registered the sight of Jennifer Weinfelt holding court in the girls' locker room at six o'clock. She was wiggling out of her field-hockey polo and adjusting the straps of her 32D purple mesh bra. And she smiled when she saw Phoebe, but it wasn't a friendly smile—more like a snicker smile.

"So what's up with you and Jason?" she said, raising one arched eyebrow—just like Rachel had. (They were all the same; they were all suspicious.)

"What do you mean?" said Phoebe, playing dumb.

"Slow-dancing at Aimee Aaron's . . ."

"We're just friends."

"Oh." Jennifer lifted her flaky chin. "Right."

———

A CROSS-EYED BRUNHILDE with a killer drop shot from Watchung Day School subsequently eliminated Phoebe in the semifinals. Understandably, then, her mood was less than jubilant when, that same evening, Roberta called upstairs, "Phone for you, cupcake!"

"What?" Phoebe called back. It was hard to hear over Beethoven's Ninth.

"Telephone," she trilled. "It's a boy."

A boy? Phoebe ran into Leonard and Roberta's bedroom, grabbed the receiver, and pressed it against her stomach before she even said hello. Then she called downstairs to them—to her incredibly embarrassing parents who refused to listen to Barbra Streisand like everyone else's parents: "I've got it—can you hang up?"

She thought they had. But when she said, "Hello?" it sounded like the inside of an orchestra pit. (She could just barely make out a human voice on the other end of the phone.) "Sorry," she told whoever it was. "Can you hold on a second?" Then she tried again. "MOM, DAD, PLEASE! COULD YOU HANG UP THE PHONE?"

"We did, sweetheart!"

Phoebe took a deep breath and tried yet again. "Hello?"

"I feel like I'm on the tarmac at La Guardia," said Jason Barry Gold the Frequent Flyer.

Phoebe's stomach fell out of her body even before he'd finished his sentence. She couldn't imagine ever forgiving her parents for bringing her into this world. She couldn't imagine how Jason had gotten her number, either. Surely there were other Fines listed in the phone book. He would have had to have known she lived in Whitehead. But how would he have known such a thing? "Jason!" She giggled to mask her shame. "I'm really sorry—my parents play their music kind of loud."

"Tell me about it." He laughed caustically. "So what's up, babe?"

Phoebe Fine a babe? "Oh, nothing," she said. "I'm just doing my math homework."

"You got Petite?"

"Yeah, I got Petite. Not that he's aware of that fact. He calls me by my sister's name every other day."

"Who's your sister again?"

Someone who didn't remember Emily? Phoebe couldn't believe it. Her sister had founded the school's nuclear disarmament club. Her sister was a card-carrying member of Amnesty International. Her sister read Noam Chomsky for fun. Her sister was the rare individual whose beauty and brains and apparent disregard for the social hierarchy of Pringle Prep had rendered her an object of fascination to the cool boy population even while she'd been essentially shunned by the popular girls. By comparison, Phoebe seemed to fascinate no one—with the possible exception of Jason Barry Gold. Though for reasons that weren't entirely clear. "Her name is Emily," she told him. "She's a sophomore at Yale."

But Jason wasn't interested. "Yeah, Petite's going senile," he agreed.

"Maybe he's got Alzheimer's," Phoebe added.

"So listen, babe, what do you say the two of us check out a movie on Friday night?"

A movie? With Jason Barry Gold? This Friday? Phoebe remembered suddenly that she'd made plans with Rachel to see *Youngblood* that night. She would have to change Rachel to Saturday. And for that, she would surely pay the price of Rachel's wrath. Oh, but it was worth it! "What time?" she asked.

"I'll pick you up at eight," he said. "Where do you live, again?"

"In Whitehead. Just follow Beachmont all the way down the hill and keep going for about two miles. It's on the corner of Beachmont and Douglass. It's a purple house with white shutters. You can just honk and I'll come out." She didn't want Jason Barry Gold coming inside. She didn't want him to see the clutter and the anachronism. She didn't want him to meet her parents.

She couldn't imagine anything more embarrassing.

THAT SAID, LEONARD and Roberta Fine were hardly the weirdest Whitehead had to offer. Yes, Roberta knitted her own sweater vests, forgot to cut the sales tags off her shirts, and managed to get food in her hair every time she ate. And sure, Leonard was wearing two different-color socks—one green and one black—the day he came to play the oboe for Phoebe's tenth-grade class. Compared with their neighbors, however, Phoebe's parents might as well have been a TV sitcom couple from the 1950s.

An avid numismatist with an Adam's apple the size of a

plum, the former Swiss ambassador to Togo lived in a split-level across the street. His next-door neighbor to the left was a World War II spy turned cookbook writer whose youngest child died in a freak accident involving a desk lamp. And who could forget the Kaminskys, a husband-and-wife magician team who mostly performed at local bar mitzvahs? Once upon a time Stan and Barbara Kaminsky had been a brand name on Broadway. The real tragedy, however, was their dreadlocked daughter, who lived at home and—despite her pear-shaped body and relatively flat chest—commuted to work at Peep World on Forty-second Street, where she danced without her shirt and (some said) pants.

Then there was Bill Cornish, the painfully shy arcade game addict who lived farther down the block with his senile grandma with the red shawl. There were rumors that Mrs. Cornish was hoarding her husband's pickled corpse in the two-car garage. She wasn't the only old lady on the block getting a bad rap. It was said of Miss Clapp, who'd lived alone in a rickety blue house on the corner since before anyone could remember, that she was actually a witch. The evidence? She dressed primarily in black. Her cat was blind. She rarely came outside during the day. And when she did, she walked with a thick wooden cane that bore a vague resemblance to the stick portion of a broom.

As for the guy who built the place to the Fines' right—a near-windowless concrete affair hidden behind a hedgerow of tall pines—it was common knowledge on the block that he'd helped build the atom bomb. Though a resident of New Jersey, he'd somehow gained access to the Manhattan Project. But that was before Phoebe's time. As she grew up, about six different families would move in and out of that gloomy bomb shelter of a manse. Phoebe's least favorite were the Glicks, a retired couple whose Rottweiler, Anselm, always made a beeline for her crotch.

And still, from Phoebe's perspective, the Glicks were an ever more welcome sight than the Bertmullers, a motherless family of three who lived two doors down. Mr. Bertmuller was a Jungian psychoanalyst. It was never clear what had happened to his "female archetype." It was hard to believe that the Bertmuller boys would ever be anyone's types. The older son, George, was a badly shaven, white-painter-pants-wearing perpetual-graduate-student type rumored to be studying mushrooms at Columbia, while his roly-poly younger brother, Gary, was perhaps best known for skinning squirrels and hanging the hides to dry on nails he hammered into prominent trees in the purlieu. The Bertmullers also found room in their house for a constantly rotating assemblage of Japanese exchange students, as well as two black Labs (Evil and Knievel) and three boa constrictors to whom Emily had the job of feeding mice one year while the gang pitched tents in Yosemite. On the day of Emily's African dance recital in Teaneck, Phoebe kindly offered to fill in. That was the one and only time she saw the inside of the Bertmullers' ranch home. Once was enough. There were wooden masks hanging from dark red walls. There were hand-woven Peruvian throw rugs draped over mustard leather couches with metal arms.

There were several piles of fossilized dog shit collecting dust on the living room carpet.

RACHEL DIDN'T BELIEVE her at first—or maybe she didn't want to believe her. It went against her entire philosophy of life that a guy like Jason Barry Gold would want to have anything to do with Phoebe Fine. "Right," she said. "You and Jason Barry Gold."

But Phoebe told her, "I'm not kidding. He called me last night. I don't even know how he got my number."

"Maybe you gave it to him?"

"I swear I didn't!"

"So Jason Barry Gold called you last night." Rachel said it over and over again until even she began to believe it. "And the two of you are going to the movies on Friday night. Which is why you want to go see *Youngblood* with me on Saturday night instead."

"Right."

"Look, Phoebe, I'm not gonna even bother making plans with you in the future if you're always, like, canceling them!"

"But I'm *not* always canceling them! I only canceled that one time when my grandfather died!"

"Do you have any idea how hard it was getting those tickets?"

"I'm sure it was . . ."

"I don't even like Genesis."

"Look, I'm sorry—"

"Whatever. It doesn't matter. We'll go to *Youngblood* on Saturday night. Do you want to sleep over afterward?"

"Sure."

"I'll rent a movie for afterward."

"You want to see two movies in one night?"

"Oh, and I'm sure you have a better idea what to do afterward?"

"Fine, we'll watch a movie afterward."

"Have you seen *Meatballs*?"

"I saw it with you. Remember?"

"Do you want to see it again?"

"Sure, why not?"

Sometimes, Phoebe found, it was easier giving in.

———————

THAT FRIDAY NIGHT Jason and Phoebe went to see *Ferris Bueller's Day Off* at the Paramus tenplex. He picked her up in his BMW convertible. And he had the top down even though it was mid-October. And he was wearing mirrored shades even though it was already dark. "Dude," he said, pushing open the passenger door. "You look really nice."

Phoebe couldn't believe her ears. The compliment thrilled her. Then she remembered Jason's shades. "How would you know?" she said.

"I can just sense these things." He shrugged.

"Are you gonna drive with those on?" she asked him, but not because she necessarily cared. In truth, she could think of worse ways to die than at the hands of Jason Barry Gold. Rachel would be really righteous about the whole thing. But Jennifer Weinfelt, Phoebe thought to herself with morbid glee, would never fully recover from the shock.

Jennifer Weinfelt would have to live with her and Jason's names linked forever in death.

"Would you like me to take them off?" he asked her.

"Okay," she answered, thinking the better of it. (Maybe Jennifer Weinfelt wasn't worth dying for, after all.)

There was traffic on Route 80. And the movie had just opened. So they had to sit in the front row. All the actors looked like fuzz, and by the end of the movie, Phoebe's neck was so sore she could hardly keep her head upright. So Jason Barry Gold, who was wearing belted blue jeans and a collarless linen shirt with balloon sleeves, massaged it in the front seat of his convertible in the parking lot after the movie. He said, "Let me," and she let him, and he squeezed her neck so hard she thought he was going to break it. And he smelled the way Roberta's déclassé brother, Uncle Sol, who worked in the glass business and didn't know Mozart from Mendelssohn, always smelled—as if he'd always just shaved and showered. Then Jason let her neck go, pressed "play" on the tape deck, moved closer, put his arm around her the way he had that night at Aimee Aaron's Sweet Sixteen. It was the Police's first album. It was that song, "Roxanne." *You don't have to wear that dress tonight.* Phoebe was wearing pants—her beige Et Vous khakis with narrowed ankles, a red long-sleeved T-shirt, and black penny loafers with original buffalo nickels fitted into each slot. "Are you still going out with Aimee Aaron?" she asked him.

"Let's just say I'm a free agent," he told her.

Then he stuck his tongue down her throat and his breath reeked of mouthwash and mustard and she nearly gagged. And she couldn't understand how you were expected to breathe and make out at the same time. Still, she had to consider it a success. It was her first real kiss.

IT WAS NOT, however, her first real date.

Her first real date had been a double date with a champion slalom skier named Chip Krupp and his older brother, Brett, who was also training for the Olympics. It was the summer after ninth grade, and Phoebe was working as a volunteer usher at one of those New England summer stock outfits populated by soap opera actors in search of legitimacy. (Leonard had a gig at a nearby chamber music camp.) During intermission one night—they were putting on that play about the invisible rabbit, *Harvey*—a guy with white eyelashes eating an oatmeal raisin cookie idled over to where she stood on the back patio and asked her if she was enjoying the show.

"Yeah," she said, even though she was bored out of her mind.

"These damn mosquitoes," said White Eyelashes, swatting at the air.

"They're really bad this summer," agreed Phoebe.

"Yeah, I got bites all over my legs."

"One summer I got bitten seven times on my left eyelid, and it swelled up like a golf ball."

"Oh, yeah?" said Chip. "That must have been really bad."

"Yeah, it was pretty bad."

"So you live around here?"

"Sort of."

"That's cool."

"I guess."

"By the way, my name is Chip."

"I'm Phoebe."

"That's a pretty name."

"Thank you."

"Do you think you'd want to get together sometime?" he asked her after the show.

"Sure," she said. Only because he'd asked. No one ever had before. It was pretty exciting.

It was even more exciting when Chip called to see if she was free that Saturday night.

She told him that she was, except she wouldn't be alone, since her friend Jody, from tennis class, was coming up for the weekend. That's when Chip offered to bring along Brett. "I'll have to check with Jody," Phoebe told him. "But it'll probably be okay."

And it was.

For the big night, Phoebe wore an old tuxedo jacket of her

father's and a pair of purple leggings with a pleated yoke. Jody wore striped jeans with zippers at the ankles and a New York Giants sweatshirt. The boys arrived in Brett's pickup. The four of them shook hands. It was the boys' idea to drive to the supermarket and buy wine coolers. The girls climbed into the back. The bumpy ride over made Phoebe's insides shake. She was glad when they got to the Grand Union.

Except then Chip backed into a wine display—he and Brett were tossing around an aerosol can of cheese food as if it were a football—and the manager came over and bawled them out. So they had to get wine coolers somewhere else. Except none of the other stores in town would accept Brett's fake I.D. So they had to settle for sodas. It was pretty embarrassing.

It was Chip's idea to drive to the top of Mount Prettyview and check out the pretty views.

The four of them sat shoulder to shoulder in the dark on a rocky ridge overlooking the valley and giggled about what had happened in the supermarket. After Jody and Brett disappeared into the bushes, Phoebe thought Chip might try to kiss her. She was relieved he didn't.

She was even more relieved when she and Jody got back to the Fines' rental A-frame, where they made hot chocolate, reviewed the events of the night, and pretended to have had more fun than they'd actually had. Or, at least, Phoebe did.

She found it so much easier making conversation with girls.

MORE RECENTLY THERE was the Carnegie Hall expedition with Eugene Lavitsky. He was the only male flutist in the history of the All-County Youth Orchestra. There were constellations of aggravated zits in the corners of his full red lips. He had the kind of hair that attracted fluff and string. He wasn't even cool in the limited context of the wind section. But he said he had two tickets to see Milstein play the Mendelssohn Violin Concerto at Carnegie Hall. And Phoebe was flattered. And she felt sorry for Eugene. And she figured Milstein wouldn't be playing much longer, since he was already close to a hundred.

Since neither of them had a car, they took New Jersey Transit to the Port Authority Bus Terminal. On the walk over to Fifty-seventh Street they talked about the ACYO. "The problem with Kwan is that he thinks he's, like, the concertmaster or something," said Phoebe.

"Yeah, well, you should try sharing a stand with Melissa Goetz," said Eugene. "She turns three pages at a time!"

"That must suck."

"It really does. But what can you do?"

Their seats were way up high and to the far left. Milstein was in profile, and the size of a pea. Most of the audience was over seventy. The old ladies were unwrapping hard candies. The old men had their eyes shut. To make the time pass faster, Phoebe and Eugene drew funny pictures of the most egregiously decrepit audience members in the margins of their programs.

After the concert they went to the Carnegie Deli, where they sat in the window and ate pastrami sandwiches. Since Eugene's father was a harpsichordist and his mother was a choirmaster, Phoebe felt comfortable talking about Leonard and Roberta in ways she didn't around Rachel. She told him about the pressure they put on her to practice; and about how guilty they made her feel when she listened to Top Forty radio. Never mind her two favorite bands, Yaz and a-ha.

"Tell me about it," said Eugene. "My father wouldn't even let me go to the Jethro Tull concert. And, you know, Ian Anderson was classically trained on the flute."

"At least your father's heard of Jethro Tull," griped Phoebe. "My father still thinks young people are doing the Charleston."

Eugene laughed so hard he drooled. Phoebe was willing to forgive that minor grotesquerie. It was when he tried to kiss her—in the back of the bus, on the way back to New Jersey— that she found Eugene Lavitsky suddenly, irreducibly creepy. It was one thing being friends with him; it was quite another imagining his zits touching her mouth. She wondered if they were infected. It didn't help that there was a scrap of pastrami stuck to his incipient beard. She was comforted by the sight of a WELCOME TO FAIR LAWN sign. That's where Eugene lived. She barely opened her mouth wide enough to say good-bye. And she ignored him at rehearsal the following Thursday night. It turned out she could be just as cruel as Jennifer Weinfelt.

It turned out being comfortable with someone and being attracted to someone were two different things.

———

JASON DROVE HER home the long way. "So whadju think of the movie?" he asked her on the back roads of Ho-Ho-Kus.

"It was okay," said Phoebe. "But you know that part where that girl does coke with all those Arab sheiks and then she freaks out? I thought that was really unrealistic."

"In your personal experience, doing coke with Arab sheiks does not produce the same type of mental freakout?"

"Come on, you know what I mean! Like, when she's quivering in the corner and they have to go rescue her. I mean, that seemed so exaggerated to me."

"Well, in my personal experience," continued Jason with a signifying glance in her direction. "That drug can definitely fuck you up *big time.*"

Phoebe didn't answer immediately. She was too busy hating herself for always talking about things she didn't know anything about.

But then, she didn't know much about anything, so what exactly was she supposed to talk about?

"Well, I guess you know more about it than me," she mumbled plaintively.

"No doubt," Jason concurred. "But hey—I'm not looking for another drug buddy."

She swallowed hard. "What are you looking for?"

He reached for the equalizer. "To tell you the truth, I'm not really looking for anything. I'm pretty much content with the way things are."

"That's cool," said Phoebe.

But it wasn't cool at all. In the days since he'd called to ask her out, she'd been harboring the fantasy that Jason Barry Gold had perceived in her a certain emotional depth—a certain affinity for the "poetry of life," as evidenced by the dog-eared copy of T. S. Eliot's *The Waste Land,* one of few concessions to "weirdness," she carried around school with her—that he'd been unable to find with a vacuous rich girl like Aimee Aaron.

BUT HE MUST have perceived something, because he called again on Sunday afternoon. "My parents are out of town," he said. "Come over and we'll rent a movie."

Phoebe couldn't believe this was happening. She couldn't understand why he liked her.

She didn't know if she could sit through another movie.

"Where'd they go?" she asked.

"Conference in the Bahamas," he answered.

"What kind of conference?"

"Plastic surgery."

"Maybe I should become a plastic surgeon."

"Probably boring."

"Probably," she said.

She didn't know if Jason was referring to the conference or the plastic surgery.

She was too embarrassed to ask.

He picked her up in his father's canary-yellow Porsche. From Whitehead, they drove to Saddle River, to a modern château with a five-car garage and several acres' worth of pine forest in back. Dr. and Dr. Gold turned out to have matching canary-yellow Porsches. Her vanity plates read FACE. His read LIFT. The Mercedes station wagon had apparently fallen out of favor. So had the Chrysler Le Baron convertible. "Check out my blow-fish," said Jason, leading Phoebe down a long hallway that led to a walk-in aquarium.

They toured the house and grounds, the indoor and outdoor pools.

Then they went up on the roof with binoculars and spied on Richard Nixon's house. "I've always thought Tricky Dick got a bum deal," volunteered Jason. "I mean, look at what he did in China."

"What did he do in China, again?" said Phoebe.

"I can't remember. But people are always talking about what he did in China. Maybe he got his feet bound or something."

"That's Japan."

"Whatever." Jason sounded annoyed.

Phoebe wished she'd let it go. Who was she to be correcting other people? Besides, maybe Jason was right; maybe foot-binding was a Chinese custom.

Maybe she didn't know shit about anything.

"What do you say we get the fuck down from here?" asked Jason, but he didn't wait for an answer.

Phoebe followed her date down a spiral staircase that led to a museum-style atrium, complete with vaulted ceiling, bubble skylight, low-lying chandelier, geometric art, and a marble side table for holding mail.

They wound up on a white leather sofa unit in a vast, sunken living room.

The carpet was white shag. The fireplace was white, too. All the lamps were made of chrome. All the tables were made of glass. Dried branches dyed the color of lapis sprouted from imitation Ming Dynasty vases. Orchids grew like grass. An original LeRoy Neiman—a colorful oil of an in-flight pole-vaulter— hung over a white piano. Another whole wall had been given over to photographs of Jason in various states of athletic dress and undress: Jason emerging from an Olympic-sized pool, Jason skiing at Vail, Jason snorkeling in the Caribbean, Jason at home plate, Jason windsurfing, Jason in full lacrosse gear holding a trophy high over his head, Jason in white gloves teeing up for a hole in one.

He'd rented *Caddyshack*.

He said he'd already seen it three times, but he wanted to see it a fourth. He put the tape in the VCR, turned off the lights, kicked off his shoes. Phoebe did the same. Then she sank her backside into the sofa, rested her sock feet on the coffee table, but it didn't last. Midway through the movie, Jason had rearranged things so she was leaning against him—against his chest and between his legs, his arms wrapped around her like a straightjacket, her legs extended before her. Then he pressed his open lips to the back of her neck. And he smelled like dandelions and beer and fresh-cut grass. Then he hit "pause" on the remote, dug his elbow into the back of the couch, and rolled the two of them over, inch by inch, limb by limb, until all 185 pounds of Jason Barry Gold rested on top of Phoebe's shapeless body, and Jason Barry Gold was breathing like an elephant.

Phoebe was hardly breathing at all.

As Jason groped the waistband of her army-surplus pants, she lay there like a cadaver, petrified that things would careen out of control—and then what? Did he think she was going to have sex with him? Would he be angry if she didn't? Had she "asked for it" by coming here while his parents were away? Would she be able to face him on Monday if she did? And what if she didn't? What if she got pregnant? She could never admit a thing like that to Roberta. If it came to that, she would have to call Emily at college. And how soon could she go home? How could she act natural when she felt anything but? How could she enjoy what was happening to her when the burden of experience—her lack of it, her need for it, her desire for it, her fear of it, her exhaustion in the face of it—was a heavier load to bear than all 185 pounds of Jason Barry Gold?

And was it okay to skip from first base to third base, or did you have to go to second base first? Phoebe pondered this last question as she steered Jason's hands down and away from the site of her shame—her nearly nippleless flat chest.

Years later, Roberta would express the belief that her younger daughter had stunted her frontal development with all the strenuous exercise she'd undertaken between the ages of eight and eighteen, when most girls recede to the couch to watch TV, snack, and talk on the phone. She postulated that Phoebe ran too many laps, played too many tiebreakers, straddled the uneven bars one too many times. Maybe she was right. Back then, however, Phoebe's flat chest struck her as just another sick joke on the part of an unjust God. Here Emily was a busty 34C, while Phoebe was flatter than a two-lane blacktop in Iowa. She felt cheated, she felt cursed. What was the point of having horrible cramps and ruining all your underwear once a month when you still looked like a nine-year-old? In the beginning of tenth grade Roberta bought Phoebe a training bra, but in that flimsy bandage Phoebe felt like an impostor. She might as well have been wearing a police badge.

She went back to her little-girl undershirts with the applique flowers on the neck.

And she let Jason Barry Gold finger her underwear instead— her white cotton panties decorated with tiny red apples. Then he lifted her underwear away, pried apart the intruding skin, and jammed a finger inside. It felt cold and vaguely constricting. It didn't feel like much else. Or maybe Phoebe was too busy wondering what Jason Barry Gold wanted from her when he could have Aimee Aaron? And did she even like Jason Barry Gold, or was she just flattered that he would pay her this kind of attention—flattered that the most popular boy in the twelfth grade would have sex with her if she were willing?

———

THE ONLY GUY Phoebe was absolutely sure she had a crush on was Coach Clay. Not that she would have admitted such a thing to Rachel or anyone else. He doubled as the trigonometry teacher. He was pushing forty-five and completely bald. His skin tone was about six shades darker than the white Mercedes sedan he heedlessly parked in one of two handicapped spaces outside the gym. He was generally regarded as a tyrannical prick.

Phoebe wanted desperately to please him.

It had been like that since the first day of practice—since he'd bounded onto Court 1 as if tennis were no laughing matter, the collar of his white polo shirt standing up, name-brand sweatbands circumscribing each of his well-defined wrists. He held his racquet by its throat. His lemon yellow shorts were so tight they made smiley faces around his crotch. He smelled of cologne and sweat and things still unnamed. He leaned his shapely backside against the white leather tape that ran along the edge of the net. "How you guys doing?" That was Coach Clay's first line—a line Phoebe and her teammates, huddled together on the service line, were too intimidated to answer—until he said it again: "I SAID HOW YOU GUYS DOING TODAY?"

Then they said, "Fine."

Then he said, "Two rules on my team. Come here to hustle, or don't come at all. Is that understood?"

They nodded.

They never heard the second rule.

"Drop your racquets," demanded the head coach of Pringle Prep's varsity tennis team. So they dropped their racquets. "I want you to touch the net, run backward to the baseline, touch it, run forward to the net, touch it, and repeat ten times. NOW GO!"

They lunged for the white leather tape. Then they started backward. Coach Clay was the size of a tennis ball by the time they hit the baseline. He seemed larger than life on Phoebe's way back to the net.

He stayed that way for the rest of the school year.

"Get your racquets, go back to the baseline, and form a line," he ordered his panting subjects upon their completion of the drill. "THERE WILL BE NO LASSITUDE TOLERATED ON THIS TEAM!"

Standing at the net, he fed them each three balls, two into the left corner and one into the right. They were to hit all of them straight down the line. Without a doubt, Phoebe had the best ground strokes of the lot. But Coach Clay wasn't one to throw gratuitous flattery around. "Racquet back earlier," he demanded her first time up.

"Deeper," he ordered on the second.

"Nice." He caved in her third time up. "I want you all to notice how—what's your name again?"

"Phoebe Fine," she told him, delirious.

". . . Miss Fine follows through."

Then he hit an extra ball to her forehand. And she hit that one perfectly as well—so perfectly that he was unable to stop himself from meeting it midair. His backhand chop volley fell to the right of her feet. She barely had time to take her racquet back—to scoop it up and off the court and then right past him. He lunged but missed. Then he turned sideways to trace its charmed trajectory—to watch her forehand drop just inside the parameters of the right pocket, before he turned back around to congratulate her on her "nice execution."

And in that magic moment it seemed to Phoebe as if Court 1—like the Garden of Eden; it was just as green—had only two players to its name: Phoebe Fine and Bradley Clay.

But it turned out there were others. "Next!" he thundered.

Whereupon Phoebe scurried out of the way of Pringle Prep's soon to be crowned first singles, Amanda Chang, and assumed her place at the back of the line. (It was always like that, Phoebe found. There were always others waiting in the wings.)

And would she ever be the star of anyone or anything?

———

WITHOUT WARNING, PHOEBE squirmed out from under Jason, expelling his finger in the process.

"What's the matter?" asked Mr. Popularity, trying to bring her back under his sway.

"I just—I can't," she said, planting her feet on the carpet.

"Can't what?" said Jason, trying to regain lost ground.

"Please!" She must have cried out a little too frantically. Now Jason sat up with a start, wiped his finger on the side of his jeans, then his mouth on the back of his arm. Then he walked over to an enormous gilded mirror, where he stood with his back to her flicking at an invisible eyelash. "Jason," she began again, suddenly as desperate to reconnect with him as she was consumed by guilt. No doubt he hated her now, hated her for leading him on. . . .

"What?" he said.

"Can I ask you a question?"

"Depends what question."

"Do you, like, like me?"

"Sure I like you. Why?"

Marginally encouraged, Phoebe readjusted her hairband, re-buttoned the top button of her army-surplus pants, took a deep breath. "Because you could be with any girl at Pringle, and I just don't understand why you're with me."

"It's not like we're going out," he said.

Then he turned back around. His face was blank. And she couldn't believe she'd ever talked to him—couldn't believe he even knew her name. "I didn't say we were going out," she said, swallowing her own words.

"So what *are* you saying?"

"I'm just saying that I don't understand why you're not fooling around with Stephanie Cohen or Jennifer Weinfelt or something."

"How do you know I'm not?"

Phoebe could see now that it was a losing battle. And she turned away, defeated, debilitated, but somehow still unprepared for the final analysis: "Look, Phoebe, I don't want to hurt your feelings or anything. But I fool around with a lot of different girls. No, I take that back. You *are* different from the other girls I fool around with." He let loose a disdainful snort. "You're more of a challenge—'cause you're a virgin."

Phoebe got her bag and called a taxi.

Jason Barry Gold didn't try to stop her at the door. He was too busy watching *Caddyshack* for the fourth time, laughing his head off at all those misfired drives.

NEEDLESS TO SAY, Rachel felt compelled to remind Phoebe that she'd seen it coming from a mile away. "I told you he was an asshole," she told Phoebe after Phoebe told her the whole story—stretched out on Rachel's sleigh bed a few afternoons later, a box of half-eaten doughnut holes resting forlornly in her lap. She was more blah than brokenhearted. She was thinking at least now she could say she'd gone to third base. She wasn't expecting to ever talk to Jason Barry Gold again.

She wasn't necessarily sorry about that, either.

But at a certain age, the past is as irrelevant as the future is unthinkable. (Only a social ignoramus, for example, would dare mention the previous weekend's parties on Monday morning.) Indeed, a week or two later, Jason waltzed up to Phoebe in the hall outside Petite's classroom as if that night in Saddle River had never happened. "Yo, Phoebster, waz up?" he said, hand raised to high-five her.

"Hey." She smiled warily as she raised her hand to meet his, thinking she had at least one thing to be happy for in life: at least she wasn't wearing her pale pink polo shirt with the mysterious bleach stain beneath the left armhole.

But he caught her hand around the wrist. "You should come by the field after tennis," he told her. "We're playing the Peddie School, and it looks to be an excellent matchup."

"Oh, really?" she said, mock-wrestling to free herself of Jason's grip.

But he still wouldn't let go—not until she'd promised him she'd be there. And she was.

She was standing on the sidelines pretending to be "psyched" when Jason scored the winning goal in the final ten seconds of the game.

After that, it was only a matter of time before the two became "really good friends." Which is to say that, much to Rachel Plotz's consternation—"he's just using you" was Rachel's personal opinion—Phoebe spent more than the occasional free period driving to and from the Pringle Bagel Emporium in Jason's BMW convertible. There was never any indication that he had the slightest interest in fooling around. In fact, he spent most of the time talking about Aimee Aaron. (They were back together, but he was still having "space issues.") And that was fine by Phoebe. She only wanted to get along, to avoid conflict, to have other people not hate her. Or so she told herself.

Maybe that was all Jason wanted, too.

Though as his graduation neared, it began to seem that his stake in his and Phoebe's friendship was larger than it had first appeared. He said he'd never met a girl he could really talk to before. He said he was really going to miss her next year. He said he'd keep in touch, and he lived up to his promise.

The following letter arrived in the Fines' mailbox the summer before he started college:

Dear Phoebe,

I'm actually writing this letter from Stratton, Vermont, where I'm attending a tennis clinic. Yeah, you're right: tennis IS a very good time. Speaking of which, when you return from summer school, I'd like to reserve a few days with you. This is so I'll have the chance to kick your petoot in tennis. And no doubles with Rachel Plotz. Nothing personal, I'll have you know, but I don't want to deal with that sob story. No fucking way.

Update. It's over with Aimee. Finished. Kaput. End of Story. I just couldn't deal anymore. But you shouldn't get the idea that I'm a cold, unforgiving louse of a person—or that I'm a legitimate heartbreaker. I'm not, I tell you, I'M NOT! But sometimes in this world, certain people take life a little too seriously for my taste, if you know what I mean. (I know you do.)

Dude—I MISS YOU!

I'll see ya soon. (I better.)

Love always,

Your best buddy,

Jason Barry Gold

a.k.a. "The Gold Standard"

Pringle Prep, Class of '87

University of Pennsylvania, Class of '91

Harvard Business School, Class of '94?

C.E.O. of the World, 2010?

P.S. Dude—what do you say the two of us get married in fifteen years if we're still single (and desperate)? Ha, ha.

Phoebe never wrote back. With his connection to Pringle severed, Jason Barry Gold no longer seemed like the expedient social investment he once had.

And she didn't appreciate the backhandedness of his marriage proposal.

Maybe, also, not writing back was Phoebe's way of getting back at him for the way he'd treated her that night in Saddle River. Somewhere along the way, she'd come to realize that neglect is the best revenge. Which is to say that the nastiest thing Jennifer Weinfelt ever uttered still couldn't begin to compete, cruelty-wise, with the silence of a phone not ringing, a letter not arriving, an overture played to an empty concert hall.

4. Spitty Clark

or *"The Gentle Date Rapist"*

CHANCES ARE THAT Phoebe Fine never would have "rushed" if Mindy Metzger hadn't persuaded her to, arguing that sororities, despite their less-than-democratic admission policies, were largely self-selecting institutions, and therefore not half as elitist as they might at first appear. And Phoebe believed her—up until the moment the Greek Committee, having summoned all the participating freshmen to the second-floor TV lounge of Alumni Hall, distributed its so-called invitations. As it happened, Mindy Metzger received her invitation first. And Mindy Metzger, upon discovering the most-revered of all Greek letters, Pi Pi Pi, printed in purple on a parchment card inside, had the decency not to scream for joy—not until Phoebe had received her invitation. But then when Phoebe did receive hers, Mindy didn't even ask if she could see it. She just leaned over Phoebe's shoulder and read it for herself. Then she whispered, "Ohmigod, I am *so* sorry," because inscribed on Phoebe's parchment card were the wrong letters, the letters of Phoebe's second-choice sorority—not Tri Pi (as it was known) but a less prestigious house called Delta Nu Sigma (or "Delta Sig," for short).

"Oh, well," said Phoebe, as if it didn't matter one way or the other.

But of course it did. She didn't want to be a Delta Sig. She wanted to be a Tri Pi. Never mind Mindy Metzger. Tri Pi was the sorority that girls seemingly too sophisticated for sororities wound up pledging. Which is to say, girls raised primarily in cities as opposed to suburbs; girls so exceedingly comfortable with their own self-construction that the act of getting dressed always appeared to have been accomplished in five minutes— even if the truth was more like two hours; girls who, even if they were Jewish, weren't "too Jewish"; girls such as Phoebe aspired to be and occasionally even convinced herself that she was.

Delta Nu Sigma was a different matter.

Blessed with the same approximate demographic as Pringle Prep, it wore its Jewishness with the same sense of duty-bound pride with which its sisters sported Larry Levine lamb's-wool overcoats in winter. And it was for this very reason that its letters added up to an infinitely less prestigious affiliation even within the Jewish sorority girl population, for whom real popularity depended on approval not just from other Jewish sorority girls, but from sorority girls in general, and specifically from a handful of semilegendary pretty girls—none of them Jewish, and all of them blessed with long blond hair, skinny asses, and solid American last names—whose friendship the rest of the Greek community coveted as small Caribbean protectorates looked to the United States for cash infusions.

But what choice did Phoebe have now? Just then, a tiny girl with rubber bracelets appeared at her side, threw a lei around her neck, and introduced herself as "your Rho Chi, Cheri!" before she tried to lead Phoebe away.

"I'll just be one second," Phoebe assured her.

Then she tapped Mindy on the shoulder to say good-bye.

"Oh, bye!" Phoebe's about-to-be-ex-best-friend turned around to fake an empathetic smile before she turned back around to continue freaking out with the other Tri Pi initiates, her mouth moving in exaggerated shapes, her eyes popping out of her skull like one of those rubber-man squeeze toys. That's when Phoebe knew Mindy had left her behind. And she hated her for it—suddenly hated everything about Mindy Metzger, from her self-deprecating humor to her desperate need to curry favor with the "right people." Maybe that described Phoebe's personality, too. Only now Phoebe was the "wrong people." Now she could stop trying to fit in. If only she had the nerve. But she didn't. She wasn't like Emily. She wasn't interested in overthrowing the patriarchy. She wasn't even sure what the patriarchy was.

She was just trying to find a place to call home so she wouldn't be so sick for the *real one.*

So she climbed into the backseat of Cheri's wine-colored Saab 900 Turbo along with a half dozen other twittering Delta Sig pledges. And she made gratuitous noises of pleasure and victory on the ride back to the House, a crumbling white elephant with a wraparound porch located in the shadow of the agriculture quad. And she was first down the stairs that led to a basement meeting room with fake wood paneling and a flocculent red carpet where a mob of her future sisters stood around hugging, kissing, shrieking, and drinking fruit punch. (She hugged, kissed, shrieked, and drank fruit punch with the best of them.) And she waited patiently while speeches were made and more shrieking achieved. Then Cheri drove a few of them over to Delta Sig's "brother house," Chi Zeta Epsilon, where Phoebe was fed brewskies at a rate of one every fifteen minutes and lifted onto the beefy shoulders of a crew team Adonis named Doug for a celebratory whirl around the pungent upper floors.

THE NEXT MORNING, the Greek Committee distributed the following memo:

Hoover University does not tolerate hazing. The following activities are therefore prohibited in your pledge programs:

1) Denying pledges a proper night's sleep (six hours per night minimum), edible meals (three per day), and access to showers;

2) Preventing pledges from attending class or otherwise interfering with pledges' academic calendars;

3) Forcing pledges to consume any amount of alcohol;

4) Requiring pledges to don uncomfortable or degrading clothing such as dunce caps, girdles, lederhosen, or undergarments appropriate to the opposite sex;

5) Coercing pledges to eat or drink any foreign or unusual substances such as saltwater, raw eggs, or raw meat (raw fish may be employed in pledge week festivities only when prepared by certified dining establishments such as the Samurai Sushi House in Spruce Creek);

6) Throwing at, pouring on, or otherwise applying eggs, paint, honey, hot wax, or gasoline to pledges' bodies;

7) Making pledges participate in any activity in which the pledge is the object of amusement or ridicule (this does not include such traditional Greek activities as putting on skits, playing charades, or serenading sororities or fraternities);

8) Kidnappings or road trips that compromise the health or safety of pledges (e.g., no hanging pledges out car windows);

9) Subjecting pledges to cruel and unusual psychological conditions of any kind (e.g., forcing pledges to spend the night standing up listening to loud music);

10) Compelling pledges to participate in any activity that is illegal, indecent, or contrary to the pledge's moral or religious beliefs and/or the rules and regulations of Hoover University, such as they are.

————————

THE NEXT NIGHT, Spitty Clark came over to the freshman dorm to "tuck Phoebe in." That's what it was called. From what Phoebe had heard, however, it tended to involve something considerably less innocent than letting an upperclassman pull the sheets tight around your neck and shoulders. But Cheri said not to worry. Cheri said Spitty Clark was a "total cutie." Cheri said Phoebe had to make sure to be back in her dorm room by midnight at the very latest. It was ten past when Phoebe heard a knock, went to the door, and flung it open onto a heavyset guy, not particularly tall but not particularly short, either.

His thick legs angled out beneath his torso like the supports of a sawhorse. His blue eyes were as narrow as the change slots on a public phone. His cheeks were pink. His curly blond hair poked through a bright red baseball cap. His meaty shoulders carried the weight of an overstuffed knapsack. He was wearing a pair of tan khaki pants and a faded T-shirt that read WHAT-EVER THE LETTER, GREEKS DO IT BETTER on the front and KAPPA OMEGA, SAN JUAN NIGHT '87 on the back. "Ho, ho, ho," he chortled like some kind of Santa Claus on spring break.

"You must be Spitty," said Phoebe.

"And you must be Pledge Fine," said Spitty.

"That's me."

"Well, it's a pleasure to make your blood-alcohol content rise," he told her.

Then he burst into the cinder-block cell she shared with Karen Kong, out as usual though no doubt somewhere nearby, wasted out of her mind with her legs spread. That's how Phoebe's roommate spent most nights—like a zoo animal recently released from captivity. During Freshman Orientation Week she'd gotten so drunk she hadn't known she'd lost her virginity to the pothead on the sixth floor, who felt so bad about the whole thing—he hadn't been able to tell if she was passed out or not—that he'd asked Phoebe to tell Karen he hadn't meant any harm. Which Phoebe did, the next afternoon. She told Karen, "Danny came down to talk to me. He's worried that you didn't know you had sex with him last night."

"I did?" said Karen. "Are you sure? Wait a second, how do you know? And, by the way, is it any of your fucking business?"

Since then, the two girls had drifted apart.

Maybe because Phoebe was still (humiliatingly enough) a virgin, and Karen wasn't.

Spitty scanned the room. Phoebe watched his eyes linger on Karen's votive candles, then shift abruptly to her buns calendar.

February's featured attraction was the Lycra-clad backside of a competitive biker. "It's my roommate's calendar," Phoebe told him, so he wouldn't get the wrong impression.

"Interesting roommate," said Spitty before he flumped himself on her desk chair and rolled it over to where she now sat—on the edge of her bed, her knees tucked inside her pink-and-green floral-patterned flannel nightgown. Then he reached into his sack, pulled out a bottle of Jack Daniel's and two plastic cups. "Thirsty?" he asked while he poured.

But it was less a question than a command. So Phoebe said nothing, took a tiny taste, and gagged before she grumbled, "I hate tequila."

"It's whiskey," he scoffed.

"Well, then I hate whiskey."

Spitty lifted his chin authoritatively. "Pledge Fine, I think Mr. Daniel deserves a little more of your respect than you're showing him at present. Otherwise stated, I'm trying to suggest that you reconsider your position on the Jimster."

Phoebe wrinkled her nose in confusion. "Who's the Jimster?" She thought he might have been referring to one of his fraternity brothers.

It turned out he wasn't. He held up the bottle. "The Jimster, my good friend, goes by many distinguished names—among them, the Jackster, Jackie D., Jackie Boy, Jack of All Trades, Mr. D., J.D., Mr. Daniel, and finally, Jack Daniel's. In short, the Jimster is what our English majors here at Hoover University might refer to as an epaulet."

"I think you mean epithet," she said. "Epaulets are like shoulder pads."

"Whatever." He shrugged off the mistake. "I'm not an English major."

"What major are you?"

"I'm in the Hospitality School."

That's when it dawned on Phoebe that Spitty Clark looked a little old to still be an undergraduate. "Senior?" she inquired.

"I'm actually still a junior," he conceded. "I took some time off last year. You know. Bummed around. Made some new friends. Saw some old ones."

"Where'd you go?"

"Where didn't I go! Jamaica, Daytona, New Orleans, the Keys . . ."

"Where the sun shines."

He seemed to like that. "Yeah—where the sun shines."

"I hate the sun," Phoebe told him.

"Hate the sun?" Spitty uttered her blasphemy out loud, as if he had to hear it again to believe those three words had ever been put together in the same sentence. "How can you hate the sun? 'Specially in this wrist-slitter of a town. I mean, it's a god-damn rain forest out here! Not that our annual 'Fun-dra in the Tundra' celebration isn't among the premier keg spectaculars of the Greater Allegheny Region. But enough about the weather. PLEDGE FINE, I ORDER YOU TO IMBIBE!"

But Pledge Fine didn't want to imbibe. She didn't want to be ordered around, either. She wanted to quit college and get a job at the airport driving one of those little green shuttle buses back and forth between the arrivals terminal and the car-rental lot until she couldn't remember her own name. Couldn't remember a time she'd ever thought she was going somewhere in life—except back to the car-rental lot. Or the arrivals terminal. That's how much she hated college. Even more than she'd hated high school. All the bathrooms smelled like puke. All the white guys spoke like they were black. All the black guys spoke like they were white. All anyone cared about was getting wasted. It was so loud in the dorm she couldn't sleep at night. All the food tasted the same. None of her professors seemed to know she was alive.

She couldn't even figure out what to major in.

She'd begun with international relations—had attended eight-hundred-person lecture courses in Greek Revival amphitheaters, read articles by Henry Kissinger, and mastered terminology like "realpolitik," "domino theory," and "détente." That was before she enrolled in "El Siglo De Oro 215." It was the theme of trickery in *Don Juan Tenorio* that turned her on to Spanish literature. But then she read a book by Emile Durkheim about suicide being a constant in every culture. It seemed to validate her own inability to enjoy "keggers." She promptly switched to intellectual history, then found she couldn't muster up any interest in Voltaire's coffee addiction—kept reading the first two sentences of Stendhal's *The Red and the Black* over and over again: *The little town of Verrières must be one of the prettiest in the Franche-Comté. Its white houses with their steep, red tile roofs spread across a hillside, the folds of which are outlined by clumps of thrifty chestnut trees.* What the hell were thrifty chestnut trees? And where the hell was the little town of Verrières? All of a sudden, Phoebe felt like crying.

Spitty must have seen it in her trembling lower lip. "Hey, look," he said in a newly compassionate tone of voice. "If you don't wanna drink, you don't have to. I mean, it doesn't matter to me. I'm just doing a favor for your Big Sister, Cheri. And besides, it's supposed to be fun."

"Yeah, well, it's not," Phoebe started to tell him, and found she couldn't stop. And then she kept going. "Sororities are really stupid. I wish I'd never rushed. I wasn't even going to do it. I thought it was really elitist. My friend Mindy talked me into it. We wanted to be roommates next year, but we got divided up. We were both going to be in Tri Pi. Only, I di-di-di-didn't get in, and sh-sh-she did."

Now she was swallowing her breath, holding back tears. She hated herself for caring. But she did care. In fact, she was devastated. Getting into Tri Pi had promised to correct all the social slights she'd suffered during her earlier adolescence. She still couldn't believe she'd been turned down. During rush, the Tri Pi sisters had complimented her on her L. L. Bean moccasins, dropped not-so-subtle references to "next year," laughed at her stories about Karen Kong, fed her juice and cookies, asked her where she'd gone to high school, and sounded impressed when they heard it was Pringle Prep. Had it been obvious that her navy-blue blazer was one of Leonard's castoffs, and that her moccasins—purchased at the L. L. Bean company store in Freeport, Maine, in a wicker basket marked "Singles"—were actually two different sizes, one a $7\frac{1}{2}$, and the other an $8\frac{1}{2}$? Had someone talked to someone else who'd gone to Pringle Prep—someone who'd heard from Jennifer Weinfelt that Phoebe used to wear weird rings?

"Sheeeezzzzz." Spitty Clark shook his head at the injustice of it. "That really sucks. BUT HEY, LOOK ON THE BRIGHT SIDE. YOU WOUND UP IN AN EXCELLENT HOUSE WITH A TRULY EXCELLENT BUNCH OF GIRLS. I MEAN TRULY EXCELLENT. And I'm not lying. Very excellent bunch, the Delta Sigs. Hey—you okay?"

Phoebe had begun to shake uncontrollably. Poor Spitty. He didn't know what to do with her. He placed a steadying hand on her upper arm. "Come on, Stein," he said. "It can't be that bad."

But it was even worse than that. "It's Fine," she moaned.

"So you're gonna be okay?"

"No, I said, 'Fine.' That's my last name—as in Phoebe Fine."

"Oh, sorry."

That's when she started to bawl.

"You want me to get a nurse or something?" he asked her when it seemed like she might never stop.

"This isn't a hospital!" Phoebe wailed. "This is a freshman dorm!"

Now Spitty was at a loss. He muttered something to himself. He said, "Come on, Pledge Stein," a few more times. Then he punched her in the jaw—not exceptionally hard but not all that lightly, either.

"Ow!" she shrieked. But the blow had done the trick. In the process of nursing her imaginary bruise, Phoebe had stopped crying and started craving something bitter—just like herself. "Where's the Jimster?" she sniffled.

Spitty's eyes lit up. His relief was palpable. "So now you like the stuff?" he said, passing the bottle. "I can't keep up with you."

"I changed my mind, okay?" She faked a little grin of her own, threw back her head, chugged, gasped.

"Yeah, well, keep changing your mind." He cheered her new-found respect for an institution he considered sacred. " 'CAUSE WE GOT A PARTY TO THROW AROUND HERE, AND YOU'D BE WELL ADVISED NOT TO FORGET IT."

Then he pulled a noisemaking instrument out of his sack and blew it in Phoebe's ear.

"Stop," she whinged.

But he kept blowing and laughing. And she kept wincing and whinging. She tried to sound like she was having fun. She wanted to believe these were the best years of her life. That's what Roberta had told her—that the friends you make in college are the friends you make for life. Except the corners of Phoebe's mouth kept giving her away, kept turning down on their own miserable accord. (She couldn't imagine there being a "rest of her life.") So she drank more and faster. She thought the Jimster would cure whatever was wrong with her—whatever made her feel like she was in a hall of mirrors, watching herself, watching herself go through the motions of having a riotous good time in her newly won capacity as Pledge Fine. She must have drunk half the bottle.

She wound up puking all over Spitty Clark and his SAN JUAN NIGHT '87 T-shirt.

But if he was mad, he didn't let on. He escorted her to the unisex bathroom at the end of the hall. And he encouraged her to "make love to the porcelain god" at the appropriate moments. And he splashed cold water on her forehead when the worst of it was over. Then he kindly positioned a garbage pail at the side of her bed, parallel to her pillow, before he pulled the sheets up and under her neck, tucked them in and around her legs and ankles, turned out the lights, and directed her to "send my best to the sandman," before he slammed the door shut, sometime around 3:00 A.M.

Pledge Week had only just begun.

———

ON TUESDAY NIGHT Phoebe was blindfolded and led off to the football fraternity, Phi Upsilon Chi, where she was ordered to lick whipped cream off the hairy chest of a tight end named Carl and eat M&M's out of the half-inch-deep navel of a half-back named Kurt. On Wednesday she had to steal one pair of boxer shorts from every fraternity on campus; there were thirteen. On Thursday she had to strip naked before her future sisters, whereupon the secretary of Delta Sig, no string bean herself, Magic-Markered the word *FAT* on those areas of her body deemed in need of toning up. (To Phoebe's absolute horror, both her thighs and buttocks were singled out for improvement.) On Friday she had to complete a so-called scavenger hunt, a further series of humiliations that concluded with her allowing a Phi Chi pledge named Bart to draw one uninterrupted line down the length of her body. And on Saturday she was presented with a fourteen-carat-gold-plated pledge pin fashioned in the shape of a harp, made to learn the mawkish lyrics to a ditty about the eternal beauty of Lake Hoover, hugged and kissed and congratulated by one hundred of her "new best friends," and declared a sister of the Hoover University chapter of Delta Nu Sigma.

Summer arrived shortly thereafter.

For most of June and some of July Phoebe played in the pit orchestra of an operetta festival on Lake Michigan. After twelve straight nights of *The Mikado* she was ready to smash her violin into a million pieces—preferably over the heads of the "three little maids."

The monotony was briefly interrupted by a piece of fan mail that arrived in her name.

Dear Phoebe Fine,

Friday night—I wore glasses, you played the violin. I thought you were stunning, but let my opportunity to speak with you slip by. Can you give me another? I'd like to take you out for dinner. Your pick, my plastic. What do you say?

Will all due regards,
Glenn Pecker

Phoebe didn't respond. Flattered though she was, she couldn't imagine anything more desperate than responding to a stalker's advances.

A few nights into *The Merry Widow*, she submitted her resignation and returned to Whitehead, where she sat around doing absolutely nothing (just like her old classmates from Riverbank) for a month and a half. Leonard and Roberta were away on their once-a-decade European vacation, visiting great composers' summer houses and the like. Emily was traveling through Latin America under the spurious auspices of some so-called Spanish-language institute. (There was reason to believe she was aiding and abetting Marxist insurgents.) So Phoebe had the house to herself—a whole house in which to contemplate the absurdity of her childhood. It was the tennis trophies that depressed her the most—their buxom tin figurines, racquets reaching, straining, striving, but for what? What was the point of tennis? Of any of it? And what possible pleasure could she ever have derived from hitting a fuzzy ball over a low-lying net? She felt like a ghost in her own life—tiptoeing through old haunts as if they were no longer hers to haunt. As if history had moved forward and left her behind—at ten past ten. Like a stopped clock in a store window. Stranded in the past present. Wondering if she had a future. Doubting that she did.

That was also the summer Phoebe lost eighteen pounds— not by accident. She worked diligently to achieve hipbones that sharp. She understood the jealousy emaciation aroused in other women. She wanted desperately to be on the receiving end of it. Maybe she was still a virgin. Maybe she hadn't gotten into Tri Pi. But she could get into a size 4. And how many Tri Pis could say that? Certainly not Mindy Metzger, who, last time Phoebe had seen her—for a reunion coffee, during which time

Mindy had suggested that Phoebe transfer out of Hoover rather than roam the campus in the company of her rejecters—appeared to be ballooning into a size 10.

———————

UNABLE TO SUSTAIN the belief that driving an airport shuttle van would be any less depressing than sharing a bunk bed with a manic depressive named Meredith Bookbinder on the top floor of a second-tier sorority house, Phoebe returned to Hoover the following September with the twin goals of reading all the Great Books that had ever been written and cultivating an elusive mystique in keeping with her newly anemic body. She was still embarrassed about what happened on the second night of Pledge Week—not just the throwing up part, but the tear-stained confessions, as well. And she certainly wasn't expecting to hear from Spitty Clark again. But when the phone rang—six weeks into the first semester of her sophomore year—she knew exactly who it was.

Maybe because he asked to speak with Phoebe Stein.

This time, she didn't bother correcting him. It seemed hopeless—just like everything else in her life. So she said, "Yeah?"

"Hey, it's Spitty. Remember me? Party 'til you puke?" He laughed raucously.

"I remember," said Phoebe, deciding whether to be insulted.

He redeemed himself with: "Did you like my postcard?"

"What postcard?" she asked him.

"I was in Maui," he told her. "Summer internship at the Ramada. You didn't get it?"

"No."

"I sent it to Delta Sig."

"I didn't move in here until last month."

"You'd think someone would have saved it for you."

"Not likely."

"Well, it was a good postcard. I can't remember the exact wording, but it went something like this. Dear Stein. You'd probably hate it here. It's really sunny. Love Spitty. P.S. You still depressed? Speaking of which, you still depressed or what?"

"Maybe," she told him.

"Well, I got the perfect cure. Me and a few of the guys are gonna be out tailgating Saturday morning."

"What's tailgating?"

"YOU'VE NEVER BEEN TO A TAILGATE?"

"Not consciously."

"What about unconsciously?"

"I wouldn't know, would I?"

"Well, it's about time you found out."

"I don't know your friends."

"You know me. Come on, Stein—you can't study all the time!"

"I never study. I hate studying."

"Then what do you do, Stein? I never see you at keggers, never see you at games, never see you anywhere. Where you been hiding anyway?"

"I'm not hiding!" Phoebe harrumphed.

But Spitty was right. She barely left Delta Sig—except when she had to go to class. Then she'd put on her Walkman (Peter Gabriel, the *So* album, especially the single "Don't Give Up," or Edward Elgar's *Enigma Variations,* in particular the variation with the emoting cellos) so if she ran into anyone from her past—anyone like Mindy Metzger—she wouldn't be forced to chat. But that was only half the story. She wanted attention, too—wanted people to notice how she was wasting away. More than a few of the Delta Sigs already had. They nicknamed her "Ethiopia Arms." They mocked her diet of rice cakes and raisins.

It wasn't the kind of noticing she'd hoped for.

In fact, with the possible exception of Meredith Bookbinder, who put all her energy into despising herself—she was still mourning the fetus she'd aborted on the first day of school— Phoebe's so-called sisters seemed to have started hating her even before she'd given them a reason to. She'd walk into the TV room where they'd be sitting Indian-style on the industrial carpeting watching *L.A. Law*, stainless steel mixing bowls of airblown popcorn lodged between their fleshy thighs, and they wouldn't even acknowledge her presence—not even during the commercial breaks. Maybe they'd found out Delta Sig wasn't her first choice. Maybe they were jealous of her thighs. Maybe it was her attitude they resented. In truth, the last time Phoebe had demonstrated any kind of sororal spirit was the first night of Pledge Week. She never baked for bake sales. She arrived late to chapter meetings. She hadn't even participated in the Fall Walkathon—couldn't even remember what it was they were walking for. Muscular dystrophy? Cystic fibrosis? Multiple sclerosis? Homeless cats? She'd spent the day hiding in the Law Library.

To think she was an outcast even among Jews!

But, then, what made her Jewish anyway? She'd probably been to temple about as many times as Spitty Clark had. And who was to say she didn't have more in common with the Roman Catholics or the ancient Etruscans? And didn't it count for something that she had the same birthday (December 25) as Jesus Christ? Maybe she was the goddamn Second Coming. Ha, ha. It was all pretty funny when you started to think about it—

about how upset she still was about not getting into Tri Pi, and here she was about to save humanity from itself. . . .

Spitty must have heard her sniveling on the other end of the phone. "That's it," he said, taking matters into his own hands. "I'm picking you up at noon!"

"But—"

"No buts allowed. Only tits. And asses." He howled with laughter.

TAILGATING TURNED OUT to consist of leaning your back against someone's Jeep in the parking lot behind the football stadium, drinking warm beer out of paper cups, and eating cold fried chicken legs laid out in picnic baskets on fold-up tables folded down in the immediate vicinity of the Jeep. Phoebe didn't know it was a dressy affair. She wore jeans and a T-shirt. Spitty was wearing pressed pants, white bucks, and two button-down shirts on top of each other—the outer one being a bizarre Brooks Brothers issue consisting of three separate striped fabrics, one pale blue and white, another pale yellow and white, and a third pale pink and white. His buddies were dressed in a similarly colorful manner. "Hey, what's up?" they nodded in Phoebe's general direction.

They didn't say much else. Then, again, Spitty didn't exactly encourage Phoebe to mingle. He stood next to her the entire time chattering on about how "Mardi Gras beats spring break's ass." Phoebe found the whole thing pretty boring. And she wasn't dressed warmly enough. And she was tired of standing, and wary of being mistaken for someone with school spirit. So right before the game started, she informed Spitty that she wanted to leave. "You wanna go home *now*?" he cried out in disbelief. "Right before the kickoff?"

"I hate sports," she told him.

"You hate sports. You hate the sun. What *do* you like, Stein?"

"Sylvia Plath's okay." (She was reading *The Bell Jar* for her new favorite class, Women Writers on the Edge 202.)

Spitty squinted through the morning mist. "Isn't she in Tri Pi?"

Phoebe rolled her eyes condescendingly. "She's a dead poet."

"How'd she die?"

"Stuck her head in the oven."

"That's no way to go. The last thing the woman probably saw was crumbs. That or grease."

"Still better than blood."

"Now, that's a matter of opinion," contended Spitty. "If it was me, I'd probably just jump off the clock tower. Maybe it's a cliché, but that's a serious last view we're talking about."

"It's also a long way down."

"Exactly. If I'm gonna go, I'm gonna go with a *bang*." Spitty pushed his right fist into his left palm. It was an impressive performance. Neither one said anything for a few seconds.

It was Phoebe who broke the silence: "I just don't think I could ever get up the nerve to jump off that thing. If it was me, I'd probably just overdose on tranquilizers or something wimpy like that."

"Oh yeah?" said Spitty, glancing sideways. He elbowed her in the rib cage. "Hey, Stein, you're not gonna do anything stupid now, are you?"

"I wouldn't rule out the possibility," Phoebe was only too happy to tell him—to imagine him worrying that she would. Even though she knew she wouldn't—couldn't bear the thought of not being alive to find out which of her mortal enemies came to her funeral. "But probably not."

" 'Cause I'd miss you," he said, his blue eyes twinkling like little stars, a goofy smile plastered across his puffy face. That's when it first occurred to Phoebe that Spitty Clark might have a crush on her.

She wasn't, at that point, interested.

For one thing, he wasn't her type. Since arriving at Hoover, Phoebe had decided that her ideal paramour was a foreign-born graduate student in architectural preservation who spoke several languages and wore his black canvas book bag slung sideways over his French-cuff shirts. For another, she preferred the idea of being admired from afar to the idea of being worshiped in the flesh. Freshman year she'd fooled around with a bunch of different guys. She always managed to get creeped out. If it wasn't the pimples on their backs, it was the wrinkled monstrosity between their legs. She'd take off all her clothes, then announce she "really had to go." For her efforts, she was called a ball breaker, a tease. She didn't bother defending herself. She wasn't horny like other girls seemed to be. She wasn't hungry either.

Or maybe she'd simply convinced herself that she wasn't hungry or horny because to have appetites was to be disappointed if and when they weren't fulfilled, and she'd suffered enough disappointment in one year on account of her rejection by Tri Pi.

But she could also be a flirt. "Would you really miss me?" she asked Spitty.

"Yeah, I would," he told her. "Come on, I'll drive you home."

"You'll miss the kickoff!"

But he was already gone—three paces ahead of her, walking briskly in the direction of his car, a chocolate-brown Crown Victoria he'd purchased at a police auction for a couple of hundred bucks. He unlocked the passenger door. Then he glanced behind him—at his buddies, now safely out of earshot. "Between you and me," he said. "I don't give a fuck about football."

"But—"

"But nothing." He climbed into the driver's seat. "I'm with you. Sports are a fuckin' bore."

Phoebe couldn't believe what she was hearing. Spitty Clark was just as much of a phony as she imagined herself to be! The revelation made him infinitely more likable, and certainly more viable as a boyfriend—assuming she'd been interested in having one. "I'm gonna tell everyone," she teased him.

"You better not," he said, index finger outstretched. "Or I'll break your neck."

"Go ahead," she said. "Saves me the trouble of breaking it myself."

"You're really something, Stein."

Now she was giggling. She hadn't giggled in months.

"So you wanna go out to dinner Friday night?" Spitty had a big smile on his face when he asked her that.

"I only eat breakfast and lunch," Phoebe told him.

"Well, you can just sit there and watch me chow down."

"Sounds fun."

"You better believe it," he said, turning the key in the ignition. "Myself, I've always been a big fan of food—eating it, cooking it, shopping for it, you name it."

"You like to food-shop?"

"Are you kidding? I fuckin' love it! All those brightly lit aisles. Everything in its place. Songs you can sing to on the stereo. You should try it sometime. Hitch a ride down to the Stop & Shop at three in the morning one night. You'll see what I mean. It's not even about buying stuff. I mean, I like the cereal aisle the best, and I don't even eat cereal." He shifted the car into reverse.

"What do you eat for breakfast?"

"Who, me?" he said, accelerating out of his space.

"Yeah, you."

"Oh, I'm not really a breakfast person."

"Me neither."

"You're not really an *anything* person, Stein," he said, chuckling as he straightened out the car.

Phoebe spent the rest of the weekend trying to convince herself that Spitty was only kidding around—and that she had interests and passions and predilections just like everyone else.

Except she couldn't think of that many.

———

FRIDAY NIGHT, JUST as planned, Spitty drove Phoebe to Billy Bob's Sirloin Saloon, a family-style restaurant across the street from the Amoco station. Oil paintings of the Wild West hung from stained-wood walls. Red-and-white checked cloths, laminated in clear plastic, covered all the tabletops. The place was filled with children—screaming, whining children cutting up their dinners into strange shapes. Phoebe and Spitty sat down at a table for two. She ordered a black coffee and a house salad with dressing on the side. He ordered a sixteen-ounce strip steak and a rum and Coke from the bar. Already significantly over twenty-one, he was only too happy to show some I.D. "So who you taking to your formal?" he wanted to know after the waiter disappeared.

"No one," Phoebe answered with a shrug. In actuality, she hadn't given the matter of Delta Sig's fall formal much thought.

Spitty couldn't understand that. His eyebrows disappeared under his hat hair. "You're not going to your own formal?" he exclaimed. "How can you not go to your own formal?"

"Very easily," she told him. "Formals are lame. And besides, it's not like I have a boyfriend."

"I'm a boy and I'm your friend."

"Are you trying to invite yourself to my formal?"

"I'm not ashamed to ask for what I want."

"Why do you like parties so much?"

"Why do you think so much?"

"What's wrong with thinking?"

"There's nothing wrong with thinking," Spitty began. "So long as you don't think too much. See, that's your problem, Stein. You dwell. It's not healthy. Sometimes you just gotta let things go, stop feeling sorry for yourself, stop trying to figure out the why and the how and the what does it mean. Because none of it means shit. You know why? Because we all die in the end anyway. Some people stick their heads in the oven. Other people just keel over in the middle of dinner. But no one gets out alive. And that's the sorry truth. And that's why you gotta enjoy yourself now. Because that's all you basically get in life—a few superior kegs, a few worthwhile hangovers, a few nights when the other crap fades into the background and it's just you and the moment and the moment is righteous." He leaned forward. "Then, Stein, you can die in peace. And if not in peace then at least knowing that you spent a few minutes of your life not just sitting around being bummed out about how and why and when it was all gonna end."

Their food arrived. Spitty's steak was so big it was hanging off the sides of his plate. Phoebe took a sip of her coffee and wondered if her date was right. Maybe thinking too much was the root of all her problems. Maybe she would start having fun the day she stopped trying to figure out why she never had any. "Okay, fine," she sighed with mainly performed exasperation. "Do you want to go to my formal or what?"

"I'd be honored," replied Spitty, not quite suppressing a cheeky grin.

———————

PHOEBE MAY HAVE thought formals were fundamentally lame. But she was also vain enough to spend most of the week preceding hers shopping for the right outfit. There were three expeditions before she found the black velvet scoop neck cocktail dress she ended up purchasing at a store called Contemporary Model in the pedestrian mall downtown. There were two preliminary trips to Shoetique before she settled on a pair of black patent-leather high-heeled Mary Janes. So vanished the meager savings she'd accumulated from her work-study job shelving books in the Architecture and Urban Renewal Library. And on the day of the big event, concerned that she would fall victim to the six o'clock crunch—the haggling over electrical outlets, hot water, and mirror space that preceded even the slowest of Saturday nights at Delta Nu Sigma—she started beautifying in the middle of the afternoon.

Randi Rugoff must have had the same idea. Phoebe was working over her hair with a round brush, a blow-dryer, and a diffuser in the second floor bathroom when Delta Sig's resident aerobics queen minced in, a magenta towel wrapped around her squat, bronzed form. "Getting ready early?" she shouted to be heard over the electric storm.

"Yeah," Phoebe shouted back.

"Remind me," continued Randi, her eyes combing the length of Phoebe's malnourished body with undisguised aggression. "Who's your date again?"

Phoebe turned off the dryer. She didn't feel like yelling Spitty's name out loud. "I'm taking Spitty Clark."

Randi smiled lewdly. "You're taking the rapist?"

"The rapist?"

"You didn't know Spitty Clark raped a Delta Sig?"

"What?"

"Why'd you think Kappa O got kicked off campus?"

"I don't know—I never thought about it."

"Well, have fun," said Randi with a gleeful smirk.

Then she disappeared around the corner, in the direction of the showers, leaving Phoebe alone with her pounding, incredulous heart.

———

OFFICIOUS THOUGH SHE tended to be, Delta Nu Sigma's president, Samantha Schwartz, seemed like a good person to talk to in a crisis. Two years could make a difference that way. She was the only senior living in the house; the rest of them were sophomores. Phoebe threw on a pair of sweatpants and proceeded downstairs to Samantha's presidential suite. Samantha came to the door with a chemistry textbook pressed flat against her ski-jump tits. It was pretty obvious Phoebe was interrupting her. "Do you think I could talk to you for a minute?" she asked her in a tiny voice.

"Come in," clucked Samantha with a constipated smile.

It was the neatest room Phoebe had ever been in. There was a Post-it note hanging over Samantha's desk that read, "Buy odor eaters." Samantha sat down on the edge of her bed. It had one of those frilly elasticized skirts fitted around the bottom of the mattress. Phoebe sank into a neon green beanbag chair and took a deep breath. "I'm supposed to be taking Spitty Clark to the formal tonight," she began, "and someone just told me he's a rapist."

Now Samantha sighed the sigh of a much older person than herself—a person who'd lived through enough personal highs and lows to have at her disposal the means to look beyond what others, younger and less experienced than herself, tended to obsess over. Then she reached for an emery board. She filed as she spoke. "It was before your time. There was a Delta Sig named Maggie Green who was going out with one of Spitty's brothers in Kappa O, a guy named Dummy Stevens who graduated last year. There was a party one Saturday night at the old Kappa O house down on Thurgood. It was four o'clock in the morning. Maggie had crashed for the night in Dummy's bed. Dummy was downstairs finishing the keg. According to Maggie, Spitty climbed into Dummy's bed and had sex with her, pretending to be Dummy, and she was too drunk to know the difference until it was too late. How late? She stayed for bacon and eggs the next morning. She didn't file a complaint until the afternoon. According to Maggie, she was still in shock. According to everyone else, she decided to call it rape only after Dummy found out she'd cheated on him. There was a hearing several months after the fact. Spitty said it was consensual. Maggie said it wasn't. There were no witnesses. Spitty walked away with ten hours of community service, but Kappa O was kicked off campus until the year 2010. For that, Spitty's brothers will probably never forgive him. As for Maggie, she ended up transferring out of Hoover—in protest, I guess. She was one of those people who always had to make a statement. To be perfectly frank about it, none of us here at Delta Sig were particularly sorry to see her go. On the other hand, the loss of Kappa O was a blow to the entire Greek community. Is there anything else I can help you with?"

"No, that's fine—I mean, I feel a lot better now," Phoebe assured her.

It was a lie. She felt like collapsing.

Her date was due to arrive in forty-five minutes.

———

THAT WAS THE first night Phoebe ever wore red lipstick. She borrowed Meredith Bookbinder's, and she wore it like a gash across her face. And she powdered her face white so her lips looked even redder. Her life had taken a dramatic turn. It seemed only fitting that her makeup should match. But what about her lines? It wasn't that Phoebe didn't believe Samantha Schwartz's version of events. But she would have to tell Spitty what she'd heard. She didn't see any way around that; she was a terrible actress. Only, how could she tell him without offending him?

Or was Phoebe the one who ought to have been offended?

Maybe Maggie Green had stayed for brunch the next morning. But if nothing bad had happened, then why had the administration thrown Kappa Omega off campus? And what was Spitty doing in his friend Dummy's bed in the first place? And was Maggie the "other crap" Spitty was talking about that night in Billy Bob's Sirloin Saloon? Was Spitty's obsession with the inescapable future just a scrim for the far more pressing horror of a past he couldn't figure out how to shirk?

"Oh, Phoebe," she heard one of her sisters trill from downstairs. "There's someone here to see you!"

She descended the stairs at half-speed.

She found Spitty in Delta Sig's communal kitchen slumped against the refrigerator. "Hi there, kiddo," he said, straightening his back at the sight of her.

"Hey," said Phoebe, smiling dimly as she leaned in to kiss his cheek. He smelled like Jack Daniel's. He looked her up and down. It was pretty clear he was attracted to her.

She wasn't, at that point, sure how she felt about that.

"You look really nice," he said.

"So do you," she lied. In fact, his tuxedo was badly in need of a press. His red cummerbund appeared to be on backward. His polka-dot clip-on bow tie was pointing northeast. He had a bad case of razor burn.

"You ready to party or what?" he asked her on the way to his car.

"Yeah," she squeaked.

It must not have been a very convincing "yeah." Spitty stopped in his tracks, cocked his head. "You sure now?"

"I'm sure," she told him.

"So how come your teeth are chattering?"

Phoebe bit her lower lip, looked the other way—toward the road, the agriculture quad, the Allegheny Mountains. A light drizzle had begun to fall. She thought fleetingly of her hair. She had spent a good half hour giving it volume. "There's something I have to ask you," she said, thinking to herself that now was as good a time as any to broach the subject. Then her eyes filled with tears. For some reason, they were always doing that around Spitty Clark.

Maybe because he was the only one who seemed to notice when they did.

"Oh, yeah?" he said. "Like what?"

"I didn't know why Kappa O was kicked off campus," she said, her voice trembling. "Not until tonight. Someone told me the whole story."

Now Spitty was the one who looked away. He flexed his lips, blew through his teeth, scratched the back of his neck, whispered, "Oh boy," before he turned back around to face her—to face up to his past. "Look, Phoebe. I don't know what you heard, but she wasn't, I mean, she wasn't complaining or anything. I mean, the thing is that she stayed for breakfast the next morning. I mean, the two of us were sitting there eating—"

"I thought you weren't a breakfast person."

"I'm not! I mean . . ." He cleared his throat. "Not generally or anything. But that weekend, I don't know, I guess I woke up hungry or something—and I guess so did she. I mean, she was sitting there eating waffles—"

"I thought it was bacon and eggs."

"So you really did hear the whole story." Spitty laughed wearily, his head waggling this way and that. "Okay, look— maybe it was bacon and eggs. I can't remember what she was eating, but she was definitely sitting there eating like nothing was wrong."

"But you had sex with her?"

"I mean, yeah, we were both pretty drunk."

"She was your friend's girlfriend?"

"She and Dummy—they were already over."

"But she wanted to?"

Now Spitty lowered his eyes, began to scrape the heel of his dress shoe backward against the tar. It was obvious he hated talking about this—hated it more than anything else in his life. He didn't say anything for a few seconds. Then he said, "Do yourself a favor in life, Stein. Don't believe everything you hear."

And in that moment, Phoebe wanted so badly to believe in him—to believe everything she heard Spitty tell her and nothing anyone else did—that there was nothing he could have said short of "I raped her" that would have prevented her from doing so.

Or maybe it was less that she needed to believe in Spitty than that she was suddenly, however perversely, attracted to him— thinking she could be with him the way Maggie Green had been with him, albeit in a more overtly consensual way. Because the thought of Spitty forcing himself on her made sex seem possible where so often it seemed impossible—impossible because it seemed to require her participation, and she didn't know if she was up to that. "Just lying there" sounded a whole lot easier. And wasn't that just what Maggie Green had been doing when Spitty climbed on top of her—Spitty, who had spontaneously mutated into the faceless, pouncing, ravenous thug of countless adolescent dreams Phoebe hadn't known how to think about when she woke up, her forehead damp, her throat parched, her legs akimbo, her sheets asunder? He'd catch her in alleys, he'd drag her into forests, he'd be waiting under the eave. It was never her fault. It was always his.

He always took her from behind.

He disappeared shortly thereafter, never to be heard from again.

Indeed, it was the aftermath of sex that Phoebe found the most daunting to contemplate. How were you expected to act normal with someone you'd been rolling around naked with the previous night? Plenty of the guys she knew—and plenty of the girls, as well—seemed to turn their sexual personae on and off at will, engaging in intimate acts one minute and idle chatter the next. By comparison, even if she'd only just kissed someone, Phoebe found conversation strained the next day. True, she'd developed a relatively garrulous friendship with Jason Barry Gold after the fact of their fooling around. But the more experience she garnered—the more eyeballs she saw lolling about their sockets like so many loose marbles—the more it seemed to her that the state of arousal and the state of amity were two distinct principalities with no diplomatic ties.

"Do you want to go to the party now?" she asked Spitty,

suddenly sick with herself for having brought the whole rape business up—and only minutes before her fall formal was due to begin! Now she was the guilty party, trying to make it up to him, worrying he hated her, grabbing on to his arm.

But he yanked it out of her grip. "Whatever," he said, on his way around the car.

He opened his own door, then Phoebe's. Then he turned on the motor. Then he changed his mind, turned it off, took her by the shoulders, pushed her flat against the gray velour seat cushions, and kissed her like a flame igniting gasoline. At least, that's how it felt to Phoebe. Then he straightened up, turned the engine back on, and proceeded to back out of the Delta Sig parking lot at a terrifying speed. "Slow down!" she shrieked.

"Sorry," he mumbled.

They didn't speak again until they got to the formal. Phoebe couldn't think what to say.

Neither, apparently, could Spitty.

DELTA NU SIGMA had rented a banquet hall on the outskirts of Hoover. There was an abandoned strip mine on one side, a home-furnishings warehouse on the other. Before it was a banquet hall, it had been a bowling alley. All in all, it was a pretty desolate spot. Spitty skidded into a parking space next to the Dumpster. Their shoulders brushing in solidarity, he and Phoebe made their way inside.

Purple streamers had been stretched from one end of a low corkboard ceiling to the other. Brass candelabras outfitted with frosted glass bulbs adorned pale peach walls. In the center of every table was a rainbow glass vase containing a single stem rose. All the band members were wearing skinny black ties decorated with keyboards. All the waiters were wearing cropped purple blazers. Phoebe and Spitty had been assigned to a table with a bunch of junior and senior guys, the majority of whom were Kappa Omegas, and their mostly younger Delta Sig dates, including Randi Rugoff, dressed in a pale mauve tube dress with a white squiggle pattern that lent her hipless body the appearance of Thuringian bratwurst. She'd come with Spitty's good buddy, Scooter, famous for having fallen asleep in the middle of his physics final. "Captain Clark!" he said, offering Spitty a manly hug.

The rest of the Kappa Omega brothers crowded around Phoebe's date in a similar fashion. If they were still sore at him for allowing their beloved fraternity to be kicked off campus, Phoebe thought to herself, they had a funny way of showing it.

"Spitty my man," declared Scummy.

"How goes it in Shangri-La?" inquired Fatty.

"Cruise Director Clark," intoned Dukes. "You ready to party or what?"

"You boys know where the bar is?" Spitty asked them. Four index fingers pointed across the room at the same time. "Excellent navigational skills," Spitty complimented his brothers. Then he turned back to Phoebe. "Hey, Stein, would you care for a cocktail?"

"I'll have a glass of red wine," she told him.

It was only after Spitty had left for the bar that Randi Rugoff got in Phoebe's face and asked her if she was "having fun yet," a malevolent grin cracking the seams of her pancake makeup.

"What's it to you?" jeered Phoebe. She couldn't believe she'd said that. She felt strangely elated by her own bitchiness.

Randi Rugoff must have felt differently. Her lips puckered like a fish, she looked like she was about to spit.

Spitty reappeared at Phoebe's side before Randi had the

chance to do so. He had a glass of wine and three gin-and-tonics woven between his thumbs and fingers. He was steadying them all with his chin. He finished off two of the g & t's even before the Oysters Rockefeller had been brought out. They were followed by Greek salad, baked chicken with raspberry sauce, rice with fresh almonds and mushrooms, and asparagus topped with cheese sauce. Phoebe ate the rice. Spitty gobbled down everything on his plate. There wasn't much conversation through dinner. Fatty and Dukes spent most of it trying to balance spoons on their noses. Dukes's date, Debbie Rosenzweig, snuck off to the ladies' room to do a line of cocaine and never came back. Randi appeared not to be speaking to Phoebe or anyone else at the table.

No sooner had the dinner plates been cleared than Spitty went back to the bar for another round. He returned just in time for the fruit flambé, and devoured his in ten seconds flat. Then he tapped his knife against an empty highball glass and bellowed, "Quiet!" over and over again until the room fell silent—even the band stopped playing halfway through a jazzy version of Hall and Oates's "Maneater." That's when Spitty stood up, steadied himself against the back of his chair, and began to weave undetectably—except maybe to Phoebe. "I'd just like to take this opportunity to say a few words on behalf of Delta Nu Sigma," he began. "A truly excellent house." There were cheers, whoops. "Comprised of a truly excellent bunch of girls." More cheers, more whoops. "I'd also like to thank my date here. Thank you for inviting me, Phoebe. Thank you for believing in me . . . Phoebe." He raised his glass. Phoebe reached for hers. She wanted to crawl under the table. She saw her private obsessions writ as large as billboards. She saw the lie she called her life about to be unmasked. Heat rose up the back of her neck. She remembered why she liked to hide. "I fuckin' love you, man," Spitty completed the thought before he fell back down in his seat.

The crowd shrieked with vicarious titillation. Someone in back yelled, "Spitty, you fuckin' whore!"

Other than her father, no member of the opposite sex had ever told Phoebe he loved her before. She didn't know if she wanted to kill Spitty Clark or marry him right then and there. "You're drunk," she whispered.

"I'm not drunk," he roared back, to the stomach-clutching amusement of his fraternity brothers. "Come on."

He grabbed Phoebe by the elbow and dragged her onto the dance floor. The band had picked up where they'd left off, and Spitty spun her round and round and round some more. Until the floor became the ceiling and the left wall became the right wall. And the "other crap" faded into the background. And it was just Phoebe and the moment and the moment was "righteous"—just like Spitty said it would be the day she stopped thinking, started living. The dance floor started to fill. One song replaced the next. Suddenly, it was two in the morning. She and Spitty were slow-dancing to Eric Clapton's "Wonderful Tonight." "You want to get out of here?" he slobbered in her ear.

"Where would we go?" she asked him.

"What about my house?"

Phoebe may still have been a virgin, but she wasn't dumb. She knew what she was getting herself into. She couldn't wait to get it over with. "Let me just get my coat," she said.

"My moat?"

Phoebe rolled her eyes. "I'll meet you out front in five minutes."

———

TRUTH BE TOLD: Spitty was in no shape to drive them home. But he swore he was up to it. And Phoebe had had a bit to drink herself. And in that particular moment, she couldn't imagine Spitty letting anything bad happen to her, for the very reason that Spitty himself seemed no realer to her just then than his blatant disregard for the dictates of the white line that separated the northbound traffic from the southbound appeared to pose a threat to her personal welfare. Indeed, Phoebe watched the world slalom in and out of focus through the side window of his Crown Victoria that night as if watching a movie version of her own life. As if she could rewind at will. As if the ending had already been decided. As if she were a spectator as opposed to the lead.

As if she had nothing to worry about.

By some miracle, they came to a screeching stop in front of the Big Boy sub shop.

Since being kicked off campus, Kappa Omega had set up shop in a sprawling apartment on the second floor of the Big Boy building. "Sorry about the mess," Spitty apologized even before they'd gotten out of the car.

There was a stereo in one corner of the living room, an old plaid couch in another. Empty pizza boxes and beer cans littered every available surface. "I don't care about the mess," Phoebe mumbled in as polite a tone as she could muster. "But it kind of smells in here."

"It's better in my bedroom," he said, leading her down a short hall into a shallow room with a narrow window overlooking an air shaft.

There was a Murphy's Law poster tacked to one wall, a PORSCHE—THERE IS NO SUBSTITUTE poster falling off another. A textbook entitled *Advanced Beverage Management* lay open on the floor next to a knee-high orange glass bong. Blue lightbulbs lent the room an aquatic feel. Phoebe was busy perusing Spitty's CD collection (the Doobie Brothers, the Allman Brothers, George Winston, Bob Marley, Ziggy Marley, the Steve Miller Band, Steely Dan, Boston, Kansas, Meatloaf, the Grateful Dead, the London Symphony Orchestra's *Hooked on Classics*) when he came up behind her, put his arms around her waist, buried his nose in her neck. Then he turned her around so she was facing him, her head tucked under his chin, her flimsy body pressed against his brawny one. "Phoebe," he began in a hoarse whisper. "I swear I didn't do anything to that girl that that girl didn't want me to do to her."

"It doesn't matter," Phoebe whispered back, because it didn't just then, except insofar as she wanted Spitty to do the same thing to her.

He seemed to be reading her mind. He lowered her onto his futon. So she was just lying there, eyes closed, waiting for him to rape her. Well, maybe not *rape* her. But do what he had to do.

How was Spitty to know? He said, "Is this okay?" with every new body part he uncovered.

"Yeah, it's fine," she told him even while she maintained the hope that he'd rip off her clothes, ask her if it was okay later.

But Spitty Clark wasn't that—or, really, any other—kind of date rapist. He kissed Phoebe on the eyes, the ears, the arms and legs, the stomach, and even between her legs. Then he took off his shoes, his socks, his cummerbund, his pants, his jacket, his shirt, his baseball hat, his boxer shorts festooned with tiny Santa Claus busts. Then he fell on top of her, wedged a knee between her legs—before he careened off to the side.

"Spitty?" she cried.

She sat up to the sound of retching. She found her formal date leaned over the side of the futon, a pool of vomit on the floor near his chin, a long string of semidigested cheese sauce swaying like a pendulum from his lower lip. It smelled so bad she had to cup her hand over her nose. But she wasn't mad. She wanted to do for Spitty Clark what Spitty Clark had done for her on the second night of Pledge Week. Thinking the least she could do was help him clean up the mess, she stumbled to the bathroom in search of a towel. She pulled a tattered blue one off the back of the door.

She found "The Weekend Lay List—Week of October 20" hanging behind it.

That's what it said at the top. Down the left side were the names of all the old Kappa Omega brothers: Spitty, Kenny, Balls, Brian C., Brian B., Fatty, Dukes, Scummy, and Scooter. There were check marks next to Kenny, Balls, Fatty, and Scooter. There were girls—"Suzy C"; "Can't Remember the Dingbat's Name"; "Jenn L."; "Randi Rugoff"—in parentheses next to each check mark. Spitty's line was still empty. But for how much longer? Never mind the fact that he hadn't actually "gotten laid." Phoebe imagined her formal date entering a nice fat check mark of his own tomorrow morning, and thinking that he was only having fun. And that there wasn't any harm in that.

There was to Phoebe.

She threw the towel down in disgust and stormed back into Spitty's bedroom. It wasn't clear he even heard her come in. He was bent over his own lap. He was staring at his dinner. She got dressed as quickly as she could.

She didn't see the point in saying good-bye.

———

A COLD, WET fog hung from the night sky like laundry on the line, occluding vision, portending danger. But Phoebe was past the point of being afraid. Her heels in her left hand, impervious to the pain prompted by the collision of stocking feet and poured cement, she started up the street in a jog—past the bagel place and the lesbian bakery, the Burger King and the bookstore, the Greek diner and the dry cleaner—DISCOUNTS ON FORMAL WEAR!—then onto campus, down the center of the humanities quad, past the Modern Languages building, the Music Library, and the Harold C. Pritchard Hathaway Hall for the Study of European Civilization and Culture, then left, in the direction of the biochemistry complex, the tennis courts, and the clock tower Spitty said he'd probably jump off if it came to that, her heart beating wildly, her head strangely clear. She could see now what she didn't want to be in life: a name on someone else's list. And it seemed like a first step—a step closer to figuring out what she *did* want to be.

But she wasn't finished with Spitty.

She found a pay phone on the corner of Thurgood and Raintree, diagonally across the street from the old Kappa Omega mansion, which had been refashioned into a graduate research center for the study of Native American arts and crafts.

"Hello?" Spitty picked up on the sixth ring.

But now Phoebe couldn't catch her breath, couldn't get the words out either. She felt the tears coming on again.

"Hello?" he croaked again.

"Sorry you didn't get laid this weekend," she finally blurted into the receiver.

"Phoebe?!"

"What?"

"You sound like you just ran the Boston Marathon. Where the hell are you?"

"Why does it matter?"

"Look, I'm sorry I got sick—"

"I don't care about you throwing up. I saw your stupid checklist in your stupid bathroom."

Spitty groaned before he spoke. "Aw, jeeez," he said. Then, "Listen, Phoebe, it's my fuckin' moron roommates. I swear I never touched that thing."

"So how come your name's up there?" she asked him.

"Phoebe, you gotta believe me!" he pleaded.

"I'm sick of believing you. All I do is believe you."

"So don't believe me. What do I fucking care?"

"But I thought you did," said Phoebe, her voice shaking just a little. "That's the thing. I thought you cared about me."

"WELL, I DON'T ANYMORE," Spitty exploded. "THERE'S NO FUCKIN' POINT. I NEVER SHOULDA COME BACK TO THIS FUCKIN' TOWN. I FUCKIN' HATE EVERYONE HERE! I SHOULDA FUCKIN' STAYED IN MAUI!"

She'd never heard Spitty so angry. She hadn't known he had it in him. She was overcome with emotion, though for once in borrowed form. "So go back there," she whimpered. "No one's stopping you."

"Maybe I will," grumbled Spitty, suddenly conciliatory, almost childlike. "Listen, I'm sorry I yelled. I just—I'm just not feeling so good. Maybe we should talk in the morning. Hey—I had a good time tonight. I mean, until the end. So I'll talk to you tomorrow?"

"Sure," Phoebe told him before she hung up.

But it was an empty promise. Everything had changed. She might have gotten past the Weekend Lay List. It was Spitty's display of fury that frightened her more than the list and the Maggie Green story put together. She wanted him to be the sunshine to her clouds. She couldn't handle the idea that he had weather patterns of his own, and that he contained within himself the makings of a downpour and possibly even a monsoon. She ran the rest of the way back—past the horses and the chickens, the stables and the coop, until she was standing on the back steps of Delta Nu Sigma, sweating and freezing and hyperventilating all at the same time, turning the key in the lock that separated her from home, as close to a home as she could find back then, back there, back when she was eighteen and three quarters.

SHE FOUND MEREDITH Bookbinder sleeping peacefully on the top bunk. Meredith hadn't even gone to the formal. She was the smart one, Phoebe thought to herself as she climbed into the bottom bunk. She fell fast asleep soon afterward, and dreamt she was skiing down the side of a steep mountain with Scummy, Dummy, Scooter, Dukes, and all the rest of the Kappa Omegas trailing close behind—with the exception of Spitty Clark. He was nowhere in sight. He was out of the picture—a piece of the past she had no trouble shirking. That's what Phoebe told herself the next afternoon when she heard the phone ring. She had a feeling it was Spitty calling to make amends, and it was. She had Meredith tell him she was out. He called a few more times after that.

Then he gave up.

She didn't know he'd skipped town until she ran into Scooter, a few weeks later, waiting in line in the bursar's office. (There were some student-loan forms that she needed to sign.) "Hey, I remember you!" he declared. "Weren't you Spitty's date at the Delta Sig formal?"

"That was me," she confirmed his suspicion.

"Did you hear about Spitty?"

"Hear what?"

"He's gone AWOL from Hoover."

"Oh, yeah?"

"Yeah, he's down in São Paulo, assistant managing beverage services at the Marriott. Spitty really liked you, I think. Stein. That's you, right?"

"It's Fine. That's my last name, as in Phoebe Fine."

"Fine—that was it. Well, anyway, before he left, Spitty told me that if I ever ran into you, I should tell you—uh, shit, what was it? Oh, now I remember! He said to tell you he was sorry he was such a bad date. Yeah, that was it. He felt really bad about that night, I think. Oh, another thing. He was gonna miss you a lot. He said that, too. He said you were a really fun girl."

"That was nice of him to say." Phoebe smiled placidly, as if her interest in the whole matter was mild at best. In truth, she wasn't entirely sure how she felt about the prospect of never seeing Spitty Clark again.

Maybe in the back of her mind she'd been holding out the possibility that the two of them would eventually make up and get married and live in a little shack by the sea in walking distance of a well-lit supermarket.

5. Jack Geezo

OR *"Roberta's Advice"*

Bebe!

*Apropos of our phone call this afternoon, I have some further thoughts
to contribute! It seems to me that you will not be attracted to the kind
of boys who frequent fraternities, where you cannot be totally yourself,
since so much of yourself is of a different, brighter, less drinking-
oriented, more sensitive, artistic nature, though obviously a part of you
is drawn to the glitter and gaiety of frat houses! The contrary sides of
you fight for your attention, and when you go to those frat parties you
find yourself acting like the others and of course that kind of boy
thinks you are that way! Then, as a relationship develops, both of you
discover that you are acting and not being yourself! The answer seems
to me quite obvious—that you may have all the friends you like
within the Greek System, but to find a boyfriend you need someone
who is not in the least drawn to that lifestyle and would never have
joined a fraternity! I think you have to give some thought to how to
get out of your rut—perhaps by joining a campus organization,
getting to know boys in your classes, or through nonsorority friends, on
blind dates or whatever, and stop trying to be what you are not—a*

typical sorority girl! The answer is in your own mixed messages and mixed priorities! Just because you are very chic and pretty does not mean that bright, less social boys are not your style! Many of them like bright attractive girls, but you probably seem so sorority-ish, even though you aren't, that they're scared off! Keep in mind that to the average kid, not wealthy, beautiful, or particularly social, the Greek system reeks of wealth, privilege, mindlessness, etc! That is what you are IN, and how your image is construed, whether you like it or not! It seems to me that the nonfrat boys probably think (untruly) that you are beyond their reach! So the answer can only be for you to make yourself less formidable, socially speaking, by hanging out with people who are not necessarily the cutest crew team types around! And when you do meet some shy people, help them out of their shells, if possible! When I met Daddy he was VERY shy! (So by the way have many of Emily's boyfriends been, and especially Jack Geezo who, as you may remember, had a minor speech impediment!) I think the kind of boy you ultimately will like will be a person you can feel comfortable intellectually and emotionally with, and who is not necessarily that sophisticated or drunk all the time! The fact is that you SEEM very sophisticated, but your lack of experience doesn't fit that image! Therefore, you need to meet a boy who shares your worldly-wise brightness without having been and done everything! You are a deep person, Phoebe—very insightful and very smart! But the average Joe College is terrified of dealing with that! He will be flattered to have you as a friend but not as a girlfriend! Therefore, look for someone BRIGHT rather than cute, SENSITIVE rather than swaggering, GENTLE rather than athletic, and you may find that the cuteness and the swagger come later! That's my little sermon for today! I think you have a very similar problem to what I had at Conservatory, where I was constantly being told to be less quick with my tongue and mind and to act sillier (à la your present-day sorority girls) so that the opposite sex would like me! After a while I began meeting older boys who did not feel so challenged by a smart, attractive violist like myself, but young men sometimes found it daunting! According to Emily, you are a real handful, probably the best-looking and smartest girl out there (I'm quoting Emily), and that is NOT guaranteed to put a shy or sensitive guy into a chase after you! (He might give up before he started!) The opposite is also true—that the guys with a lot of self-assurance but without the other qualities you like are the only ones who are not frightened off! Ultimately, you will probably find an older guy more to your liking because you can be more yourself! I hope you don't think this letter amiss! It is what I was thinking after I hung up! So I suggest that you think about the campus literary magazine, the political clubs, and even (God forbid) some of the shy oboists!

> *Love and kisses!*
> *Good luck with all your papers!*
> *Call soon!*
> *Love always!*
> *Mom!*

P.S. I had a similar conversation with Emily during her sophomore year when she was very discouraged at not finding anyone she liked who liked her at the same time, the only difference being that she had loads more confidence than you, and didn't find the boys her own age sophisticated enough, which is why I suggested she date graduate students!

6. Humphrey Fung

OR *"The Anarchist Feminist"*

NOT TWO WEEKS after she and Phoebe met—in Introduction to Biological Sciences 101, a prerequisite for graduation—Holly Flake drove her baby blue Dodge Dart over to Delta Nu Sigma in the middle of the night and helped load up the back with Phoebe's possessions (plastic milk crate after plastic milk crate of shoes and books, posters and towels, hangers and diuretics). Then she squired the lot of it back to her off-campus apartment, one half of a two-family house next to the Leafy Bean Café. Conveniently for Phoebe, Holly's roommate had moved out the month before. It didn't surprise Phoebe. As a general rule, Holly didn't get along with most other girls. She was too jealous (even though she was positively gorgeous). She was too possessive (even though she wasn't the slightest bit materialistic). Her mother had been a model. Her father was a well-regarded neurosurgeon. She had a learning-disabled, identical-twin sister inexplicably named Jim. She was exactly what Phoebe needed. Just as Phoebe was exactly what Holly needed. Indeed, the two girls compensated for each other's failures—Holly's failure at friendship, Phoebe's failure of experience. Not that Phoebe ever actually got up the nerve to admit to her new best friend that she was still a virgin. But there was never any doubt about which of the two was the bigger slut. In fact, Holly Flake was a self-identified slut.

Never mind the used condom she kept in the bottom of her book bag—"in memoriam for all the lost nights." Holly Flake was convinced she'd invented a new sexual position—she called it "tantric doggie" and was only too happy to demonstrate on her stuffed pig, Wilbur, for anyone willing to watch. And when she was bored, which was all the time—daily life was never quite exciting enough for the Lake Charles, Louisiana–bred redhead—she'd make lists of her thirty-two ex-lays. (A math major, she had a natural affinity for numbers.) Sometimes she'd rank them by the size of their personal fortunes, sometimes by the size of what God gave them. Sometimes she'd alphabetize them by last name, sometimes by first. If she couldn't remember either—if, for example, she'd screwed them in the parking lot at a Grateful Dead show—she'd give them code names like Deadhead 1, Deadhead 2, and Deadhead 3. Whatever list she made, her differential equations T.A., Anton Abrams, wound up at the top of it. She said he was the heir to a big-name paper-towel fortune. She said he was worth ten million at least. She said it was as wide as a poster tube and as long as a ruler. She said she broke his heart, but Phoebe read through the lines that it was really just the opposite.

At least Holly had a list.

Phoebe wanted a list of her own, and she wanted Humphrey Fung at the top of it—she knew it the moment she saw him, across the porch at Gerald Stevens's Fuck Spring party, leaning back against the balustrade, a cigarette fastened between his lips. He was tall enough and slenderly built. And he was dressed in a tartan kilt fastened with a pewter pin, tube socks pulled up to the knee, and a black T-shirt that read, I DESPISE EVERY-THING YOU STAND FOR. And yet, even despite that outfit, he was easily the most beautiful boy at the party, and possibly in all of Hoover University. He had tawny skin and sculpted cheeks, permanently flared nostrils and impossibly long lashes. But he wasn't just beautiful, he was tough. He looked like nothing could touch him. That's probably why Phoebe wanted to. She was thinking some of Humphrey's audacity might rub off on her. She was desperate to lose her virginity. And she was testing the limits of her newly discovered powers of attraction. In the four-and-a-half months since Spitty had left town, she'd somehow managed to reinvent herself as the darling of the Eurotrash crowd, most of whom spoke scant English, which meant that all she had to do was stand there looking sulky and half starved. Except it got a little boring impersonating an actress in a Godard film.

Especially since she didn't speak French.

She dragged her new best friend into the corner for a second opinion.

"What do I think of Humphrey Fung?" squealed Holly Flake. "Aside from the fact that he's got the dumbest name on the planet, he's wearing a skirt, and he's a humorless poser?" She dragged Phoebe across the porch, stuck her head in Humphrey Fung's magnificent face. "I think he's perfect. Oh, hi, Humphrey! Do you know my new best friend?"

He looked up slowly from behind a mantle of silky black bangs. "What happened to the old one?"

"What happened to your pants?"

"What happened to your face?"

"Well, I'll let you two get to know each other. . . . Oh, Gerald!"

"Yo, Flake," said a doughy-faced giant in a trench coat and matching bowler. "Have you ever seen *The Lawnmower Man*? I swear the fractal patterns in that movie are designed to induce a narcotic high."

"Gerald, you'd probably get high watching *Bambi*." Holly disappeared after the party host.

A few semiexcruciating moments of silence passed between Humphrey and Phoebe before she thought to ask him, "So how do you know Holly?"

"She donated powder for one of our demos," he told her.

"Demolitions?"

"Demonstrations."

Phoebe breathed an inaudible sigh of relief. It was one thing to deactivate from Delta Sigma; it was quite another to fall in love with a terrorist. "So what was the powder for?" she asked him.

"A few of us dressed up as ashen corpses," he answered. "You know, black capes, Kabuki makeup. It was a right-to-smoke thing."

"I'm sorry I missed it."

"Yeah, it was a pretty serious scene out there. We were up against a pretty substantial counterrally—a bunch of vegan assholes complaining about secondhand smoke. They can eat my secondhand shit." He took a final, furious drag on his cigarette before tossing the butt into the adjacent bushes. "Anyway, my slogan really put them to shame."

"What slogan was that?"

"Keep your hands off our self-destructive impulses," he said, exhaling in Phoebe's face.

"It's a good slogan," she said, waving away the mushroom cloud.

"Yeah, it's almost a shame I gave up on anarchy. I was a genius at the signage."

"So why'd you give it up?"

"I'm too rule-oriented a person." He shrugged before withdrawing a hard pack of Parliaments from a zippered compartment down by the waist of his black leather motorcycle jacket.

"Would you mind if I had one of those?" Phoebe asked him.

Humphrey extended the pack in her direction. "I wouldn't have guessed you smoked."

"Only at parties," she lied.

In fact, she'd only smoked six cigarettes in her entire lifetime, and the first two had been just the week before—at a local bowling alley where she and Holly Flake and two filthy-rich foreign students—one from Venezuela, one from Monaco—had passed a leisurely evening gawking at the tattooed forearms of Vietnam vets. Everyone else had been smoking Gauloises blondes. Phoebe hadn't been able to think of a good reason why she wasn't too. That's how she started. And now that she had, she wasn't interested in stopping. She liked the way smoking made her feel—as light and jumpy and vaguely nauseated as a buoy tossing in the high seas.

And she wanted to impress her own self-destructive impulses upon Humphrey Fung, who struck a match with one hand and pressed the resulting flame to the tip of her cigarette. But it didn't take, it wouldn't take. The flame crept closer and closer to his finger. She didn't understand what she was doing wrong. She regretted ever asking for a light. His scowl on temporary hold, Humphrey looked like he was about to crack up. "You have to inhale on it," he told her finally before he ripped the thing out of her mouth, stuck it in his own, lit it, inhaled on it, handed it back to her.

"Thank you," she whispered in defeat.

But she had it backward. She learned that soon after—that her incompetence made Humphrey feel useful. Just as her naïveté fueled his fantasies of having seen and done it all before the age of fifteen, albeit in a backwater college town in central Pennsylvania. A native of Hoover, Humphrey Fung was the son of Jack Fung, distinguished professor of parasitology, and Greta Fung, a yoga instructor at a nearby New Age retreat. He barely tolerated either parent. He found their back-to-nature values abhorrent. His idea of "alternative" had less to do with smiley faces than it did with alienated frowns.

Beyond the facial expressions, however, he had yet to identify a subculture that met the needs of his own anomie. He'd tried them all—Goth, punk, surf-punk, skinhead, sk8 (skateboarding), D&D (Dungeons and Dragons), SCA (Society for Creative Anachronism), and just plain "A," as in Anarchy, his latest incarnation. None of them ever satisfied. All of them felt like costumes—costumes he slipped in and out of with the ease of a beauty-pageant contestant. Maybe his perpetual identity crisis had something to do with his being half Chinese and half Swedish. Maybe his beauty was to blame. Whatever the case, life had been too easy for Humphrey Fung.

In most ways, it still was.

"What do you say we get the fuck out of here?" he asked Phoebe with an insouciant lift of his cleft chin.

But it was less a proposition than a declaration. He was already zipping his jacket and walking down the front steps. He must have known the answer would be yes, and it was. She threw her arms around Humphrey's narrow waist while he revved the motor of his vintage Norton. The accordion pleats of his kilt billowed out on either side of him as they pulled away from the curb.

It wasn't clear if he was wearing anything underneath.

———

"SO HOW COME I've never seen you before?" he wanted to know over a cheeseburger deluxe at the twenty-four-hour greasy spoon.

Phoebe took a deep breath. With his black Doc Marten tie-ups with yellow overstitching, Humphrey was bound to be a harsh critic of the Greek system. (College was easy that way. You could tell everything about a person's politics based on his or her footwear.) But then, she couldn't lie about everything— or could she? "I was in jail—I mean a sorority," she said, trying to make the best of the truth.

It must not have been good enough. Humphrey made a face as if he'd just tasted something rotten. "You were in a sorority?"

"Until three weeks ago," she confessed. "That's when Holly kidnapped me. Now I'm living at her place."

"Well, congratulations on getting out alive. Aside from rendering heterosexuality compulsory, sororities promote a nefarious kind of intragender rivalry—all under the deceptively magnanimous guise of fraternity and philanthropy."

For a moment or two Phoebe was speechless. She'd never heard a guy speak this way. It was so uncool it was cool. It was Spitty Clark's worst nightmare. In light of her recent deactivation from Delta Nu Sigma, it only made Humphrey Fung that much more attractive to her. (The crowning blow had been Homecoming Weekend, during which time Phoebe had found herself upside down in a miniskirt being carried out of Chi Zeta Phi by an irate bouncer who'd taken umbrage at her lack of a hand stamp.)

"It sounds like you know a lot about sororities," she offered.

"I recently became a women's studies major," he told her by way of explanation.

"A women's studies major? You're joking."

"I only joke when it's funny, and there's nothing funny about gender discrimination."

"Maybe not. But I didn't know you were even allowed to be a male women's studies major."

Humphrey shrugged. "It hasn't been easy. A lot of the women in the program don't take me seriously. They think my politics are a front. They think I'm a total poser just 'cause I'm good-looking."

Phoebe didn't let on that Holly had used the exact word. "I don't dismiss you as a poser," she sought to reassure her prospective devirginizer. "I mean, I wouldn't even know who you were posing as."

"Well, thanks," he said.

"People don't take me seriously either," she added. "Then again, I'm not sure if I want people to take me seriously. I mean, to be perfectly honest, I don't take myself very seriously."

"You should," said Humphrey.

"Why?"

"Otherwise, people will step all over you. And besides, for too many years women have been treated as entertainment, objects, decoration, wall hangings, toys, tools, playthings . . ."

Humphrey's talk excited her. She liked the idea of aligning herself with a male feminist—if only because she couldn't imagine going to a tailgate with one. But the idea of being a plaything aroused her even more. She wasn't ready to grow up and become a player, never mind a woman. She was just getting used to being an object of desire—just starting to enjoy it.

And wasn't that what she was to Humphrey Fung—an object of his desire? It certainly seemed like it on the way out of the greasy spoon. It was on the sidewalk out front that he first asked to kiss her. She didn't say yes, she didn't say no. She thought her closed eyes and parted lips would speak for themselves.

But Humphrey wasn't the kind of guy who felt entitled to presume. He said, "For too many years men have read women's silences in a self-interested way. So I'll ask you again. Do you want me to kiss you before I drive you home? Or do you want me simply to drive you home?"

"You can kiss me," she told him.

At which point he felt entitled to lean her up against a telephone pole and press his lips into her lips, his hands gripping her butt, his kilt brushing her thigh. But the moment was short-lived, thanks to a carful of drunken Tau Upsilon Gamma brothers who throttled by to the tune of "Dyke it up!" and "Leave it to Beaver!" They must have thought Humphrey was a girl. Phoebe quailed in embarrassment. She was the only one. "Sexist homophobes!" Humphrey screamed back at them at the top of his lungs. Then he turned back to Phoebe with a self-satisfied grin on his face—he seemed to thrive on conflict—and asked her, "Would you like me to drive you home? Or would you like me to drive you back to my bivouac and tent down for the night?"

"Okay," she whispered.

"Okay what?" he said.

"Okay the latter."

"Okay cool."

LAKEVIEW HOUSE WAS the only anarchist cooperative at Hoover. Humphrey lived on the second floor. The walls were painted black. The bookshelves were filled with Nietzsche and Conrad. Fugazi played on the stereo. Or maybe it was Fishbone. A hand-painted banner reading IF THERE'S NO DANCING, I

DON'T WANT TO BE PART OF YOUR REVOLUTION extended from one side of a marble fireplace to the other. The line was attributed to Emma Goldman. She was one of Humphrey's current heroes. Phoebe sat down on a plaid couch, pulverizing several renegade Cheerios in the process. Humphrey sat next to her. There was no sign of a bed, but there was a deerskin teepee in the corner. "How come you live in an anarchist cooperative if you're not an anarchist anymore?" she asked him.

"Convenient to campus," he answered. "Plus, the chef's superb. Also, I signed a lease through June."

"If you were a real anarchist, you wouldn't mind breaking it."

"We live by our contradictions. Would you mind if I took off my shirt?"

"That's fine."

He took off his shirt. He had a runny, half-bitten-looking *A* tattooed in blue on the small of his back. "I'm having it reworked," he said. "By next week it'll be a sideways *F.*"

"For *fuck you*?" said Phoebe, suppressing the urge to giggle.

"Actually, *feminism,*" Humphrey corrected her. "However, should I ever become closely aligned with the antifur movement, I figure I'll be covered."

"Or the country of Fiji."

"Less likely."

"Why?"

"Tropical climates make me break out in hives. By the way, I'm extremely attracted to you. Would you mind if I took off your shirt?"

"That's fine."

"What about your pants?"

"That's fine, too."

"And my kilt?"

"Sure." Phoebe couldn't believe her bad luck. It was Spitty Clark all over again—asking permission with every new body part he uncovered. She half expected him to start throwing up his bacon and eggs.

But he managed to maneuver her into his teepee without further incident, pausing only once to ask, "Just out of curiosity, have you ever done this before?"

"There was this guy I used to go out with, Paul," she mumbled in terror, because she'd waited so long for this moment it had taken on the quality of a dream.

But it wasn't like a dream at all; it was blinding like the first glimpse of morning.

And because she couldn't bear for Humphrey Fung to know the truth about her lack of sexual experience. But it wasn't just Humphrey. It was everyone. And everything. She considered herself undercover. Always in costume. Just like Humphrey. Though if Humphrey feared his good looks rendered him a poser, Phoebe feared she was good-looking only because she was posing as such—as a dandelion blown sideways in the suburban breeze, resigned to a life spent watching her flower turn to dust, if it wasn't first truncated by the ruthless blade of a lawn mower. That was the romance of her waifdom: that her fate was an essentially tragic one. That she'd accept what was given her. That you could cut her down and she wouldn't complain. She'd keep growing back for more.

In fact, behind her ditsy demeanor, she considered herself a calculating bitch, a murderer in the making. At night she dreamt of strangling each and every last Tri Pi with her bare blue hands. During the day, meanwhile, she tried to have no discernible personality at all. And wasn't that what guys, even anarchist-feminist guys, wanted—a projection screen for their own delusions of grandeur? And didn't everyone like the sound of his own voice the best? "Whatever," said Humphrey. "For too long, women have been identified by the company they keep."

As if he didn't believe her. And why should he have? She was just lying there waiting for it to be over. It wasn't that easy. It took three tries before he even got it in. That's how much it hurt. It hurt so much it sent shivers up her spine. And the pain it provoked seemed to be mocking the significance she attributed it—a significance that had nothing to do with the present and everything to do with its future completion. Such that when it was finally over—it seemed to go on forever—she breathed an audible sigh of relief.

How was Humphrey to know the reasons for her joy? "It's been a pleasure pleasuring you," he declared.

"Same here," Phoebe told him before she slid out from under his dead weight and disappeared into his anarchist bathroom, where she lifted one naked thigh onto his toothpaste-encrusted sink, rinsed off what little blood there was with a damp piece of toilet paper, caught her reflection in the mirror, found she looked the same, and experienced a wave of bittersweet regret at the thought that now she was just like everyone else.

Just another girl who'd had sex.

EXCEPT ONCE YOU had sex, Phoebe found, you had to keep having it. And you had to enjoy it. You had to make little noises to let the other person know how good it felt. Even if it only felt okay. Even if you'd just as soon be having a cup of tea or reading or smoking or talking on the phone. And you had to say, "Yeah," when the guy asked you, "Did you come?" Even if you'd never had an orgasm in your life. And you had to worry about getting pregnant, and getting cheated on, and getting all kinds of weird diseases with acronyms instead of names.

But having sex with Humphrey Fung—it wasn't something Phoebe was inclined to say no to. Because it turned out that a lot of girls in Gerald Stevens's circle were hot for Humphrey. And he wanted Phoebe. And that made her hot by association. And she'd always dreamed of being the girl who other girls dreamed of being. Except that being hot turned out to be as stressful as sex—maybe more so. Because once you were hot, you had to stay hot twenty-four hours a day. So you wouldn't be found out for the dreary blob, the unmitigated dork, the drooling dullard you really were.

Oh, but he found out anyway, Humphrey did. "Where'd you say you grew up?" He was always asking her that. He asked that the night Phoebe lit the wrong end of her cigarette. It made a terrible smell, a chemical, rancid smell. He already knew the answer.

She told him anyway: "New Jersey."

"That's a fucked-up state," he said. "I mean, what's with those jackboots the troopers wear? And why can't they call them towns? *Townships.* That's what they call them in South Africa. A coincidence? I don't think so."

"Canada has townships, too," offered Phoebe.

"Canada is a special case," objected Humphrey.

Phoebe let it go. She'd spent enough time with Humphrey to know that he grew surly when others called his opinions into question, even though he himself called those same opinions into question every six months or so.

Oh, but it was worth it—worth placating Humphrey Fung, Phoebe found—and not just on account of the status he conferred upon her, but (ironically enough) on account of the opportunity to conform to age-specific conventions he allowed her. At nineteen she'd never been anyone's girlfriend before. Which is to say, she'd never partaken in the corny pleasures of holding hands on the streets; of buttering two bagels instead of one; and of wearing *his* sweaters (and occasionally skirts) over her own. And she took to the job with all the gusto of a drag queen— spent half her waking hours primping and prettying herself for Humphrey Fung; always made sure her underwear matched, and that her stomach was flat, her legs skinny, her skin soft, her aplomb undeniable. Just as she found the photographic record of his childhood endlessly revealing and hopelessly endearing, and sat through countless hours of soporific home videotapes dating back to his competitive karate days.

EXCEPT THE MORE doting Phoebe became, the more distant Humphrey grew. Though his frostiness was often difficult to disentangle from his feminism. Take, for example, the breezy April morning Humphrey's pathologically jealous housemate, Dave Injun, walked up to her right in front of Humphrey and said, "You know you want me to fuck you."

"You're disgusting," Phoebe told him. What else could she say?

But the rattle in her voice only fueled Dave Injun's rage. "Hey, Humphrey, my dick is hard," he carried on. "Let me fuck her. You won't mind, right?"

At which point Phoebe looked over to Humphrey. But he wouldn't even look up. "For too many years, men have tried to rein in women's sexuality," he mumbled from inside his comic book. "So don't let me be the one to stand in the way of anyone's fun."

And later, when Phoebe tried to talk to Humphrey about it—about how she was wondering if he wouldn't mind telling Dave to leave her alone—he made it out to be her problem. He said, "That's just Dave. It's you who have to change. You've got

to learn how to defend yourself. Here, let's practice. Go ahead.
Tell me to fuck off. Go ahead."

"Fuck off," she obliged.

"Try it again."

"Fuck off!" Now her frustration was real.

"That's a lot better," said Humphrey. "Try it once more."

But this time, Phoebe didn't respond. She was too busy wondering if wishful thinking—at least, on Humphrey's part—wasn't at play.

AS THE SPRING progressed, it began to seem more and more
that way—that Humphrey would happily have dispensed with
her like an old razor had his politics not prevented him from
doing so with a clear conscience. But he'd never come right out
and admit it. Then he stopped admitting anything at all. It
happened shortly after school had let out for the summer, on the
Fungs' tiny, private island off the coast of Maine. Humphrey
and Phoebe had driven up for a long weekend. It was a ten-
minute speedboat ride from shore. Dr. Fung greeted them at the
dock. He was a short, trim man in a Katmandu T-shirt and
belted safari shorts.

"Do you think I could use your bathroom?" Phoebe asked
him.

"Why, of course you can," he answered, steering her gaze
toward a gabled shed on the edge of the woods. "It's right over
there."

There was no toilet paper inside, and there were spiders
everywhere. And you were supposed to cover your excrement
with peat moss. Phoebe couldn't get out of that outhouse fast
enough. By the time she did, Humphrey was gone. In his place
stood a broad-shouldered blonde in a patchwork caftan. She in-

troduced herself as Greta Fung. Then she led Phoebe inside a two-story clapboard cottage with no electricity or running water.

The Fungs were so casual about sex, they'd assigned Phoebe and Humphrey the same room, a bare-bones attic partition right next to their own. Maybe that was the problem. There wasn't enough in their way; there wasn't enough for Humphrey to rebel against. He was busy unpacking his toiletry kit. He didn't even look up when Phoebe walked in. "That outhouse was so scary," she began, recalling how Humphrey relished every opportunity to mock his parents' Peace Corps idea of a good time. "There were only, like, a *million* spiders in there!"

But to her shock and dismay, Humphrey shot her a withering look and spat, "Spiders have just as much right to be in there as you do!"

He spent the rest of the weekend reading Simone de Beauvoir's *The Second Sex* on a flotation device off the dock, pausing every now and then to burst into obstreperous laughter.

So Phoebe played badminton with Professor Kling, a biology department colleague and friend of Professor Fung's. And she helped Mrs. Fung peel potatoes and shuck corn. And she fielded insults from Dave Injun, who was nicer to her that weekend than he'd ever been before (or ever was again). And she talked agrarian reform with Joanne and Jacob, a mother-and-son marijuana-farming duo. And she went canoeing with Humphrey's robotic older brother, Harry. Saturday turned into Sunday, Sunday into Monday. Then it was time to go.

Phoebe and Humphrey drove the eight hours back to Hoover in virtual silence. (Dave Injun was continuing on to the resort town of Kennebunkport in his own car; he said he had a few things he wanted to relay to President George Bush about what President George Bush could do with his, Dave Injun's, genitalia.) Indeed, it was only after Humphrey struck down a small, furry creature that ran out in front of their rental car on a local road near Harpswell that he deigned to open his trap in any significant manner—though not (horrifyingly enough) to speak. Mouth-to-mouth resuscitation proving futile, however, he climbed back into the driver's seat with tears in his eyes and resorted to his earlier sullen incommunicativeness.

"Do you want to stop for something to eat?" Phoebe asked him.

"Doesn't matter," he muttered back.

"Do you want me to read you the crossword puzzle?"

"Not particularly."

"Do you want me not to talk to you, is that it?"

"Do what you want."

It went on like that.

NOR WAS THE situation improved back in Hoover, where Phoebe sat on Humphrey's plaid couch in Humphrey's black-painted bedroom, leafing through Humphrey's junk mail, trimming a pencil point with a plastic sharpener in the shape of a boat, watching the shavings disappear into his coffee-brown carpet, wondering what she'd done wrong, while Humphrey, seemingly oblivious to her presence, picked out Smiths tunes on his guitar ("Girlfriend in a Coma"), the heat festering around them, the fan blowing hot air in their faces.

"Why are you being like this?" she finally got up the nerve to berate him.

"Why am I being like what?" he said, lowering his instrument onto the floor.

"Like a jerk," said Phoebe, gulping at her own display of gutsiness.

"I don't think you've ever insulted me before." Humphrey smiled patronizingly. "I have to say, Phoebe, I'm really very impressed."

But it wasn't clear he was. Rather, Phoebe suspected that he liked her better before—back when she was the kind of girl who wouldn't have dared tell him what he'd done wrong. In fact, being Humphrey's girlfriend had given her the confidence to love the sound of her own voice as much as she loved his. "Are you really?" she pressed on.

He didn't answer immediately. First he reached for his cigarettes, then his lighter, his dark eyes flickering in the flame. Then he sighed wearily. "Look, Phoebe," he began in an unctuous tone. "You're a nice girl. We're just different, you and me. I'm just a simple guy, a quiet guy, the kind of guy who's content to exist on the margins, resigned to the knowledge that Homo sapiens are just one eco in the ecosystem. And you—you always need to be the center of attention."

"But you were the one who encouraged me to assert myself!" Phoebe cried out in her own defense.

But Humphrey had already completed his closing arguments. He rested his cigarette in an ashtray by his feet. Then he lifted his guitar back into his lap and proceeded to pick out the opening chords of his new favorite Smiths song, "Meat Is Murder."

———————

IT WASN'T LONG afterward that Humphrey made the decision to drop out of the women's studies program in order to double-major in zoology and political science. Shortly thereafter, he broke his lease at Lakeview House and moved into Hoover's so-called nude macrobiotic house, where every night of the week a different member of the co-op was on tofu duty and the proceeds of the composting toilet were used to fertilize the herb garden out back. It was around the same time (early August) that Phoebe found out about Kera, the aspiring anti-fur activist from the local high school. According to Holly, who'd spoken to Gerald Stevens, who'd spoken to someone else, Humphrey had been two-timing since at least mid-May. Needless to say, Phoebe was devastated by the news. It was left to Holly to try to persuade her not to be.

Holly told Phoebe that Humphrey wasn't the kind of guy you fell in love with so much as you "fucked around with," and that for future reference it was best to leave while *they* were still crazy about you. That way *they'd* never get over you. But it was never clear to Phoebe just how Holly knew. Because for all her ex-lays, she rarely had a guy around for longer than a week—that was the truth about Holly Flake. Which may have explained why she seemed as elated as she did by the news of Humphrey and Phoebe's breakup. Not that Phoebe was in any position to complain. She needed her best friend too much right then. She needed Holly to keep reminding her that she'd been using Humphrey all along. And maybe she had been.

That didn't mean she wasn't heartbroken to see him go.

And yet, it wasn't Humphrey Phoebe wanted back so much as it was a vision of herself that seemed to have vanished along with his feminism—never mind his anarchy. Where once she'd pictured herself floating eight feet above the earth, now she felt plodding and pedestrian. It didn't help that her dyed red hair had turned orange in the sun. Or that she was suddenly famished all the time, and gaining back weight. She couldn't imagine ever feeling hot again.

She couldn't imagine a time in life she'd ever aspired to going anywhere—except maybe back to sleep.

7. Claude Duvet

OR *"Semester-Abroad Claude"*

HE'D HAVE A name like Claude Duvet.

He'd be twenty-six, unemployed, and staying with a friend.

He'd be a tortured artist.

He'd be wearing eyeliner.

His parents would live in Brittany, or in the suburbs—in Roissy.

She'd meet him on the rue de Something-or-other.

He'd walk up to her in the middle of a crowd. He'd say, "Are you American?"

They'd take leisurely strolls along the banks of the Seine.

They'd hang out at O'Niel.

He'd drive a Vespa, and he'd take her on the back of it through the serpentine streets of the Left Bank. She'd lean left when he leaned left, and right when he leaned right.

They'd have dramatic fights in public.

They'd spend the weekend in Normandy.

They'd do Ecstasy in crowded nightclubs.

He'd tell her he loved her.

She'd only laugh.

She'd walk around barefoot in mint-green tap pants and a

matching mint-green lace brassiere. It would be the morning, and the velvet drapes would keep the sun at bay.

The hair on his chest would be dark blond.

So would the hair *down there*.

They'd plan a getaway to Florence. They'd have a huge fight about when to leave. She'd throw his *Guide Routard* into the Seine. It would be very dramatic.

It would be a foreshadowing of things to come.

In the sleeper car, he'd undress down to his boxer shorts in front of four other passengers.

She'd find it beyond gauche.

They'd have a bad time in Florence.

She'd tell him, "So long."

He'd cry bitterly. She'd walk away unfazed.

She'd have her eye on someone new—the guy who tended bar at O'Niel.

He'd have a name like—Guy. He'd wear a leather jacket. He'd have a criminal record.

They'd have meaningless sex—at least, it would seem meaningless to Phoebe.

She'd come home with definitive views about the superiority of French birth control pills.

She'd come home dreaming in French, and wearing too much eyeliner, and smelling of clove cigarettes and underarm sweat.

You know how they think American girls are promiscuous? They'd be talking about girls like her.

She'd come home smelling of sex, sex, sex, and more sex.

She would.

Really.

But she didn't, truth be told.

She came home smelling of vomit—gamy, verdant, vertiginous, verisimilar vomit.

With a blotchy face.

And no adventures to recount, no snapshots to stimulate impromptu approbation of the "Ohmigodhe'sSOcute!" variety—only this sinking feeling in her heart that she was just one of those people who would always and forever be standing on the outside of things looking in, her nose pressed to the glass, a perpetual tourist, an Ugly American par excellence, a drooling, pink-eyed monster stuffing brioche into her mouth until she thought her stomach would burst, her heart give out. And then it did. She couldn't share that; she couldn't tell them about how, somewhere between Here and There, the world divulged itself in all its various shades of gray and brown, and it was disappointing, to say the least.

She came home haunted by the gleeful cackle of a stingy landlady with stiff black hair, who took her to task for using too much strawberry jam on her brioche, too much hot water when she bathed, too much toilet paper on her bottom. And (it's true) Phoebe occasionally forgot to turn off the forty-watt bulb that served as the only artificial light in the windowless attic bedroom she shared with Jo Ann Jones, her Mormon roommate from Brigham Young University with the fat ass and the enormous floral underpants. ("I'm just a poor old widow," Madame Bertrand would moan—even though her husband was upstairs, albeit in a wheelchair, paralyzed from the neck down.)

And as if that weren't bad enough, Jo Ann Jones left her diary out on the bed. And Phoebe couldn't stop herself from reading it. And, well, it turned out that Jo Ann Jones thought Phoebe lay under the covers at night masturbating to the comforting twang of her Midwestern truisms. She'd written, "Dear

Lord, Please save me from Phoebe Fine's devil sex and evil ways." Is it any wonder she came home ten months early?

Her doting, adoring, distraught, moderate, moderately attractive parents were waiting at the arrivals gate.

She saw them before they saw her. She saw Roberta gripping the metal barricade, and she saw Leonard *just standing there* fingering the nadir of his beard, the way he always did—as if palpating a wound that refused to be diagnosed. And then she saw them see her. She saw that panicked look in her mother's eyes that made her want to pretend nothing was wrong, even though it clearly was. She had to tell Roberta, "Stop looking like someone died!" even before she said, "Hi, Mom."

"I'm not looking like someone died!" (Roberta)

"Hello, Crumpet." (Leonard)

"Hi, Daddy." (Phoebe, breathing, but only barely there was never enough time no sooner had she breathed in than it was time to breathe out it was a vicious cycle really it was the same with the hairs down there she plucked them one at a time and it was an arduous process and sometimes it hurt but it had to be done but they always grew back it was the same thing over and over again there was never any progress never any resolution just this ringing in her ears just this chorus behind her eyes singing Handel's *Messiah* in the basement of an Episcopalian church in Mahwah Hallelujah Hallelujah Haaaa—leeee—lluuuu—yyyaaaahh necks jutting out like rapist swans she told them to be quiet but they kept singing they never stopped singing they never shut up Haaaaaa—laaaaaay—looooooo—yaaaaaaah it was a nightmare from which she never woke and maybe she never would she could already hear them I remember Phoebe Fine back when her legs were long and shapely her tits were small but perky she was the Nelly Bly of the Bedroom the Wicked Waif of the West the Mylar balloon dangling from the ceiling of a muscular dystrophy benefit she came with no strings attached boys she'd expound even when they were 30 40 50 60 70 to be perfectly frank about it was getting a little old such delectable creatures then she'd light another cigarette and another one after that and then another one after that and then she'd raise one eyebrow exhale it's all par for the course darling even though her golf skills were nil and she always remembered to blow the smoke out through her nose no matter that her skin was already losing that certain youthful dewiness she kept smoking darling because nothing got in her eyes that's the kind of girl she was a fearless girl a fun girl a damn fun girl just about the funnest friggin' fraulein in all of greater Fort Lee but the teeth so young and such bad teeth so many cavities such a tragedy really so sad for the parents they did what they could.)

"Phoebe, I have a little tea for you." (Roberta standing in the doorway at home in Whitehead.)

"Oh, thanks. Thanks for everything." (Phoebe, avoiding her mother's eyes. At that moment, they scared her more than she scared herself. So she looked away—out the window, at trees with no leaves, and a kid on a mountain bike doing wheelies in his driveway, and everything hush-hush beneath thick white sky. And then a car went by—a low rider with his brake lights on. And then she thought of Claude Duvet, who never was. And it made her pretty sad that he hadn't been.)

8. Bruce Bledstone

OR *"The Visiting Professor of Critical Theories"*

IT WAS HOLLY Flake who found Bruce Bledstone's picture in the local paper, in a photo spread called "New Face on Campus." There were twelve pictures, a hodgepodge of students and faculty. He didn't look like either one. He was wearing a checked scarf that caught the tips of his overgrown hair. And he was squinting as if he'd lost his sunglasses, smiling as if he had a few secrets. He looked like a man who'd been around. Phoebe already knew one place he'd gone. "A Visiting Fellow at the Center for the Study of the Periphery, Bruce Bledstone recently returned from the hinterlands of Glasnost Russia," read the caption beneath the photograph. " 'Contrary to popular opinion,' claims Professor Bledstone, 'Siberian winters are actually quite mild.' "

The same could not be said for Hoover winters, Phoebe thought to herself with a glance out the window of the corner booth where she and Holly sat chain-smoking Camel Lights over tepid coffee. Not that she could see much; it was snowing too hard. It was snowing so hard you couldn't tell where the sidewalk ended and University Avenue began. As if the weather mattered! She was just happy to be back. Back at school. Back at the twenty-four-hour greasy spoon with her best friend. Just like old times. Just like everything was back to normal, except it never really was, and it especially wasn't now. Now that she wasn't even supposed to be here. Now that she'd come back ten months early from her junior year abroad that never was.

Now that she wasn't half the girl she used to be, not so many months ago.

For one thing, she was devastated by the scope of her failure. For another, she felt strangely liberated by her own admission of defeat. She was through with keeping up appearances. She was feeling somewhat self-destructive. It wasn't precisely love she was looking for. She had this feeling that Bruce Bledstone would understand. "Maybe we should take his class," she said, turning back to her best friend.

But her best friend had an even better suggestion: "Maybe *you* should take his class."

"Oh, please," Phoebe cried out in a protective show of false modesty.

"Why not?" postured Holly.

"He's probably married!" protested Phoebe.

"So?"

"So forget it."

"Do what you want." A triad of expertly spaced smoke rings filtered out of Holly's puckered lips. "In my personal experience, married guys are even hornier than regular guys."

This time Phoebe didn't bother arguing back. Whatever Holly knew about married men, it was bound to be more than *she* knew, what with her own list of ex-lays still being no list at all—still just one name, Humphrey Fung. (Holly's list currently numbered thirty-eight.)

But then, it was one thing to have sex with "anyone," and it was quite another to sleep with "someone"—someone who wasn't supposed to want you, wasn't even allowed to want you but couldn't help himself from wanting you. To Phoebe, that seemed like the ultimate test. And she was sick of failing, flailing, floundering like some kind of spastic fish laid out on the dock to die.

———

BUT HUMPHREY FUNG had to go ruin everything. At least, that was Phoebe's first thought upon entering room 324 for the first day of Hegemony 412, a graduate level seminar open to juniors and seniors. There she found her beautiful ex-boyfriend seated at the far end of a long oak table. He was decked out in a sky-blue mechanic's jumpsuit with the name Joe scripted on the breast. He must have been over animals and back into workers. Pretending not to know him, Phoebe sat down at the near end of the table and surveyed the rest of the competition: a bunch of political science majors in plaid shirts and ill-fitting jeans; a girl in a hairband with visible gums; a guy in a Star Trek T-shirt with an enormous, protruding Adam's apple; some pretentious-looking graduate students in black overcoats and cat-eye frames. Phoebe was wearing her best black miniskirt, a cropped turtleneck sweater, and a pair of knee-high black suede boots that zipped up the side. She'd spent a good deal of time selecting that outfit.

She wondered how long Professor Bledstone had spent selecting his.

He arrived ten minutes late in a black blanket-wool suit jacket, a pair of black jeans, and a dark red button-down buttoned to the neck. And he was a big man, somehow bigger than she'd expected. And if he wasn't precisely cute, he was certainly formidable. His eyes were luminous and green. His blond-brown hair was flecked with gray. There was a transparent quality to his skin. He removed his jacket and walked toward the only vacant chair at the table, two seats away from her own. He didn't seem all that happy to see them. "My name is Bruce Bledstone," he began, "and I'd be happy to give every one of you an A this semester, provided you complete the necessary course work and make regular contributions to class discussion. I'm not much interested in grades."

Then he droned on about the syllabus—about the major concepts they'd be covering (genealogy, resistance, territorialization, the state apparatus, the political unconscious, the poverty of everyday life) and the major thinkers they'd be reading (Foucault, Fanon, Deleuze, Althusser, Jameson, and Debord). And Phoebe did her best to concentrate, but found her attention drifting anyway. She was thinking about how, growing up, she'd force herself to look at the sun. Just because you weren't supposed to. Just to prove she could. Except she couldn't.

She couldn't stop torturing herself with that blistering impossibility.

It took what seemed like an eternity for the visiting professor to notice her. She had to tap her nails against the table and stretch and yawn and recross her legs about one hundred times and blurt out, "Excuse me?" at two minutes to two. "I was wondering if you wouldn't mind—um—defining 'hegemony'?"

"Hegemony," Professor Bledstone corrected her pronunciation, inciting giggles from the graduate-student contingent and a belly laugh from Humphrey. (She wanted to strangle all of them right then and there.) "And who are you?"

"I'm Phoebe," she must have whispered out loud. "Phoebe Fine."

She watched the visiting professor scan the class list before he scanned her. "In answer to your question, Phoebe Fine, it was the preeminent Italian Marxist, Antonio Gramsci, who coined the term *hegemony* to explicate the moment when the ruling class is able not only to coerce a subordinate class to conform to its interests but also to exert total social authority over subordinate classes. You'll be hearing a lot about hegemony this semester."

Phoebe couldn't wait. Humphrey must have felt differently. He was out the door at the stroke of two, and he never came back. The rest of Phoebe's classmates huddled around Professor Bledstone like dogs near a carcass, mouths gaping, heads wagging in agreement with whatever it was he was saying. Phoebe stayed in her seat, doodling hearts and flowers and high-heeled shoes, hoping to be mistaken for an overeager taker of notes, wondering what she would say when she was the only one left. Then she was. She stood up. She was going to ask the visiting professor where he was visiting from. But he opened his mouth before she had the chance to open hers. "Phoebe Fine," he said. "Would you mind doing me a favor?"

"What will you do for me?" she asked him back. (Those were the days before she understood the value of fear in love.)

He smiled cautiously before producing a book. "I'm actually on my way out of town. Assuming you're walking through the quad at some point this afternoon, would you mind dropping this off at the Political Philosophy Library?"

"Why would I mind?" she said.

Then she walked toward him. Maybe it was her imagination. She could have sworn he held on to that book for a second longer than he had to. (She could have sworn he was looking at her like she was more than just another stupid undergraduate.)

They left the classroom together. On the footpath outside, they exchanged pleasantries about the unseasonably warm temperature.

"Well, bye now," was the last thing he said before he left.

He left her standing there holding a book by Gramsci called *The Prison Notebooks.*

———

HOLLY THOUGHT HE was trying to send Phoebe a message. "Maybe he's trapped in a bad marriage," she speculated over frozen yogurt later that evening.

"Maybe," said Phoebe. But inside she was wondering if the only reason the visiting professor asked her to return *The Prison Notebooks* was that she was the last one standing there after class.

Conversely, it could hardly be called an accident of fate that Phoebe ran into the visiting professor the following Monday in the Political Philosophy Library. That he conducted his research there wasn't hard to figure out. Sure enough, he was standing by the checkout desk, his arms piled high with books. She was standing behind him. "Hi, Professor Bledstone!" is how she began.

"Phoebe!" he said, whipping around, a startled expression on his ghostly face.

That he remembered her name! "Hi," she said again. (She hadn't meant to repeat herself; it just happened.)

"What are you doing here?"

"Just studying," she shrugged.

"For my class?"

"Not today. I have to conjugate some verbs today." She waved her French book in his face.

"The language of the colonizer . . ." he trailed off. "I always regretted not learning Spanish."

"I already know Spanish," she assured him.

"I see," he said.

But it wasn't clear he saw anything. And Phoebe wondered

if he wanted to get away. (She wouldn't have blamed him if he did.) But she wanted him to stay. And when he advanced in line, she matched his steps, asked him if he had had a "fun weekend." (She didn't ask him where he'd gone.)

"Not particularly," he told her.

"Me neither," she told him. "I had really bad cramps." (She thought he'd care if only he were given the opportunity.)

"I'm sorry to hear it," he said.

That he was sorry! It made Phoebe weak with joy. "So how do you like it out here in the boondocks?" she asked him.

His eyes traveled someplace she'd never been—maybe Siberia. "It's fine for the moment," he said. "In general, I prefer the city to the country."

"What about the suburbs?"

"I've never lived in one, but I can't imagine I'd want to."

"You probably wouldn't," she agreed. "I grew up in New Jersey, and it wasn't even fine for the moment."

The visiting professor nodded like he understood. But he didn't laugh. He didn't even smile. Phoebe was hoping he would. In fact, she was all but counting on it. "By the way, I'm looking for a job," she said, begging for resurrection, thinking maybe she could help him keep track of all those books. "If you hear of anything . . ."

"What can you do?" he wanted to know.

She looked straight at him before she answered: "Anything you want me to do."

He ignored the innuendo. "Actually, I'm supposed to be writing a book."

"About hegemony?" She made sure to pronounce it right this time.

"Something like that," he said. Then he paused. Then he looked straight at her, straight through her—or so it seemed to

Phoebe. "If I got approval from the Center, I could probably hire you as my research assistant."

"You're kidding!" she squealed. "I mean, that would be amazing."

"I probably wouldn't be able to pay you much."

As if money mattered. (Those were the days before money mattered.) "That's fine—I mean you don't even have to pay me," she spluttered. "I mean not that much or anything." She smiled.

He smiled, too. Then he set his books down on the counter and said, "Talk to me after class on Thursday."

And it was, just maybe, the happiest moment of Phoebe Fine's entire life.

But she had one more question. "Professor—" she began.

"Please," he broke in. "Call me Bruce."

She couldn't believe he'd said that. It filled her heart with something like pride. "Okay, Bruce." The name stuck to the roof of her mouth like peanut butter. "Can I ask you a question?" But she didn't wait for an answer. "Do you like to teach?"

He laughed then, an old studied laugh, and said, "Not very much, but don't tell the other students in our class."

"I promise," she told him.

It was their first secret.

It wouldn't be their last.

———

ONCE SHE BECAME his research assistant, every Thursday after class, Phoebe would follow the visiting professor up the three flights of stairs that led to his office in the colonial mansion that housed the Center for the Study of the Periphery. Unruly stacks of books and clippings littered his desk. The walls were bare, the carpet imitation Persian. A little window under the eave offered scenic views of the lake and outlying mountains, except when the fog was so thick you couldn't see past the pane of glass, which was all the time. It was there Bruce Bledstone would present Phoebe with her research assignment for the week. And Phoebe would present Bruce Bledstone with a carefully edited version of her tragicomic life. She'd leave out the part about how she'd become this *drooling pink-eyed monster*. Instead, she'd regale him with horror stories about suburbia— about the rich idiots she went to high school with and the wacky parents she grew up in the same house as.

She'd tell him about how Leonard and Roberta recycled paper towels and tinfoil and loved Handel's *Messiah* even though they called themselves atheists. And her older sister, Emily, thought she was hot shit because she was going out with this suspected member of the PLO who also managed to be on the guest lists of all the coolest nightclubs in New York. And her best friend, Holly, was such a slut she couldn't remember the names of half the guys she'd slept with. And her ex-boyfriend, Humphrey, had turned against her after she'd insulted the spiders in his peat-moss outhouse. And France wouldn't have been so bad if it weren't for her landlady, Madame Bertrand, who spent all her waking hours poring over photos of yachting royals in *Paris Match* and took Phoebe to task for using too much jam on her brioche. (Is it any wonder she came home ten months early?)

But New Jersey was even more of a nightmare. Her mother, Roberta, couldn't say the word *psychiatrist* out loud. (The *food doctor* was as close as she'd gotten.) Even though Roberta was the one who took Phoebe to see an Indian man in a brown suit in a high-rise building in Fort Lee who asked her a lot of nosy questions about her mother. (Wasn't that ironic?) And speaking of eating, sometimes she couldn't. But sometimes when she did, she made herself sick. And the truth was that it wasn't just sometimes, it was all the time. It was almost every day, sometimes twice a day. It started during her junior year abroad that never was. It was all pretty terrible. It was all pretty tragic.

Bruce Bledstone made it less so.

He never dispensed advice. That wasn't his style. And he never told her much about himself other than the fact that he'd been born and bred in Kansas and hadn't been back there since. But he'd listen—he'd listen!—one leg propped up on his desk, the other planted on the floor. And he'd hand her a box of tissues when she started to choke up. And he'd smoke her cigarettes while he listened to her rave. And sometimes, between the inhale and the exhale, he'd tell her about the "late-capitalist pigs who run this country," *her* country. (He didn't identify as a citizen.) And still other times they'd just be sitting there, neither of them talking. And he'd be staring at her as if she were his, even though she wasn't. And she was young, and she was stupid—but she wasn't that stupid: she knew what some looks meant.

She knew it was okay to visit even though it wasn't Thursday.

———————

AT FIRST SHE'D make up excuses. Then she ran out of excuses. Then she'd just show up, sit down, and start babbling. The visiting professor never told her to leave. He never told her to stay, either. But he gave her keys to his office, so she could leave the books and articles he'd asked her to find him in a neat pile on his desk. She'd stick a note on the top of every pile. She signed them all, "Faithfully, P." She thought that was a pretty ironic way to sign off. She assumed he'd know what she was getting at.

It was hard to imagine that he wouldn't have.

"I was thinking of dropping out of your class, or at least changing to pass-fail—you know, for ethical reasons," she informed him one afternoon at Pita Paradise. They'd stopped in for some lunch on their way back from the Political Philosophy Library.

"Drop out?" He wrinkled his brow, narrowed his eyes quizzically. "Why would you do something like that?"

"Some people in the class, well, you know . . ."

But it wasn't clear he knew anything. "No, I don't know." He played dumb, or maybe he really was.

Maybe he was the naïve one after all.

"Some people in the class are starting to get the wrong idea about us," she mumbled into her chickpea salad. It wasn't exactly true. It seemed like a good way to introduce the "right idea"—namely, the idea that Bruce Bledstone might be falling madly in love with her. Now he performed a single, protracted nod and said, "I see."

"Well, what do you think I should do about it?" Phoebe asked him.

"That's not for me to say," he answered. "Though as a general rule, I would advise against worrying about what other people think. Especially since other people are usually wrong. On the other hand, there are no absolutes."

"Right, of course," she chirped, her disappointment bottomless.

BUT THERE WERE encouraging signs on other fronts. For example, one Thursday after class, the visiting professor informed Phoebe, "It's no secret that my marriage is in crisis."

She tried to act surprised. In fact, she'd done her research. "I didn't even know you were married," she lied. "I mean, you don't seem like you're married."

He shrugged. "It's not something Evelyn and I go around publicizing."

"Of course not." Phoebe shrugged back.

As if to keep your marriage a secret were the most natural thing in the world, when the only married people she knew intimately—her own parents—seemed perfectly comfortable having others regard them as a single, state-sanctioned entity.

"To be perfectly honest, neither of us actually believes in the institution of marriage," he continued. "We have a marriage founded in convenience—financial as well as collegial."

"But do you love her?" It came tumbling out of her mouth. She didn't mean to pry; she was just curious. Curious if people really married for the tax break.

"Love her?" Bruce Bledstone repeated Phoebe's question as if he didn't understand—as if it were a pretty naïve question to be asking. "I guess I love her. Why would you ask something like that?"

But she didn't have an answer for him just then. And she tried to meet his eyes. But he looked away, toward the window. There were no scenic views of the lake or mountains that afternoon. It was raining too hard, and the fog was too thick. And she could tell he was mad, and it nearly destroyed her. "I'm sorry," she murmured. "It's none of my business."

"Marriage is a complicated institution," he told her—or maybe them both. "Not to mention a bourgeois construct."

Then he asked her for a Camel, and she was more than happy to oblige—nearly ecstatic for the opportunity to offer him something that he wanted. Because somewhere along the way, his happiness had become the measure of her happiness. And because somewhere along the way she must have perceived that he didn't need her the way she thought she needed him.

She had this idea that he would.

She had this idea that he would find her beautiful, and that would be enough. She didn't understand then that the world is filled with beautiful girls. Or that beauty fades—even in youth. Which is to say that once you get to know people, they stop looking like anything in particular.

———————

IT WASN'T SO many weeks later that the visiting professor called to say he wasn't feeling his best—something about a bad cold—*and would Phoebe mind dropping off this week's research assistance at his rental house downtown?* "It's a forty-minute walk from campus," he said, "but there's also a bus."

She told him walking would be no problem—she could use the exercise. And besides, it was a nice day, nicest one so far this year. She wrote his address on her hand. She told him she'd be over after French. It was dinner-hour by the time she arrived at 84 North Route 11, a sky blue saltbox dating back to the 1950s.

There was more crabgrass than real grass in the front yard. And the porch was leaning to one side, and the shutters were hanging off their hinges. Phoebe couldn't quite believe that a man of Bruce Bledstone's stature would live in a house in that kind of disrepair, but it was he who came to the door, so he must have. He must have wanted to see her. He greeted her with a toothy smile and a jocular pat on the back. "Well, hello there, Phoebe," he said. "Come in, come in."

So she came in. She was wearing the same black miniskirt she'd worn to the first day of Hegemony 412, along with black tights, a green top, and chunky black shoes. He was wearing white jeans and a brown sweater and socks with no shoes. He didn't look particularly sick. He hadn't lost his appetite, either. He turned to her midfoyer. "I was about to order a pizza. Do you eat pizza, Phoebe?"

She was thinking she should have worn her hair down. "As long as you don't get pepperoni or sausage," she told him. "I don't eat red meat."

The living room wasn't much to look at. There were no pictures on the wall, no carpet on the floor—just a striped sofa, matching easy chair angled toward an oversized TV, and a blond-wood coffee table situated between the two. The visiting professor took Phoebe's coat, asked her if she'd like something to drink. He said he had vodka and gin. She asked him for a screwdriver. He disappeared into the kitchen. While he was gone, she arranged herself on the sofa, kicked off her shoes, inspected her chronically mutilated cuticles. (They had looked worse in the past.) It was another five minutes before he returned with her drink, which he set down on the coffee table at her feet. Then he sat himself in the easy chair to her right and pressed the power button on the remote.

There was a big war going on halfway around the globe, in the Persian Gulf, and his TV screen was fulgurating as if in the throes of some kind of firefly convention. "This is your government in action," he offered during a commercial for some do-it-yourself pregnancy test.

"It's not *my* government," she protested. "I didn't even vote in the last election!"

"You should vote if you believe in democracy," he told her. "I don't know if you do."

The problem was: neither did Phoebe. And she made a mental note to find out. By which she meant, *ask Bruce Bledstone if he believed in democracy at some later date.* In the meantime, he refilled her glass. He kept refilling it. Then the doorbell rang. From the sofa, she listened to the visiting professor chewing out the delivery boy for being so late. That's when it first occurred to her that Bruce Bledstone wasn't necessarily the nicest man.

But, then, what did she care? He was nice to her—nice enough to let her sit on his sofa and watch his all-news station and eat his pizza and ramble on about all the inconsequential people who'd passed through her inconsequential life. It never occurred to her that he might have fed on her attention the way she fed on his. Or that visiting professors of critical theory got lonely just like everyone else. She thought they had bigger things to worry about—bigger, better things that ended with the suffixes *ism* and *ony.*

He returned with a flat box balanced on his uplifted palm, like a gentleman waiter in an old-fashioned Italian restaurant. He sat the box down next to her drink, then sat himself down next to her body. "You should have told me you didn't eat pepperoni," he scolded her between bites.

She told him that she had; she acted annoyed.

Secretly she was relieved.

She wanted to be empty for him—empty so he could overwrite her. So she was not herself—someone else. Because she'd had enough of Phoebe Fine, the sorority-reject nervous-breakdown bulimic with the bloated face. And because she was seeking escape from a life that seemed like no life at all—just a mind-numbing alternation of work and play; and day and night; and beds made and unmade; and bodies soaped and sweated and soaped; and empty stomachs filled and emptied and filled all over again.

And because she wanted to be so empty that her recent

past—her recent failures and rejections—would become ir-relevant. So she could start from scratch—a blank slate, pure unadulterated epithelium, two-dimensional and in no hurry to become three. So all you saw was all you got. So ordinary peo-ple couldn't get under her skin. (There'd be no skin to get under.)

And because Bruce Bledstone was to be her getaway car. That was the master plan.

Phoebe picked the crust off one slice. He ate the rest of the pizza. The scud missiles didn't stop. "Do you think a lot of civil-ians are dying?" she asked him at half past nine.

"It's a fucking bloodbath over there," is what he said.

At which point she tried to imagine what it would be like to lie in a bathtub full of blood. But it was the image of a warm bed that dominated her conscious thought. She must have started to yawn.

"It's getting late," said Bruce.

"It's getting late," agreed Phoebe.

"I should drive you home."

She didn't answer.

He drove her home in his dark red Chevy Caprice with the beige acrylic-knit interior, and he said good night before she'd even gotten out of the car.

———

BUT IT WASN'T so many nights later that the visiting pro-fessor rang Phoebe up to see if she might be interested in join-ing him and a few of his colleagues for a drink at a local cocktail lounge.

"Sure." She tried to sound casual even while she was prac-tically bursting with gratitude for the invitation. That Bruce

Bledstone thought she was worthy of associating with actual faculty members!

That Bruce Bledstone wasn't embarrassed to be seen in the company of Phoebe Fine.

He said he'd swing the Caprice by at nine.

She dressed in a black leather skirt and a fake-fur coat.

He was wearing a gray suit jacket and a navy blue Mao cap.

"Hello there," he greeted her from behind the wheel.

"What's this music?" she said, fastening her seat belt.

"It's Bulgarian folk."

"I didn't know they had bagpipes over there."

"You don't have to like it."

"It's okay. I mean, it's not really my taste."

"What's your taste?"

"More like Madonna, Lisa Stansfield, that kind of stuff."

"I like Madonna."

Phoebe couldn't believe her ears. No matter that his tone was equivocal. It made her think he understood. It made her want to reach over and hug him. "You like Madonna?" she squeaked with joy.

"I like that one from a few years back," he continued. "What's it called? 'Material World.' "

"You mean 'Material Girl'?"

"That's the one—it's a very clever song."

"Yeah, it's a good song," Phoebe concurred. "But I think a lot of people misinterpreted it. I mean, they thought Madonna was celebrating being materialistic. But I think she was actually making fun of it. Don't you think?" She turned to the visiting professor for validation.

But he had none to offer. "It could very well be," he said, smiling cryptically, his green eyes glinting in the headlights of a passing camper.

Then she didn't know whether to feel like a genius or a jackass—not until she got to Pete's Tavern.

Then she felt like a genius.

———

"THIS IS MY tireless research assistant, Phoebe Fine," he said, introducing her to the assembled crowd.

They were a motley group—an AIDS activist with pock-marked skin; a raven-hared graduate student of indeterminate sexuality who was writing her dissertation on eighteenth-century witchcraft; a British guy named Todd who'd been in-vited to Hoover to deliver a paper on the Hegelian infinity in relation to the British pop-rock act the Pet Shop Boys; a Mary Shelley scholar with a large flat butt, and her semiestranged husband, Ron, a labor-history guy with a comb-over. Phoebe found their company riveting—if only because they treated her as if she were one of them. As if there wasn't anything strange about her being out with her professor on a Tuesday night. They shook her hand warmly and asked her what she was studying. And she returned the favor by asking them about their own par-ticular fields of expertise and showing interest in their answers, even while she couldn't have cared less. Even while her primary interest remained the mirror over the bar—a mirror by which she was able to evaluate if and how Bruce Bledstone acted dif-ferently with the Mary Shelley scholar from the way he acted with her.

Alternately, if he was standing right next to her, how the two of them looked together. (*Like father and daughter,* Phoebe shud-dered to herself before banishing the thought from her head.)

"Your friends are really cool," she informed him an hour into the whirlwind. He'd come over with another drink. He was al-ways coming over with another drink.

"Glad you think so," he said, grinning. He seemed to find everything about her amusing that night.

She asked him, "Would you rather I thought they were losers?"

"Not at all," he answered. Then he took a drag on his cigarette, turned sideways to release his dragon plume through his patrician nose. "I've promised to give Todd a ride back to the Holiday Inn."

Phoebe wasn't sure how Todd's plans affected hers.

But that they affected hers at all! "That's fine with me," she said with a dishonest shrug.

The bar was closing. More hands were shaken, double cheek kisses exchanged. The three of them walked out into the parking lot. Bruce was in the middle, Phoebe on his right. The temperature had dropped, but there was a stillness to the air that foretold spring—and bred restlessness. "I can't believe this town shuts down at midnight," whined Todd.

Phoebe remembered suddenly what Spitty and his fraternity brothers used to do after last-call in Hoover. "We could always drive over to Altoona," she piped in.

She hadn't meant it as a joke.

Bruce and Todd seemed to find the suggestion hilarious.

"No, thanks," gagged Todd.

"Next weekend," choked Bruce.

"It was just a joke," Phoebe said, cringing. She couldn't tell if they were laughing at her or with her.

"Well, it was very funny," said Bruce.

"Thanks," she whispered, but not loud enough for anyone to hear.

She felt suddenly ridiculous in her own body—as if her feet were too short for her legs, her hands too big for her arms. As if her *essential boring blahness* were on display for all the world to see. She climbed into the front seat, rolled down the window, lit her umpteenth Camel of the night in search of the levity cigarettes occasionally precipitate, though rarely beyond the first one of the night. Todd got in the back, but he hung over the front. Arms outstretched over the backs of their seats, he chattered on about his boyfriend's mother, his mother's boyfriend—Phoebe couldn't say for sure. She was too distracted. She was too busy wondering *what next*. But she didn't want Todd to leave—not yet. She found his presence strangely comforting, the way the presence of a third person sometimes is.

She was sorry when the Holiday Inn came into view and Todd sprung from the backseat.

"Sweet dreams," said Bruce.

"It was nice meeting you," said Phoebe.

"Nighty night," said Todd, leaning into her window with what seemed to her a leering smile, but maybe she was over-interpreting the curl of his lips. Maybe he was just smiling. It was hard to say for sure.

Then he was gone, and it was just Phoebe and Bruce. They were pulling out of the circular driveway, turning left on McGuire in full view of the hippie kite store, when he asked her, "Should I take you home? Or do you want to come in for a nightcap?"

She swallowed hard before answering, "I'll have a nightcap."

They parked down the block. There wasn't anyone else on the street. But the stars were out—millions of them. And to Phoebe they seemed like coconspirators in their fantasy; to Phoebe the stars seemed to be lighting the way to Bruce Bledstone's bedroom. He walked a few feet in front of her, his head bent forward over the crabgrass. She couldn't tell what he was thinking about. She wasn't thinking about anything in particular. She was too busy holding her breath, trying to stop her teeth from chattering.

———————

SHE DIDN'T REMEMBER his house being such a mess. There were books and newspapers and half-empty mugs strewn all over the floor. The visiting professor made two screwdrivers, one for Phoebe and one for himself. Then he joined her on the striped sofa, reached for the remote. They watched a little news. They watched a rerun of *Married with Children*. He said it was his favorite sitcom. She asked him why he didn't have any children. He said, "That's a very provocative question to ask."

She told him, "I'm a very provocative girl."

He grimaced, said nothing. But when the show was over, he glanced at his watch and announced to no one in particular, "It's getting late."

Just like last time.

But it wasn't like last time at all. It was different. Phoebe could tell by the way the visiting professor was sitting—awfully close to her, his legs splayed on the coffee table, his elbow digging into her arm. She was sitting on her calves. "It's getting late," she seconded the observation, the ball of her stocking foot brushing the side seam of his jeans. (It was an accident—just like the Political Philosophy Library.)

He didn't take his eyes off the TV. He rattled his ice against the side of his glass. Then he asked her, "Do you want me to drive you home, or do you want to stay here tonight?"

She didn't answer immediately; her heart was beating too fast. And besides, she wasn't sure Bruce Bledstone wasn't inviting her to spend the night on some pull-out cot.

She wasn't sure until he reached for her hand.

He squeezed it so hard she thought her knuckles would break. Then she knew. Then she turned to him. He wasn't smiling but he wasn't frowning, either. He was looking at her as if she had something he wanted. And she was looking at him as if she was looking at the sun. She couldn't keep her eyes open so she closed them. That's when he unsnapped her barrette. Her hair tumbled over her shoulders and onto his hands. Then he took one tendril, wound it behind her ear, brought her to his lips. And his breath was hot like car exhaust. And his kiss felt less like a surrender than a coronation. She had to open her eyes to make sure it wasn't all a dream.

She found the visiting professor exactly where she left him— sitting there, waiting for an answer.

"I guess I'll stay," she managed. "I mean, if you don't think it's too weird."

"Why would it be too weird?" He spoke to her in the same flat, affectless monotone he used in class. And it unnerved her just enough to send her fleeing from the room.

"Could I borrow your phone?" she asked him mid-flight.

"It's in the kitchen," he said.

She took the phone into the broom closet with her. Then she dialed home. Holly picked up halfway through the first ring. It was pretty obvious that she was alone. And that she was disappointed it was only Phoebe. And that her thirty-ninth lay had yet to materialize. "Guess where I am," Phoebe whispered into the receiver.

"Don't tell me," said Holly—as if she meant it. As if she didn't want to know. No matter that seducing the visiting professor had been *her* idea. She couldn't bear the thought of its actualization. She couldn't bear the idea that she was losing her quasi-virginal sidekick. At least, that's how it seemed to Phoebe. Here she'd called in search of reassurance. All Holly had to offer was sarcasm.

Or was Phoebe kidding herself?

Had she called to warn her best friend that she was "catching up"? And what hope was there for a friendship that competed for attention with sex? Or was it rather that sex was the stage upon which she and Holly competed for each other's attention, with men mere props in their own psychodrama? (Was it Holly who she loved the most, always had?)

"Fine, I won't," said Phoebe.

"Do what you want," said Holly. "Just make it quick. I'm expecting company."

"I'm sure you are."

"Oh, so now you're the only one who gets to have a sex life?"

"What are you talking about?!"

"Forget it."

"Fine, I will."

"Fine."

The two girls hung up as worst enemies. Though at that moment Phoebe couldn't have cared less. What did she need Holly Flake for when she had Bruce Bledstone waiting for her in the living room?

Except he wasn't there when she got back. Her panic lasted only a few seconds. Then she heard the floorboards creaking overhead. She climbed the stairs one at a time. She found the visiting professor standing at the top of them.

He didn't have to say, "Come here."

She went to him. She fell between his arms, and he held her there—against his chest, against his heart, against his groin. And it felt safe and dangerous all at the same time to be engulfed by this massive warmth—this pulsing stranger—in whom she had decided, for unclear reasons, to place her bets for salvation. And they stayed like that for who knows how long. At which point he took her to his bed and pulled her on top of him, his hands gripping her hips, his mouth ajar but no sounds coming out, not until it was all over, and he was lying flat on his back, a single, languid leg tossed diagonally over her own. Then he said, "Well, that was fun."

"Yeah," she whispered back.

———

BUT IT WAS so much more than just "fun." Or so it seemed to Phoebe that next afternoon after class on the third floor of the colonial mansion where she and Bruce Bledstone sat in weighted silence, the rain candy-striping down the little window under the eave, the air between them not quite robust enough for two simultaneous breaths. At least, it felt that way to Phoebe. She'd never been so proud. She'd never been so aroused, either. Which is mostly to say that she could tell that Bruce Bledstone was aroused.

And was there really any difference?

"I'll be in New York this weekend," he told her.

"Whatever," she told him.

Because she could tell he'd just as soon have stayed in Hoover with her. In fact, he came back early. But first he called to say he was on his way. He said Evelyn was out shopping for a new raincoat.

She said, "I hate raincoats."

He said, "The sound of your voice makes me hard."

She said, "I like your hard-on. Can I like your hard-on?"

He said, "You can like anything you want."

He said, "It's time we reclaimed the relations of reproduction."

He said, "The fucking thing wouldn't cooperate."

He said, "It was really very embarrassing. When I tried to fuck my wife, I could only think of you."

And Phoebe took it as the highest form of flattery. She didn't see how else to take it. Especially since good sex was what kept couples together, just as bad sex was what drove them apart. That's what Bruce Bledstone said. And Phoebe had no reason to doubt him. Experience didn't suggest otherwise.

Experience didn't suggest anything.

She waited for him on the porch of his falling-down house. At the sight of his approaching car, her stomach collapsed like a Japanese folding screen. "I missed you," he said before he pinned her against the front door. He smelled like cheap cologne; he smelled of sandalwood and burning leaves.

"I missed you, too." She could hardly get out the words.

She could hardly believe that, of all the girls in the world, it was Phoebe Fine he wanted the most.

———

SO THEY RARELY went on real dates. (He said it was a small town and you know how people in small towns talk.) And he balked at the prospect of attending the Hoover Symphony Orchestra's Spring Concert, in which Phoebe currently played (what else?) second violin. (Classical music he deemed elitist.) But he picked her up after the show and took her back to his falling-down house, where she sat face forward in his lap and played him Beethoven's Romance no. 2 in F Major, op. 50. She told him it was his punishment for being a bad husband. And he seemed to take the insult in stride. But she hadn't made it through the first page before he yanked her violin out from under her neck, then her bow out from under her fist. And then he carried her upstairs, where he offered her his own version of romance. And she kindly accepted. She couldn't get enough of Bruce Bledstone. He couldn't get enough of watching TV. Sometimes they watched sitcoms while they had sex. Maybe it doesn't sound that romantic.

It was to Phoebe.

It was as if she were seeing the world for the first time. Which is to say that she saw nothing at all, so blinded was she by the spectacle of their passion—a passion that rendered the humdrum routines that had once marked her daily existence mere background noise. She kept forgetting who'd called. She kept leaving the keys in the door. She'd finally, triumphantly, lost her appetite. Even conversation came to seem superfluous. What words could begin to live up to the gravity of their lust? And who, for that matter, had the energy to talk?

Oh, but it wasn't just the passion. To wake against Bruce Bledstone's sleeping chest, her hot cheek rising with his every breath and the morning sun casting oblong shadows across the light blue floorboards in his bedroom on the second floor and everything quiet and calm and contained within this one shimmering bubble of space and time, their very own and no one else's—that was as close to bliss as she'd ever known.

During class time, they'd revert back to teacher and student—well, almost. The visiting professor would do everything in his power to avoid eye contact. But sometimes he'd fail. Sometimes he'd be caught speechless in the middle of his speechifying. Then he'd have to clear his throat and start all over again—as if nothing had happened, even though it clearly had. That's when Phoebe felt the most powerful.

That's when she felt the world was hers, and she was the world.

———

IS IT ANY wonder she almost forgot about the existence of Evelyn Nuñez? The visiting professor rarely mentioned his wife's name except to complain that she stole all his best ideas. (She was a critical theorist herself.) Then the phone rang. It wasn't that early. It wasn't that late. They were still asleep—not for long. Phoebe knew it was Evelyn calling because the voice on the machine said, "Hey, Honey, it's me." And while the tape rewound, she sat up on her elbows, opened her mouth to speak. She wanted to let Bruce Bledstone know she wasn't half as stupid as she looked. She wanted to tell him that his marriage sounded "pretty convenient."

She didn't have the nerve.

Somewhere along the way, she'd gotten scared, if not of the visiting professor himself, then of the possibility of losing him. Which is to say, the possibility of saying the one thing that would make him realize that she was more trouble than she was worth. And that he didn't need her the way she thought she needed him. No matter that she'd walked and talked, inhaled and exhaled, before she met him. Without him, she was nothing, no one—that's who she'd become. Or, at least, that's who she thought she'd become—the image of his desire: nothing more, nothing less.

So she just lay there waiting for him to make it better. She waited until she couldn't wait anymore. Then she rolled over onto her side, curled up in a little ball. That's when he called out her name, but she didn't answer. She wasn't that easy. Even shadows have to be cast. He must have understood that. He came toward her then—pressed his nose against her neck, his cock against her ass, and told her she was a very lucky girl, and did she know that—*did she know how lucky she was to have youth and beauty, among the two most prized commodities in a late-capitalist economy*? (She wanted to tell him that she didn't know—that she'd rather have had age and experience.)

But that he found her beautiful! It made her sick with pleasure. "You're old and ugly," she gurgled into her pillow.

But he must have known she was only kidding. (He must have known he had her right where he wanted her.) He ran his hands down the outside of her hips and then across her thighs until they met in the middle and she started to melt. Then he pushed himself back inside. Then she was glad she hadn't said anything stupid. That's how weak she was in the face of sex— not even half as strong as she was at the age of eleven, back when boys were just a side project to be slotted in between scale models and sit-ups.

At the age of twenty, they'd become the centerpiece of her life.

———

NOT SURPRISINGLY, THEN, when Phoebe did finally broach the subject of Evelyn—one night, one phone call—it was with extreme trepidation. "Shouldn't you tell her about us?" she asked Bruce Bledstone. "I mean, don't you think she deserves to know?"

"Why would I want to punish Evelyn like that," he asked her back, "when she's not the one who's done anything wrong?"

He had an answer, it seemed, to everything—even "I love you." That's what she told him in his sweltering arms one freezing, raining day in April. He pushed the hair out of her eyes, told her she was the sweetest thing since brown sugar—even sweeter than saccharine; no contest with NutraSweet. But he couldn't return the sentiment. Not right now. Because "To do so would be to imply a commitment I'm not currently in a position to make," he said. And he didn't want to mislead her. Not to mention the fact that he wasn't entirely sure what those three words meant, love being, arguably, "the most culturally constructed of all cultural constructs."

And Phoebe appreciated his concern—his reticence in the face of such lofty matters, his reluctance to make promises he couldn't keep. But it was not okay that she had fallen in love with Bruce Bledstone and that Bruce Bledstone had not fallen in love with her. It didn't seem possible, either. Not while she was the very definition of lovable—never got in his face except when she was, *well, you know.* Then she was a whole lot of face, mouth open wide like a toilet with the seat up. She had that much enthusiasm for life. She was the *joie* in *de vivre.* She left promptly in the morning. She never once insisted on prophylactics. She rarely mentioned the "other woman." She never even asked if there *were* other women. She was just meek enough to be malleable. But she wasn't so meek that she couldn't take it up the, *well, you know.* She was nice, too.

Then she got mad.

Then she started showing up twenty minutes late for Hegemony 412, if only to make the point that she wasn't just another name on the visiting professor's class list. But the visiting professor would keep lecturing as if she were exactly that—only late for his seminar. It made her so mad that, after class, she'd follow him up the three flights of stairs that led to his office in the colonial mansion so she could ask him if he was planning on giving her an A this semester. *And was that the grade he thought she deserved for keeping her mouth shut—for not calling his wife, his friends, the university administration and telling them all he was a lying piece of shit?*

Once upon a time, they'd spoken of politics and art. Sex

changed all that; sex turned their gazes inward. Now they talked almost exclusively about themselves and the crimes they had and had not committed at the other's expense.

He'd say, "That's a very hurtful thing to call me."

He'd say, "I can't understand why you make me out to be so callous."

Then he'd make a face, clutch his back. ("Excuse me, I was lifting some boxes last night. You know, Phoebe, I'm not as young as I used to be.")

Then he'd explain his grading policy: "As you know, I'm happy to give all my students A's this semester, provided they complete the necessary course work and contribute regularly to class discussions. I'm not much interested in grades."

That's when Phoebe hated him the most. She'd hate him so much she'd follow him all the way back to his falling-down house—all the way back to his bed. Because he loved her there if he loved her anywhere. That he loved her nowhere—that their relationship was as much a matter of convenience as his marriage—was a concept she was unwilling to entertain.

———

"IN LIFE, WE always hurt the people we care the most about."

That's what Bruce Bledstone told Phoebe one late May afternoon in his bed, in his arms, in his thrall. He was leaving Hoover in a week—returning to the city he always did prefer to the country. And she saw there was no hope. (He'd given her a B+; he said it was less suspicious that way.) And she tried to shut him out. She saw him only three times that summer; wrote him only one accusatory letter; accepted only one plane ticket to the Caribbean resort where he was "interrogating postcolonialism" while his wife was away in El Salvador visiting family and friends.

She spent the summer waiting tables at Pita Paradise and overidentifying with the torch songs of Patsy Cline.

It was Evelyn Nuñez's arrival on campus the following September of Phoebe's senior year—by strange coincidence, Evelyn had a one-year appointment with Hoover's German studies department—that brought Bruce Bledstone back to life. When Phoebe looked at Evelyn, she saw him. Not that they looked much alike. She was a petite woman with dark eyes and red lips. There was a swoosh of white in her straight black bob. She wasn't what Phoebe was expecting. She seemed way too sexy to get cheated on.

She had no idea who Phoebe was.

Phoebe was hoping she'd find out.

She had this fantasy that the two of them would end up united, if not in love, then at least in revenge. Not that Phoebe had any intentions of confiding in Evelyn Nuñez. She wasn't ready for Bruce Bledstone never to speak to her again. But she didn't see the harm in following his wife around town and around campus, and waiting in the shadows outside her office door. Small talk, sneezes—she was happy for anything. Nothing was fine, too. It was enough to be near her—near the woman Bruce Bledstone "guessed he loved." (Phoebe guessed she loved her, too.)

She got so far as knocking on Evelyn's office door.

"Come in," said his wife.

"Professor Nuñez?" Phoebe began. "I was wondering if I could, um, talk to you for a second?"

"Please, sit down," she said.

So Phoebe sat down. She sat there staring at Evelyn Nuñez, at the crow's feet that flanked the far corners of her eyes, thinking how someday, as impossible as it now seemed, crow's feet would flank her eyes as well. Then she said, "I'm Phoebe Fine, and I just wanted to tell you that I read your article on commodity fetishism in the *Old Left Review*—"

"You mean the *New Left Review*."

"Right, the *New Left Review*. And I really admired it, and I just wanted to tell you that in person." She gasped for air.

"Thank you for telling me." The woman smiled sweetly. And it gave Phoebe hope and made her feel like dirt all at the same time. What if, by virtue of her involvement with her husband, Phoebe was hurting Evelyn every bit as much as Bruce Bledstone was hurting Phoebe? Or was the truth the only culprit amongst them? Phoebe hadn't figured that one out. Bruce Bledstone was of the latter opinion. "Have you seen my new book?" asked Evelyn.

"Not yet," admitted Phoebe.

"Well, if you're interested in the intersection of Freud and Marx, you might be interested in checking it out. In fact, if you wanted to stop by my house later, I'd be happy to give you a copy. I'm living down on the lake."

"That's okay, I can buy it in the bookstore," exclaimed Phoebe, overwhelmed by the inequality of their respective bodies of knowledge.

Because it wasn't merely that she already knew where Evelyn lived; she'd already helped herself to both Evelyn's peppermint-flavored toothpaste and Evelyn's henna conditioner. Because it wasn't two weekends before that Bruce Bledstone had arrived in Hoover with the express purpose of visiting them both. He'd spent Thursday and Friday with Evelyn. And then, upon her departure on Saturday for an academic conference, he'd invited Phoebe to spend the remainder of the weekend in Evelyn's house on the lake (he'd told Evelyn he was looking forward to spending a few days by himself in the country unwinding after a stressful week) with the minor proviso that Phoebe bring her own sheets. And Phoebe had accepted the invitation—even consented to bring along her own bedding—though not before ranting and raving for a good half hour about his "complete and utter disregard for other people's feelings."

Oh, but the truth was more complicated than that. The truth was that Phoebe derived more than a modicum of pleasure from scenes such as those—scenes that made her life seem important, where once it had seemed merely insipid. To think that not-quite-two years ago she'd been sharing a bunk bed with Meredith Bookbinder on the top floor of Delta Nu Sigma, worrying about which baseball hat to escort to the fall formal and what color pumps to wear with her dress! Now she was the student mistress of a renowned professor of hegemony, the subject of graduate students' gossip, the other woman as opposed to *just some girl.*

And what an other woman she was. "I want this," she'd tell him, and "I want that." And "Fuck me," and "Fuck you," and "Harder," and "Faster," and "More." And she never cried in front of him, never threw up in front of him—not even in the same house as him. She was too busy smoking two cigarettes at once. As if she were not quite human. As if she were made of steel, indurate to barbs and bathos alike.

An iron maiden you got to torture yourself.

ON FRIDAY AFTERNOONS she'd take the Greyhound to the city he always did prefer to the country.

"It's nice to see you," Bruce Bledstone would greet her at the door of his West Village tenement apartment. But it was increasingly unclear just how nice. "I've got a little work to finish up," he'd inform her on his way into his study. "There's beer in the fridge."

"Oh, great, thanks," she'd say, straining to keep her voice up-beat.

She always looked forward to those weekends.

They were always more romantic in theory than they were in practice.

He'd take his time finishing his work while she sat there flipping through magazines. Then he'd take her out to dinner at one of the fashionable bistros in his neighborhood—one of those places where all the women have long necks and thin noses and toss their heads back when they laugh. And all the men are perfectly unshaven and rest their elbows on the backs of the women's chairs and keep their mouths closed even when they talk. And she'd be sitting there pushing her red snapper filet around its eggplant and bell pepper sauce stifling yawn after yawn born of the grueling, ritualistic workout to which she'd subjected her never thin enough, never hard enough, never invincible enough body in the twenty-four hours preceding such visits. And she'd be trying to think of relevant things to say. And the visiting professor wouldn't be helping out. He'd be sitting there looking like he was just biding time while she dredged up old jokes that had long since lost their punch lines.

He was probably waiting for her to disappear.

In the meantime, he'd take her out for the requisite after-dinner drink. The cigarettes always burned out too quickly. The glasses couldn't be refilled fast enough.

It was never entirely clear what they talked about.

Afterward he'd take her home, where he'd take her from behind as if he were doing her some kind of favor. And he wouldn't remember to kiss her first. And there was a part of her that didn't mind. There was a part of her that may even have liked it—liked the way Bruce Bledstone took what he wanted, and to hell with humanity! It was so stolid, so confident—so unlike herself. What she couldn't accept was that his eyes no longer lit up like Christmas lights at the sight of her. Maybe he'd seen her too many times. Maybe that was the problem—he already knew the contours of her naked thighs. There was no fancy new garter belt that could change that.

There was no fancy new position they hadn't already tried.

IT WAS THE second-degree rug burns with which she arrived back at Hoover one Monday after a certain weekend in New Haven—Bruce Bledstone was giving a paper at Yale on counter-hegemonic strategy—that inspired Phoebe to reexamine her commitment to depravity. Not that she wasn't proud of those suppurating wounds. They seemed like final proof of her liberation from suburbia. They seemed like tangible evidence of her victimization at the hands of Bruce Bledstone, as well. And she was sick of lying on his behalf. Which is maybe why she felt compelled to show off those battle scars to at least half the student body, as well as the campus health center nurses, who shook their heads disapprovingly and asked her if she didn't want "another kind of checkup," *if you know what I mean.* (She knew exactly what they meant, but she wasn't interested in a gynecological cure.)

She was still thinking Bruce Bledstone would make it better. Still thinking it was his responsibility to do so. Still thirsting for the subjugation he alone seemed capable of delivering. Because as much of a mess as she made, it was never messy enough—it was always too clean. Which is why she called him up and demanded an explanation for the night in question—a night for which she claimed to have no memory, such was her state of intoxication. It was only partially true. She hadn't been that wasted.

Neither, apparently, had he. "You were crawling around on the floor like a little slut," he seemed to recall. Then he laughed. As if it were all pretty funny. And maybe it was.

Maybe life was all a big joke, and the last to laugh was the first to lose.

Moreover, who was Phoebe Fine to object? Here she'd gone to great lengths to join the ranks of the sluts—as she understood it, a subset of self-realizing gender warriors not ashamed to take full advantage, economic or otherwise, of their prodigious sex drives. (She'd learned so much in Recontextualizing Madonna 316.) That said, in that particular moment in time, she would have preferred to have been crawling around her crib. She wanted her mommy, too. But she didn't have the kind of mommy who could bear to hear about such things. She had the kind of mommy who drowned out all her sorrows—and everyone else's, too—with the ordered legerdemain of Bach's *Goldberg Variations.* And besides, Phoebe was getting a little old to be running home. She was almost twenty-one. That was the really terrible part.

Now that she was all grown up, all she wanted was to be a kid again.

———

AN UGLY PERIOD of Phoebe's life was to follow. She chewed her fingernails into bloody pulp. She showered infrequently, she cried incessantly, she smoked relentlessly. She wore the same outfit every day, her "fat outfit": black palazzo pants and a men's extra-large brown cardigan. She couldn't keep down her breakfast (twelve tablespoons of brown sugar), never mind her lunch (a blueberry muffin). She played Brahms's *Tragic* Overture, op. 81 until she couldn't play it anymore. Then she started up with Air Supply's *Greatest Hits*. ("I'm All Out of Love" was the song that really hit her in the stomach.) And she lost the ability to concentrate on any academic topic that could not directly be connected to Bruce Bledstone. For example, she became a minor expert on Italian Marxism.

She was flunking French.

And she was calling the no-longer-visiting professor's city number at odd hours of the night. Not because she had anything to say. She only wanted to know he still existed—only needed to hear him say hello in that somehow-still-reassuring narcotic drawl of his. The familiarity of his voice would comfort her in the split second of its actuality. It was only after she'd hung up that she'd experience this vast, strangulating nothingness swirling around her. Then she'd feel like she had nothing to look forward to in life. She'd feel as old and jaded and washed-up as only a twenty-year-old can feel. Then she'd cry so hard her lovely, spacey new apartmentmate with the pink hair and the 1950s calico housedresses, Sabine Walinowski, would come knocking to see if she was okay and did she want any homemade miso soup? (She didn't, thank you.)

The time had come for medical intervention.

At least according to her shrink, Nancy Patchogue, it had.

She put Phoebe on these little yellow pills designed to abate her desire to binge on Mint Milano cookies when she felt sad or anxious—as if there were never any resolution, just this ringing in her ears, just this chorus behind her eyes, just this terrible hunger gnawing away at her insides, begging to be quieted with something, anything, mineral or vegetable, food or sex, fish or fowl, anodyne or cyanide, it didn't really matter in the end. In the beginning, Nancy Patchogue told Phoebe, she might get head rushes when she climbed stairs. And she'd almost certainly wake up with a dry mouth, feeling groggy and listless. And it was best if she avoided alcohol.

Even better if she avoided Bruce Bledstone.

It was the opinion of Nancy Patchogue that Bruce Bledstone was the "punishing father" Phoebe never had, her "real father" being a mild-mannered, nearly egoless fellow who preferred *Masterpiece Theatre* and gardening to contact sports and cigars. Oh, she wasn't entirely wrong about Leonard Fine, Nancy Patchogue wasn't—he *was* mild mannered. Phoebe never bought the rest of her doctor's proto-Freudian palaver, preferring to believe that the difference between Bruce Bledstone and guys her own age she might otherwise have dated was that guys her own age had zits, were really insecure, only talked about themselves, and had nothing to teach her. Whereas Bruce Bledstone was a *fucking genius*.

However, she'd come to understand that he "affected her adversely." That was Nancy Patchogue's phrase. And, so, with her doctor's encouragement, she called him up and told him she was "still in love with him," which was why she couldn't see him anymore.

He said, "The two sentiments don't seem to fit together."

He said, "I was never able to express deeper feelings for you, but you've permanently eroticized the topography of my bedroom."

Then he said, "Only time will tell what I've lost. To be perfectly honest, you've always been seventy-five percent phantasmagoric."

But he didn't sound all that upset to hear that Phoebe was leaving him. If anything, he sounded as if he were reading off a TelePrompTer. Is it any wonder she called him back not two weeks later to say she wanted to see him, needed to see him, and it couldn't wait? (Without him, she was just Phoebe Fine with the Fat Face—that's what she kept trying to explain to Nancy Patchogue, but Nancy Patchogue didn't seem to understand; Nancy Patchogue had a fat face herself.)

"Are you sure that's what you want?" he asked her.

"I'm sure," she reassured him. Because she thought she was. She didn't see any other way around it—around her vanity. Bruce Bledstone still made her feel beautiful. He made her feel sophisticated, too. He made her feel as if she were living out some case study from one of those self-help books she'd see women twice her age leafing through in bookstores around town.

"Well, it's always nice to see you," is what he always said.

The desperation lays continued on a sporadic basis.

BUT THERE WERE marked improvements in other areas of Phoebe's life. Thanks to those little yellow pills, she wasn't throwing up half as many times a day as she had been. And she'd settled on a new major—German studies. She even had a weekend affair with a budding Hegelian from Massapequa— followed by another one with a Brazilian drama major who seduced her with his well-honed directorial techniques. ("Relax," he kept saying. His hands started on her shoulder blades and moved south.) And she had a new best friend, Audrey Cone, who encouraged her to channel her excess energies into perfecting her body. That's how Audrey channeled hers. She and Phoebe went to aerobics every day at five. They were religious about eye cream. They ate fat-free muffins for lunch and fruit salad for dinner.

They turned twenty-one three days apart.

Phoebe was in no mood to celebrate. She told as much to Roberta and Leonard. But they didn't listen, they never listened. It was always the same thing. They yelled, "Surprise!" when she walked in the back door. And they made her eat chocolate cake even though she told them she wasn't eating dessert anymore. And they gave her presents she didn't want— Wilkie Collins novels she'd never read, Telemann CDs she'd never listen to. And she had to say, "Thank you," and "I really love it." Even though she *really hated it*—would have been happier with a check for twenty bucks. But at least they'd remembered the date. It was more than she could say for Bruce Bledstone. Not that the oversight particularly surprised her. She was past the point of imagining that he cared. She figured he was probably busy anyway—busy pondering the collapse of the Soviet Union, declared officially defunct with the resignation of Mikhail Gorbachev, the very same day.

IT WAS A mild winter as Hoover winters went.

The spring was short and rainy and torpid—even as it reminded Phoebe of an earlier spring, when the stillness in the air gave way to a certain restlessness that for one fleeting moment seemed to have found its match. But that time was now over. That time now seemed like a distant memory. Phoebe wasn't even the same girl. She was wiser now. She was somehow less sure of herself.

Now she understood the value of fear in love.

Graduation day came and went.

Then it was summer, though not in any ordinary sense, what with school being out forever, and Phoebe having not the faintest idea what to do next. She didn't even have a place to live. It was pretty scary, and she was trying not to cry. (She'd made that mistake the night before.) And she was leaning against a parking meter outside Bruce Bledstone's Upper West

Side sublet. (He and Evelyn had separated. "Trial Deterritorialization" was the phrase he'd used only half in jest. Not that it mattered now. It was too late in the day for Phoebe to imagine she'd been a causative factor.) And she was getting ready to say good-bye after another pointless night, another sporadic lay, when he turned and looked at her from behind a pair of expensive-looking sunglasses that made eye contact all but impossible, and said, "Do me a favor—don't come around here next time you're in a bad mood, with the burden of your problems, expecting to be entertained, to the complete disregard of my life and plans."

And his anger so shocked her that she forgot about her tears. "How can you tell me I'm a burden?" she sputtered. "I thought you were my friend!"

"We were never friends," he demurred. "I mean, we're different from friends."

Then he leaned over and planted a kiss on her cheek as if she were some distant relative to whom he felt obliged to pay his respects—that or some casual acquaintance he might or might not see again, it didn't really matter either way. Then he walked away and she watched him go. She watched his hulking form loping up the street until he was the size of a dot. Then he started to blend in with the others dots. Then he was gone, and she was alone with her thoughts. And she was thinking: Bruce Bledstone was right about one thing at least: he never was her friend, never would be. And the realization left her strangely relieved. It was easier hating him than loving him.

If only she could have held on to her anger!

But she couldn't. She couldn't bear to imagine herself a mere detail of a pattern. Which is how she imagined herself when, a month or two later, she learned through a mutual acquaintance that she hadn't been Bruce Bledstone's first sleep-over student, and she wasn't his last, either.

———

WHICH WAS MAYBE why, one, two, not quite three years past those first tremulous barrette unsnappings, when she and Bruce Bledstone were living barely twenty blocks from each other, she was still, occasionally, quixotically, calling him from downtown barrooms at half past midnight. She wouldn't be drunk, but she wouldn't be sober either. She'd be riding that middle wave of inebriation where the *poverty of everyday life* seems at the very least irrelevant, in many ways comic, and at rare moments charmed. "I want to see you," she'd shout-whisper into the receiver in her best sex-toy voice—two parts pure bravura, one part little girl lost in the mall.

Because, even with her competitive-tennis days long over, she hated the idea that she'd lost. Because in the distant reaches of her convoluted brain, she was still thinking she could make him love her. Because, thanks to Bruce Bledstone, now she knew the difference between the "putting out system," as in a preindustrial system of production marked by pride in individual achievement and encapsulated by the weavers of Silesia, and the regular old twentieth-century version of "putting out," as in "for a good time, call . . ." And because, at that particular moment, her life was so distinctly unglamorous—her main connection to New York City being the Class Act Temporary Employment Agency—that even the most degraded of lays had come to seem like compensation. Not to mention the fact that her campaign to rid herself of the final vestiges of her sheltered upbringing was as yet unfulfilled—i.e., in so many ways, alienation was its own reward.

He'd let a meaningful little wisp of a silence pass between them—at least, it would seem meaningful to Phoebe. Then he'd ask her, "Are you sure that's what you want?"

Just as he always had—as if the whole thing had only ever been her idea, and her sex drive that had required servicing. And he had only ever succumbed unwittingly and abjectly to the near-impossible task of trying to service it. "Unfulfillable Phoebe." That had been his nickname for her. And he wasn't entirely wrong: rarely had she been anything other than "in the mood." But only because sex had been the one thing she'd had to offer that he'd never seemed to tire of.

But that he still wanted it—that he was still willing!—somehow amazed her. Apparently, Bruce Bledstone couldn't say no to sex—not even sex from his worst nightmare. "How soon will you be here?" he'd want to know.

"Ten minutes," she'd promise. "Fifteen at the very most." Because, despite everything, she was still loath to make him wait.

Feigning illness or exhaustion, she'd part company with her friends—step out onto the street, onto Broadway or Second Avenue, Grand Street or Lafayette, the cityscape scintillating before her eyes like some kind of sequined tube top circa 1979, somewhere between tacky and profound. And she'd have an acid burn in her stomach from all the cheap wine and bummed cigarettes. And she'd be wearing a pair of high-heeled mules that gave her cause to imagine her reinvention as the Nelly Bly of the bedroom complete. And she'd be trying not to look at the street people—at their fallen faces and taped sneakers and misspelled, block-lettered signs: I CAN'T NOW LONGER FEED MY FAMMILY IF YOU BELIEF IN GOD PLEASE HELP ME GOD BLESSES YOU. That whole lives could be reduced to one illiterate sentence—it was shocking, it was inconceivable.

It was too close to Phoebe's own failure to ingratiate herself with the professional class, and therefore not her problem, at least not right now, maybe someday.

In the meantime, she'd hail a cab—even though she couldn't really afford it, what with her temp jobs bringing in barely ten bucks an hour. But this would qualify as a special occasion. This was better than nicotine. That's how she'd justify the expenditure. That's what she'd tell herself while she watched the blocks scrolling by, one after another after another, just like the paper filmstrips she and Emily used to pull through the windows of empty noodle boxes back when they were young, not so many years ago.

MAYBE HIS LATEST tome, *The Praxis of Theory,* had sold a lot of copies. Maybe he'd come into some family money. Whatever the case, Bruce Bledstone had come up in the world. After the divorce, he moved into a two-thousand-square-foot loft on the western edge of Chinatown. There was a fish market on the first floor. He lived on the third.

He'd open the door and smile at her, but he wouldn't say hello. He'd say, "Can I take your coat?" and Phoebe wouldn't refuse.

Then he'd offer her a drink, and she wouldn't refuse that either. Then he'd turn on the television. But it wouldn't be like it used to be—when the picture on the screen was just a momentary distraction from their own melodrama. Now they'd sit there staring straight ahead, watching and waiting for the right time—there never really was one—to go through the motions. That's all they were now: physical sensations she was far too self-conscious to experience as pleasurable.

It was enough to have recorded the event—enough to be

offered proof that she and Bruce Bledstone were still capable of producing certain fluids in each other's company. Or, at least, it was better than being forgotten. That's what Phoebe would tell herself in the morning. He wouldn't say good-bye and neither would she. She'd make her exit just as she'd made her entrance the night before—without explication, but for the occasional joke regarding her distaste for swallowing.

What more was there to say?

LETTERS. PHOTOGRAPHS. GIFTS. Bruce Bledstone didn't believe in any of them; Bruce Bledstone didn't have a senti- mental bone in his body. ("In a late-capitalist society," he once opined, "everything exacts a price.") So he came and went with few traces: a signed copy of his book ("For Phoebe," he'd writ- ten. "Best wishes, Bruce"); a handful of disintegrating petals left over from a generic get-well bouquet he'd sent her when she was holed up in the hospital during the fall of her senior year (let's just say she made a rapid recovery); a ninety-minute cas- sette tape with only one song to its name. He'd left it in her mailbox at school that same winter—the winter she kept pre- tending to break up with him. He'd written "Phoebe's Song" on the cardboard insert. It was a clarinet, accordion, drum, and bagpipe number by the Rhodope folk troop of Bulgaria. It was the same one he was playing in the car that night—the night they first got together under all those stupid stars. The visiting professor seemed to have forgotten that it "wasn't really [her] taste." Or maybe he hadn't forgotten at all. Maybe he was rewriting history to suit his own needs. Maybe he was coercing a subordinate class to conform to his interests.

Maybe he was just trying to be funny.

She liked a guy with a good sense of humor.

9. Kevin McFeeley

OR *"The Romantic from Ronkonkoma"*

LEONARD FINE WAS the first to point out that Kevin Mc-Feeley bore an uncanny resemblance to Frédéric Chopin. And he wasn't wrong: with his long skinny face, dark wavy hair, slightly bulbous nose, and haunted blue eyes, Kevin McFeeley always did look a little like the famous Delacroix portrait of the so-called poet of the piano. Oh, but the similarities didn't end there! As with Frédéric, Kevin both wrote and performed his own compositions, albeit on a Fender Stratocaster. And while he wasn't exactly tormented by gloomy visions of his war-torn homeland—as a general rule, things were pretty calm in Ronkonkoma, Long Island—his romantic impulse (let it be said) was formidable.

Never mind the Valentine's Day card he rendered out of three-hole-punched scrap paper culled from the Kinko's copy shop, where he earned his daily keep. Not long after he and Phoebe met—a few months after graduation, at an ironic pinball dive on the Lower East Side featuring Elvis lamps and underground porn flicks starring Japanese waifs getting duct-taped to upright chairs—Kevin McFeeley showed up at the door of her East Village studio sublet to declare himself. He had a towel thrown over his rubberized Fonz T-shirt. He was gripping an econo-sized, generic-brand shampoo. He was staring at his Converse sneakers. "I don't want to impose or anything," he began. "But do you think I could, like, borrow your shower? For some reason, there's no, like, hot water in my building. And to be perfectly honest, I'm smelling kind of, like, bad."

"Go ahead," Phoebe told him. "Just don't, like, leave any hair on the soap." (She like, had a thing about that.)

"No problem," said Kevin. "Oh, and thanks. Thanks a lot." He disappeared into the shower.

He emerged twenty minutes later with wet hair.

"Well, I guess I'll be going," he said about twenty separate times.

"Do you want a beer or something?" she eventually acceded.

"Maybe just one," he happily agreed.

He had a beer.

He stayed for seven months.

But then, Phoebe never actually asked him to leave. New York City could get pretty lonely, especially when the weather turned cold and wet, and the wind off the Hudson left the sidewalks littered with broken umbrellas that looked like wing-clipped birds.

And, in all honesty, Phoebe never actually gave all that much thought to being Kevin McFeeley's girlfriend. She fell into their relationship the way others fall asleep at the wheel.

And, Kevin McFeeley rubbed her feet, and brought her cupcakes, and illegally wired her apartment for cable, and let her make him up like a girl—with eyeliner, mascara, lipstick, and blush. She hadn't known guys could be that sweet. She thought all men were more or less like Bruce Bledstone and Humphrey Fung.

Or maybe it was that it had never occurred to her before that she might be attracted to someone who didn't treat her like a mild irritant.

And he told her he loved her, Kevin did. He told her that about sixteen times a day. And the only other guy who'd ever said that to her was Spitty Clark, and she'd always assumed he was too drunk to mean it. Moreover, there were times when she thought she loved Kevin, too. Though what she probably loved even more than Kevin was the idea of someone being in love with *her*. It seemed like a radical notion. It seemed like the "real thing."

But it got pretty tiring reminiscing about TV shows from their youth. ("Remember Rose on *Zoom*?" "Remember Letter-Man on *Electric Company*?" "Remember that *Twilight Zone* where that guy sees that other guy standing on the wing of that airplane?" "Remember that *Brady Bunch* when Alice becomes a drill sergeant?" "Remember that *Gilligan's Island* where Gilligan wants to be the skipper?") Especially since she'd never seen half the shows Kevin reminisced about—only heard about them secondhand from Brenda Cuddihy.

And there were only so many Saturday afternoons she could get stoned and go to the Museum of Natural History and find the gem room a "total mind fuck"—only so many Saturday nights she could muster up the energy to go hear the Sun Ra Arkestra play at Tramps.

And while she was happy to serve as muse to all those potential grunge anthems Kevin was writing about life, love, and suburbia—"Gated Community" was, perhaps, her favorite— neither his singing nor his songwriting ever impressed her. The lyrics she found derivative ("Are you having a ball / Living behind a wall / In the shadow of the mall?"), the chord progressions simplistic (tonic, dominant, tonic, dominant).

And it made her jealous that he got to be the creative genius—she, merely, the girlfriend of the creative genius.

And he wasn't just poor, he was penurious. The one time in six months he took her out to eat—at Dojo, a New York University hangout specializing in inexpensive vegetarian fare— she ended up paying. She ordered brown rice and steamed vegetables. To save money, he ordered the carrot soup. But when the check came, he didn't even have enough cash to cover his portion of the bill.

And he had this annoying habit of calling everything he liked "raw." He'd say, "The new Neil Young album is so unbelievably raw."

To which she'd reply, "Sushi is raw. The new Neil Young album is cool. I mean, *you* think it's cool. I'd rather listen to Deee-Lite any day."

And he left his smelly socks on her kitchen counter even though she asked him not to.

And he spoke so slowly.

And he smelled like pickles when he didn't wash.

And he never read the newspaper.

And he never left home without a dog-eared copy of *Naked Lunch.*

And he was so skinny he made her feel fat.

And he got so sweaty during sex.

And he wanted to do it three times a day. And when she wasn't in the mood, which was all the time—it turned out Phoebe was fulfillable after all—he went and jerked himself off. He said he couldn't fall asleep without coming. He said it really relaxed him. Little wonder that having sex with Kevin McFeeley came to seem about as special as flossing.

And he was always complaining about all the "sellout cellphone phonies" in Soho even though he was not so secretly obsessed with supermodels—called them all by their first names as in, "Did you see Kate in *Harper's Bazaar* this month? She's so skinny it's disgusting." When what he really meant—Phoebe was sure of it—was that he got a boner every time he laid eyes on Kate Moss.

And he thought musicians lived above politics. He thought musicians had no business voting. Phoebe told him not voting was a political statement in and of itself, but he refused to see how.

And there were times she thought the love Kevin McFeeley had to offer was right out of some corny movie from the 1950s, where the guy worships the girl just for being so pretty to look at and so agreeable to his advances, and not because there's anything intrinsically compelling about her. In truth, Kevin McFeeley never seemed all that interested in learning anything more about Phoebe than he already knew, which wasn't all that much. For example, he never thought to ask her what she wanted to do with the rest of her life. (She was currently deciding among the professions of feminist film theorist, high-class hooker, and night watchman—anything to avoid waking up early.)

And he never shut up about his band, Mr. Potato Head. "I swear to God that dickweed in Falstaff's Nostril stole my fuckin' pedal technique!" he'd declaim while she tried to read Jacques Lacan.

Not to mention the fact that her and Kevin's relationship was a comparatively stable one, and Phoebe had yet to outgrow her attachment to self-destruction. She kept an oral history of Edie Sedgwick by her bed. She secretly suspected that being well-adjusted was the greatest sickness of all. And at the same time it drove her crazy that Kevin thought he was so dissolute and demimonde just because he'd snorted heroin a few times.

(There were limits to Phoebe's interest in self-immolation, after all.)

Just as she could never stop doubting that Kevin McFeeley, who'd dropped out of State University of New York at Fredonia after the second year, was good enough for her. Which is to say, important enough and well-enough read and great enough a talent to be deserving of her importance, her greatness, her talent.

And at the same time, there must have been something wrong with Kevin McFeeley if he loved her, an essentially meritless person. Could he be that crazy? Didn't he know that she used to throw up brown sugar, and occasionally still did?

But, then, Kevin McFeeley was the kind of guy one got used to having around. He was really good at fixing things that broke. He didn't mind going to battle with water bugs. He'd take out your trash if it was filled with maggots and you were too grossed out to touch it yourself.

And it was nice having someone socially acceptable to bring home to Whitehead for dinner. Obviously, Leonard and Roberta would have preferred it if Kevin had been about to make his debut at Carnegie Recital Hall as opposed to some Avenue A beer-and-burger joint with an open-mike night. ("Have you ever thought about learning to read music?" Roberta asked him one night over London broil, knowing full well the answer would be no.) But at least he was the right age. At least he wasn't married. And he was always very polite. He always helped clear the table. Once he even came to dinner bearing a crate of tangerines.

And then, one day, none of it mattered. One day, circumstances overrode character. Poor Kevin. It wasn't his fault.

At a certain moment in time, Phoebe felt strongly that it was all hers.

10. Arnold Allen

OR *"The Man in the Sheepskin Coat"*

"EXCUSE ME, MISS. Excuse me. Miss. Miss. Excuse me. Miss . . ." That's how it started; that's what he said—at the end of the winter, in the middle of the crosswalk, on her way home from work. She didn't answer. She figured whoever it was probably only wanted a handout. And she was hungry, and tired, and stingy. And it was getting dark, and she was eager to kick off her shoes and put up her feet. And everyone knew you weren't supposed to talk to strangers. Just like you weren't supposed to chew gum when you played sports. Or smoke if you were on the pill. Or drink when you drove. It wasn't safe. And look how far playing it safe had gotten her—all the way to Toffler Associates, a medical-textbook supplier on East Forty-third. And tomorrow it would be something else: the NYU Dental School, the Boys Club of America, *Roofer's Monthly* magazine, the private banking division of Chase Manhattan.

Every morning Phoebe rode the subway to another glass-and-steel monolith, another high-speed elevator that led to another set of frosted-glass doors, behind which another moon-faced receptionist leafing through that morning's tabloids would avert her eyes just long enough to punch in the three-digit extension of Debbie or Barbara, Denise or Louise Ann, any one of whom would emerge from behind a simple wooden door with a simple wooden smile only to lead her back through that same wooden door—down one hall, then another, then another, past the ladies' room, the water cooler, the microwave, and the minifridge—"If you brought your lunch, you can put it in there"—to another corkboard cubicle "humanized" by another chimpanzee calendar, another petrified-wood placard proclaiming the benefits of friendship, another phalanx of Smurfs sitting atop another beige computer on which she'd be asked to compose another set of inconsequential memos for another fake-cheerful executive—if she wasn't already copying the Greenwich, Connecticut, phone book into a database, or filing color-coded purchase orders into a gargantuan black ring binder.

It was curiosity that made her glance sideways—curiosity and maybe a little of something else. Arnold Allen was attractive in a fatherly way. Not that he looked like Leonard Fine— far from it. He was a light-skinned black man in early middle age, with a slender face and glassy brown eyes floating in pools of bright white. And he was dressed in brown wide-wale corduroys, tassel loafers, and a sheepskin coat, the soiled collar of which seemed incongruous with his otherwise elegant demeanor. "Miss. I'm sorry to bother you." He walked at her side as he spoke. "But I couldn't help noticing you on the street. And. Well. Look." Here he laughed lightly, as if the absurdity of the situation had not escaped him. "I don't do things like this very often, but you have a rare sort of beauty." With that, he reached into his jacket pocket and pulled out a business card. Phoebe didn't so much take it as have it thrust into her palm. *Arnold Allen, Vice President, Atlantic Pictures, Burbank, California,* she read as she walked. Could it be true? Things like this didn't happen every day.

"Thank you," she said, stunned and flattered and wary all in the same breath. She paused on the corner to drop the card into her bag. "I'll definitely give you a call." With that, she turned to walk away.

"Miss! Please!" It was the urgency of Arnold Allen's supplication that made her stop in her tracks and turn back around. So the two of them were standing three feet apart, blocking the way, commuters pushing past them. She thought she'd let him finish his sentence. It seemed like the least she could do. "Please don't go yet," he importuned. "Arnold Allen. You haven't heard of me? *Mother of the Bride, Last Day in Heaven, You're the One I Want.* I've produced more hits than you are old." He extended his arm. "We haven't even been properly introduced."

Phoebe took a step forward, met his hand halfway. She didn't see the harm in that. And besides, maybe she had heard of Arnold Allen. It sounded vaguely familiar, the way most names do. "Hi," she said, "I'm Phoebe."

"Well, it's a pleasure to meet you," he said, laying a second hand on top of the pile, like a visiting dignitary in the act of concluding a peace accord. "I just—I can't get over your face!" His eyes danced, his brow furled. Phoebe turned a cheek, smiled in embarrassment. "For God's sake, tell me—are you a model? A student?"

Suspicion seized her. She reasoned it away. Why would this man lie? Unless he only wanted a date. But he didn't seem like that kind of guy. He was too old, the wrong race. "I work in documentary film," she told him. It was a lie but not an unrealistic one.

She'd been wondering lately if real life wasn't, ultimately, beyond the reaches of theoretical paradigms.

"So you already know a little about the business . . ."

"Sort of, yeah, but I should really be going," she twittered, her discomfort level rising at the thought that already her lie was catching up with her. "I have your number. I promise I'll give you a call."

Arnold Allen released her hand, grimaced dolefully. "I understand. Maybe . . . could I just walk with you for a few blocks?"

What did this man want from her? This man made Phoebe nervous.

Oh, but the request seemed innocuous enough. And she was concerned about offending him. She figured he probably got attitude from all kinds of white people who didn't believe a black man could hold such an important position. And she considered herself different, progressive. And besides, Kevin McFeeley had been just a stranger once, too—just a face and a voice before he became her boyfriend.

And wasn't most of life a calculated risk? Wasn't even crossing the street a kind of gamble with the gods? There were brakes that could fail, drivers who could fall asleep at the wheel. And she hated disappointing people. And she was starved for attention. And she was vain—quietly, pathologically vain. Which is to say that she felt somehow compelled to reward Arnold Allen for having identified in her a "rare sort of beauty."

"Okay," she found herself agreeing. "But just a few blocks. Then I really have to go."

"No problem," he said. "Whatever you want. That's cool with me."

———

AS THEY MADE their way up Second Avenue, Arnold Allen ran down an extended list of his Hollywood credits, told her he was the brother of a famous weatherman and that he'd been raised in Brooklyn but now made his home in Beverly Hills.

"Speaking of home," Phoebe interjected on the corner of Ninth Street. "This is where I head off."

"Listen!" he clucked, as if a brilliant idea had suddenly come over him. "We're taping a pilot, and I just know you'd be perfect as the sexy, young schoolteacher. It's not a big part, but it's a great place to start. Would you be willing to read a few lines for me?"

"Now?" she croaked. She was worried she'd perform poorly, ruin her chances. "I mean, maybe I should practice first. I mean, I've never really acted before. I mean, not professionally or anything."

"Don't worry about it," he said. "You'll be fine. This'll be your practice. Then when you show up Friday, you'll know what to expect."

Friday? Everything was happening so fast.

But, then, wasn't that just life—a series of stultifying lulls interrupted by great bursts of activity? And what if one day she would look back on this meeting with a kind of disbelief that it had all been so easy? "I mean, I guess I could do that," she started to say. "It's just that—it's getting kind of late."

"Hey, where do you live—do you live near here?"

"Yeah, but—"

"Great—why don't we go to your house?"

"My house?"

Arnold Allen prodded her upper arm playfully. "Hey. Listen. Don't be scared of me. I'm old enough to be your father. You're a beautiful woman, but I'm not after that. Call my secretary. Go ahead. Ask her if I'm a nice guy. Three hours difference. She'll still be there."

"Maybe we could go to a restaurant?"

"Listen. I'd say yes, but we're going to need a little privacy, and there's not much time." He cocked his head in the direction of uptown. "I got a dinner date in an hour, and I'm clearing out of here tomorrow morning." He lowered his chin, narrowed his eyes. "Arnold Allen. You sure you've never heard of me?"

Maybe she had. But he was still a stranger. And having him up to her apartment—it didn't seem right, it didn't seem safe.

But she was sick of collating and faxing and filing and phoning and transcribing. And she wouldn't have minded a little extra cash for shoes. She wore the same pair of black suede platform sandals every day. The toes were worn and gray, the platforms were melting away to ground level. And the daily stress of shoplifting—she could have done without it, frankly. Someday she meant to pay back the Fifth Avenue Epicure for all those lovely premade grilled vegetable sourdough baguette sandwiches she'd sneaked into her handbag of late. In the meantime, she couldn't persuade herself to spend an entire hour's wage on a piece of bread and three zucchini rounds. She would rather have skipped lunch. She always planned to skip lunch. She always planned to revert back to her earlier starvation diet of frozen yogurt and muffin crumbs. But she always got hungry. That was the problem.

She was human, after all.

And whether or not they could actually afford it, she'd convinced herself that the three hundred dollars Leonard and Roberta shelled out every month to help cover her rent was a sacrifice they were making at the expense of their own comfort. Oh, but it wasn't so much the money; it was the failure to live up to her promise that their beneficence implied. It had been said in the Fine family since before anyone could remember that if anyone made a fortune it would be Phoebe. And it had been said with a tinge of condescension, since the expensive tastes she'd been shown to possess (beginning in high school, with her purchase of Guess overalls) were considered fundamentally incompatible with the values her parents subscribed to—values defined not by the vagaries of the stock market but by the crescendos and decrescendos of a mad genius's last symphony.

Condescension or not, however, Phoebe was determined to prove Leonard and Roberta right—and wrong. She wanted to show them just how much happiness money could buy. Later they'd whisper between themselves, "Isn't it amazing?" And "Could it be true? Could she really have made it that big, that fast?"

And she'd pretend not to hear.

And there was something about walking the streets of Manhattan when you were nobody, nowhere, nothing. Even the homeless guys mocked you: "Smile, honey—things ain't that bad." What did you do then—smile? If you smiled, they won. If you didn't smile, they won, too. It was television's fault. It was all those glossy magazines with their preternaturally radiant cover girls. Every idiot on the street saw herself as a celebrity in the making. Was that it? Or was it rather that Phoebe Fine in particular had been reared to believe that she was special and others ordinary?

And what if she was to pass up her one big chance in life to be rich and famous? How would she ever forgive herself for something like that? Not that she necessarily aspired to be rich and famous, and she certainly didn't see herself as an actress type. She was far too self-conscious, not quite enough of an exhibitionist. But she wanted to be on TV; she wanted people to see her on TV. She wanted all the naysayers from her past to find her transmogrified into a glittering, impenetrable amalgam of pixels they had once known as flesh and blood, back when she was a mere mortal. They would be looking and she would be laughing, privately, somewhere far from the camera's lens. And that distance—that divide—would be enough poetic justice for one lifetime.

"Alright, let's go to my house." She looked at Arnold Allen.

"Terrific," he said. "You're a great girl. Really. I can tell."

THEY RODE THE elevator in silence, Arnold Allen air-whistling at the ceiling, Phoebe staring at her shoes. She wasn't so much nervous as she was anxious to get the whole thing over with. She wanted the results without the effort. "This is my apartment," she said, fitting the key in the lock and flipping on the lights. "It's actually a sublet. I have to get out once a month. That's how I can afford to live alone."

"Not bad," he said, circling the tiny living room. "I bet you get nice light in here."

Gripping the sill, he leaned his head out the window, extended one leg behind him in a crude approximation of an arabesque.

"It's okay." She found it odd that he wasn't wearing any socks. "Can I take your coat or anything?"

"Oh, that's okay—thanks." He bounded over to the upright piano and straddled the bench. "You play?"

He ran his hands up and down the keys but not hard enough to make a sound.

"Not really," Phoebe mumbled. "I studied the violin."

"The violin? Great instrument. Very romantic."

"So what should I read?"

"Oh, right." Arnold Allen stood up. "This is the thing. I don't have the script on me, but the setup is this. You got a room full of disobedient children, okay? And you come in, you're wearing something tight and sexy, and you tell them to quiet down. And they all shut up and you start giving them a lesson. You got that?"

"So I have to improvise?"

"Exactly." He paused. Then he said, "Hey, you got something cute to put on? It'll make the whole thing more believable. A short dress maybe? A silk top? Something like that?"

Phoebe's breath left her body. Was a change of outfit really necessary? There were always so many obstacles. And she was always so exhausted—exhausted before she'd ever exerted herself. "I mean I guess so," she faltered, her eyes grazing the hemline of her knee-length beige skirt, her corporate skirt. How hideous it looked to her at that moment! "I mean—if you think it'll help."

"Hey, come here." Arnold Allen walked toward her. Up close, he smelled vaguely medicinal. Like rubbing alcohol. Or maybe floor wax. "You're not nervous, are you?" He threw an avuncular arm around her back. " 'Cause there's nothing to be nervous about."

"I'm fine." She smiled wanly before she slipped out from under his arm and disappearing into her tiny bedroom, where her cheap, trendy clothes hung between a stranger's suits. "I'll just be one minute," she called out into the living room. Then she scanned her wardrobe, settled on a raspberry wraparound miniskirt and an off-white satin-polyester blouse. She was a little embarrassed about her legs—she hadn't shaved them in three days—but she didn't have the patience to put on stockings. She wanted to get her debut over with. She didn't like having this man in her apartment. But she wanted the part in the pilot; she wanted it badly now. Just as her reality seemed suddenly, pitifully, inadequate. She hated sharing a closet with a phantom.

She came back out in the miniskirt and blouse.

"Wow!" bleated Arnold Allen. He was sitting on the sofa now, his legs crossed like a woman, his coat still on but open to reveal a maroon V-neck sweater and the gentle swell of a beer belly. "You look hot!" Again he stood up, walked toward her. "Don't be scared," he said, reaching for her blouse, which he unbuttoned to the height of her bra, while she stood there frozen, stranded, strangely calm. As if her own paralysis rendered her inviolable. "There, that's better," he said. "That's even hotter." Then he went back to the sofa. "Okay, so I want you to walk in from the bedroom—imagine you're walking into the classroom from the hall—and then I want you to tell the kids to quiet down."

As directed, Phoebe disappeared back into the bedroom before sauntering back out to the tune of "I want quiet in this classroom!" The image of Mr. Spumato coursed across her brain. "One more peep, and you're outta here! Is that understood?" She swung her hips as she made her way over to an imaginary blackboard—actually a framed poster of a Monet painting. The water lilies. She grabbed a ruler off the desk, tapped the glass. Now she was Mrs. Kosciouwicz. "Today you'll be learning about the Pilgrims. I want you all to open to page two-sixty-three in your social studies textbooks." She looked at Arnold Allen.

"Bravo," he said, clapping in slow motion. "You're a natural, Phoebe."

"Thank you," she said, smiling fraudulently, thinking maybe that would satisfy him, maybe he would leave her alone now.

"Hey, come here," he said, patting the seat cushion next to him.

She didn't move. He patted the seat again. She didn't see that she had a choice. Or did she?

She walked over to where he sat, took a seat next to him on the edge of the sofa. "Hey," he said, reaching for the back of her neck. "You seem tense."

"I'm fine," she said.

But she no longer knew if she was. She was suddenly seized with terror, not so much of Arnold Allen but of the trajectory she felt herself to have put into motion—a trajectory that seemed to have a momentum of its own. Such that there was no escape, only capitulation. Every night, right before she fell asleep, she would feel herself falling, and she would lurch in her bed. It was like that now, except there was no corrective frame that followed, no return to stasis, just a terrible feeling in her stomach that she was getting exactly what she deserved—that she'd been a *very bad girl*.

"You sure?" Arnold Allen wanted to know, his breath on her neck, his hands fanning out to her shoulders. " 'Cause there's nothing to be scared of. Hey, you got any lotion? Your legs look dry. Let me put some lotion on them. It'll relax you—I promise."

In that moment, Phoebe felt strongly that it was wrong to let this man touch her. But Arnold Allen was attractive in a kind of fatherly way. Was that it?

Or was it rather that she was so intent on the job he dangled before her that she would have submitted to any number of degradations in order to secure it, lotion being the least of them?

"I'll be right back," she said on her way to the bathroom.

She came back gripping a large squirt-top bottle of moisturizer—"for sensitive skin" it read in large red capitals. Then she sat back down next to the man in the sheepskin coat. "Hey," he said, tapping his knee twice in rapid succession. "Stretch your legs out. Come on. Don't be shy."

Slowly, diffidently, performatively, Phoebe turned sideways, positioned her back against the arm of the sofa, extended her legs across Arnold Allen's lap, and closed her eyes—while he ran his greasy hands up and down the length of her calves. And when he moved farther up her legs, to the top of her thighs, she didn't mind. Or maybe it was rather that she was willing not to mind—willing to live with this bargain with which he seemed to be presenting her. So long as things didn't go any further. That's what she kept telling herself.

So long as he didn't touch her "there."

Oh, but who was she kidding? There must have been a side of Phoebe that wanted to be there, watching herself, watching herself go where no nice girl from Whitehead, New Jersey— no self-respecting student of Wolfgang Amadeus Mozart— was supposed to go. Just as there must have been a side of her that understood the mistake she was making, and relished the lapse. Wasn't she far from home now? Wasn't she *really living* now?

Wasn't it disgusting?

To think she'd only known this man for forty-five minutes!

And when would it be over? When? When? When? When would she find peace?

———

IT MUST HAVE been five minutes later that Arnold Allen jumped up and onto his feet, dislodging Phoebe's legs in the process. "I almost forgot about dinner!" he squawked.

Phoebe stood up, too. She was energized by the prospect of his imminent departure. "So anyway," she said, yanking on the back of her miniskirt. "Where do I show up on Friday?"

"Oh, right," he said. "You got a piece of paper and a pen?"

She brought him a notebook and a pencil from the desk.

In a large, childish scrawl, he wrote down a low-number address on Broadway.

"Do you know the side street?" she asked him.

He squinted at the ceiling. "The side street? It might be Eleventh. Yeah that's it. It's, like, Eleventh or Twelfth or something. I'll write it down for you." He looked up in the middle of his 2. "Oh, hey," he said. "I almost forgot. You're a member of the Guild, right?"

"The Guild?"

"The Screen Actors Guild."

Phoebe's eyes fell to the floor, her ribs contracted around her heart. She felt the omission was somehow her fault. In her zeal to impress Arnold Allen, she must have led him to believe that she was someone she wasn't—an aspiring actress, a member of his tribe. "I've never really acted before," she mumbled miserably.

Now Arnold Allen squinched up his face, sighed through his teeth. As if it were a big problem, a huge problem, an insuperable problem. "Damn," he swore. "I shoulda thought of that." Then he fell silent, lifted his chin, squinted critically at the ceiling as if deep in thought, his lips folded down in a frown, his eyebrows knit into one, while she stood there waiting, watching, about to be disappointed. Just as she always was. At least, it seemed that way to Phoebe—as if her whole life had been a series of near misses. She thought back to the Counties, sorority rush. Even Hoover had been a disappointment; she'd wanted to go to Yale but hadn't gotten in.

"Look, I'm going back to L.A. in the morning," Arnold Allen began again. "I can probably sign you up out there—I got some friends I can call, some strings I can pull—and if we're lucky, they'll get the application processed by Friday." He nod-ded his head up and down. "Yeah, I think that's what we're going to have to do." Phoebe's breath returned to her. Maybe the situation was salvageable, after all. Maybe this time she'd get lucky. "Yeah, I think it's all gonna work out," Arnold Allen continued. "But I should tell you that it's five hundred bucks to join."

"Five hundred bucks?" she whispered in disbelief.

"And it's gonna have to be up front."

"Can't they bill me?"

"I'm afraid not, sweetheart," he said with a knowing chortle. As if it were an old problem, a familiar problem. "I mean, you can try and do it yourself in New York. Go ahead! But it'll probably take a week or two to process. That is, unless you want to try and pay someone off." He winked and laughed some more.

What was to be done? She didn't feel it was polite to ask Arnold Allen to lay out the cash himself. Except five hundred dollars was the sum and total of her checking account. And she didn't have a savings account.

And yet, to have come this far only to be back to square one all because of a little money! And what was money, anyway, but a false promise, a flimsy rectangle that passed from hand to hand, and man to man, like some kind of airborne virus? "I mean, I guess I can give you the cash," she found herself saying.

"Listen," he began again in a newly sober tone of voice. "I'll write you a receipt for the amount just in case there's any prob-lem, which I'm sure there won't be." He put the pen back to the paper. "Five hundred dollars received from Phoebe Fine," he wrote at the bottom of the page. Then he signed his name.

"Shouldn't you date it?" she asked him.

"Oh, right," he answered.

The phone was ringing. "Excuse me," said Phoebe, lifting the receiver to her ear, thinking she should have let the machine pick up. But what if it was Kevin? He would start to worry if she wasn't home. She'd told him she'd be home by seven. But it wasn't Kevin. It was Emily calling from the West Coast. Emily was in her last year of law school. Emily was engaged to be married to an independently wealthy Argentinian Jewish human-rights activist. "Oh, hi," said Phoebe. "Listen, I have company. Can I call you right back? I actually can't just talk for a minute. I'll tell you later. Emily, please. Look—I'll call you back in ten minutes!" Out of the corner of her eye, Phoebe saw Arnold Allen motioning at his watch, mouthing the words, "I have to go." She felt yanked in every direction; she felt like a marionette manned by competing puppeteers.

She somehow blamed her older sister—for always being so suspicious. And for never giving her the benefit of her doubt. And for never having had to resort to desperate measures like this. Indeed, things came easily to Emily, always had. At least, it had always seemed that way to Phoebe— it seemed to Phoebe that Emily thought you only had to ask for what you wanted in life and you got it. Whereas, in Phoebe's experience of the world, sometimes you had to grovel.

"EMILY—PLEASE!" she lashed out at her sister before she hung up.

———

THERE WAS A twenty-four-hour banking center on the corner. Arnold Allen waited on the sidewalk out front. A homeless guy with an eye patch opened the door. It was the same homeless guy with an eye patch who always opened the door. "Pretty lady," he said on Phoebe's way inside. "Can you spare some change on the way out?"

She didn't answer. Just as she always didn't answer. She felt she worked too hard for her money to be giving it away.

After every hundred dollars she withdrew, the screen flashed, "For security purposes, please reenter your secret code." (They were all the same, they were all suspicious—even the bank machine.)

She told the homeless guy, "Sorry" on her way out. Then she handed over her life savings to Arnold Allen, who tucked the wad in his back pocket and kissed her carelessly on the forehead. "Thanks, love," he said. "I really gotta run. I got a dinner at Elaine's in twenty minutes. Listen, you get nervous, have any questions, just call. I'm staying at the Carlyle. I'll be back in L.A. tomorrow night. I'll call you Thursday. You got my card. And don't forget—Friday, ten A.M. sharp. Don't be late. You're gonna be great. Hey, that rhymes!"

Then he turned his back, flagged a cab, and sped off into the New York night. And Phoebe watched him go.

———

AT FIRST THERE was relief—relief to be alone again. Relief to be unharmed. Relief that things hadn't gone any further than they had. Of course, she felt somewhat guilty about the lotion. But Kevin wouldn't have to know. And besides, it wasn't like she'd had *sex* with Arnold Allen. These were her thoughts on the short walk back to her apartment—that it was a small price to have paid for success.

She rode the elevator wondering what she would do about dinner. She was suddenly starving, almost faint with hunger. She could make spaghetti. She could have breakfast cereal. But she didn't have any milk, and she was too lazy to go buy some. Maybe she would celebrate with some takeout from the Thai restaurant on the corner, she thought to herself as she turned the key in the lock. She was in the mood for Khao Soi.

It was the sight of Arnold Allen's proof of payment—"Dollars," Phoebe now noticed, had been spelled with just one *l*—that left her suddenly uneasy. Would a Hollywood executive really not know how to spell such a simple word? And now that he was gone, the evidence of their transaction seemed suddenly, queasily, insubstantial. Upon closer inspection, Arnold Allen hadn't even written a floor or suite number next to the Broadway address of her tryout.

In need of reassurance, she called information for the Carlyle Hotel, then the Carlyle Hotel itself. "I'd like to leave a message for Arnold Allen," she told the woman at the front desk.

But the woman at the front desk told her, "No one by that name is staying in this hotel."

But how could it be? Had she gotten the name of the hotel wrong? But no, he'd said the Carlyle. She was quite sure of it. "This is the Carlyle Hotel?" she felt compelled to double-check.

"Yes it is," the woman replied. "May I be of any further assistance?" But her tone of voice belied her words; her tone of voice was hostile.

Phoebe hated her for it.

Her whole life, it seemed to Phoebe, she'd been made to feel guilty for asking too many questions. She thought again of old Mrs. K, who only liked answers. "Has trouble following directions," the old battle-ax had written in the comments section of Phoebe's report card. And Emily—at some point during her adolescence, Emily had nicknamed Phoebe "N.P." (short for "Nosy Parker"), and all because she'd once caught her younger sister flipping through her diary, trying to find out what really happened at Emily's junior prom. (Not much, as it turned out.)

And Bruce Bledstone—she hadn't been able to ask him any-thing; she'd learned so much the day she made the mistake of asking if he loved his wife. Only Kevin seemed oblivious to her "curiosity problem." But then, she could never think of any-thing to ask him that she didn't already, intuitively, know the answer to.

She hung up the phone convinced that the woman at the front desk of the Carlyle Hotel was just another naysayer from her past. But where was Arnold Allen? Phoebe remembered now that he'd left her his business card. She fished it out of her purse and dialed the ten-digit number printed in the bottom right-hand corner—the number she was supposed to call if and when she had any doubts whatsoever as to whether or not he was a nice guy, a good guy, the kind of guy you could trust with five hundred dollars.

But it wasn't his office at all. It was no longer in service. That's what the automated recording said. But it wasn't possi-ble. That's what Phoebe kept telling herself. That everything would make sense in the end. Except doubt had begun to infil-trate the equation, throwing up X's and Y's where once there had only been digits. Why had he told her he was staying at the Carlyle if he wasn't? And why had his phone been disconnected? And what about Friday? What about her big break?

In the lamplight now Phoebe could make out writing on the back of the card. Flipping it over, she found a name, Jill Lewis, handwritten in a different-color ink but in the same, barely legible chicken scrawl. And next to Jill Lewis's name was a number with an outer-borough area code. She dialed blindly. A gruff-sounding man answered the phone. "My name is Phoebe Fine," she said in her best executive-secretary voice—the one she'd used that very afternoon at Toffler Associates. "And I'm calling in reference to a man named Arnold Allen. Jill Lewis's name and number were printed on the back of a business card he left with me."

Now the gruff-sounding man let out a furious laugh. "Arnold Allen tried to con my wife out of a large sum of money today. We've already filed a complaint with the police. You should call them, too. Tell them it's the same guy. Did you give him anything?"

"No—I—," Phoebe started to tell him. But she couldn't finish the sentence, couldn't begin to admit that she had. She couldn't even breathe. "Thank you," she whispered into the receiver before she hung up.

———

SHE MUST HAVE stood there for ten minutes, the receiver pressed to her blouse, the truth defying her grasp like one of those superbouncy rubber glitter balls from a five-cent machine. She couldn't bear to believe it had all been a scam—couldn't bear the idea that a girl like her would fall for something like that. She couldn't cry, either—not until she'd gotten to the Italian bakery where Kevin McFeeley currently made his living shoveling cannoli into white paper bags. (The copy shop had fired him for printing Mr. Potato Head flyers on the company bill.)

It was the image of Kevin's sallow face reduced to wearing that two-foot-high white paper hat that pushed her over the edge. Two idiots in love—that's what she was thinking, but she couldn't say it out loud. She needed Kevin McFeeley too much right then. She needed him to make it better, and he tried. He took one look at Phoebe's twisted face, threw down his cake server, sideswept the counter, laced his arms around her quivering frame, and whispered, "What's the matter? What is it, baby—are you okay?" Like the wonderful boyfriend that he was.

So she could tell him between gasps, "Something really awful happened."

So he could tell her that he still loved her, always would, no matter what mistakes she'd make in life.

Then he got permission to leave work early. And on the walk home, Phoebe told him as much of the story as she could bear to tell him. (She left out the part about how the man in the sheepskin coat came awfully close to touching her where only Kevin did.) And for a moment or two, in the act of recounting, she imagined herself a blameless victim of a random crime. That's what Kevin kept saying—that the guy was a professional; that she couldn't have expected to come away unscathed; that she was lucky to have gotten away as cleanly as she had. It was the sight of that half-empty squirt-top bottle of hand lotion leaned up against the leg of the sofa that made her curl up in a little ball by the stove and rock herself back and forth against the linoleum until her spine was bruised.

That's how much she loathed herself. She loathed her vanity. She loathed her gullibility the most. The money was only part of it. The greater theft was of her ego. Here she'd thought she was so sophisticated—what with her downtown address, her black leather jacket, her married ex-lovers, her intimate knowledge of Italian Marxism. She turned out to be a fool. A country bumpkin. A hayseed. A clodhopper. A yokel. A naïf. It was as if her very identity had been snatched out from under her. She couldn't believe she'd let Arnold Allen touch her. It didn't matter that he hadn't touched her "there." She felt ravaged, shattered, filthy, wretched. And there was nothing Kevin McFeeley or anyone else could say or do to make her feel better.

Oh, but he tried. He lifted her up off the floor, took her in his arms, stroked her hair while her nose ran down his neck. "Baby, it's gonna be okay," he kept saying. He held her closer and closer. She felt his chest rising and falling, then a similar cresting below the waist. That he wanted her now—it sickened her to the very bottom of her core. And she cried harder and louder. She was crying so hard she couldn't get out the word *no*. Or maybe she couldn't bear to say it. To disappoint him. It was the same problem all over again. Or was it? Maybe she wanted it, too—even as her mind was repelled. To think she could be aroused at a time like this! But she must have been. She must have wanted to be punished. She must have wanted to be loved.

She put up no struggle when Kevin McFeeley laid her down on the sofa, lifted her legs into his lap. "Sh!" he kept saying. "Close your eyes."

She did as she was told. She lifted her palms to her face, left her body to its own devices. His hands were greasy. His hands felt good. Just as they had last time, with Arnold Allen—maybe better, maybe about the same. "Sh!" Kevin kept saying. Then he climbed on top of her. Phoebe kept her palms over her eyes the whole time—just like she used to during the scary parts of *The Wizard of Oz,* like when the Wicked Witch of the West locked Dorothy in that room with only Toto for a friend. Except she always cheated. She always peeked through the slats of her fingers. She could never resist the temptation to look. But tonight there was nothing to look at.

Tonight the horror was behind her hands.

It could have been anyone on top of her that night. Phoebe didn't tell that to Kevin McFeeley. She didn't want to hurt his feelings. It wasn't his fault. At that moment in time, she felt strongly that it was all hers.

———————

SHE WOKE TO the phone ringing. It was Lisa from Class Act Temps. "Hey, hon," she said. "I got a job for you at First Bank of Yemen. Eleven bucks an hour. Can you be there by ten?"

"Sure," Phoebe told her.

"And don't forget to dress corporate."

"I won't."

She showered and dressed in ten minutes—in a pale blue blazer, white blouse, gray nylons, and the same platform sandals and sensible, grotesque, knee-length beige skirt she'd worn the day before. Then she poured herself a glass of orange juice, brushed her hair back into a neat ponytail. Kevin was still asleep when she closed the door behind her. It was sunny outside. A nice day, she thought. She felt sad but in an unspecific way, a mundane way.

Maybe not so different from the way she felt almost every day.

What compelled her to take a seven-block detour on her way to the subway, she couldn't say. Maybe it was simple curiosity. Maybe there was a part of her that still believed it might be true—the Guild, the pilot, the audition, the street address on Lower Broadway.

Except it was a professional dry cleaners. BRING US YOUR TOUGHEST STAINS boasted the sign over the door.

For fifteen or twenty seconds Phoebe stood frozen on the sidewalk gazing through the scratched window at the overhead racks of disembodied shirts and coats, their arms frozen beneath their plastic sheaths, their collars bleached and starched and pressed like new. Commuters rushed by her at various oblique angles. Her head felt light. Her stomach convulsed. Twenty minutes later, stepping off the 6 train at Grand Central, she vomited all over the platform. She wiped her mouth on her newspaper.

Then she went to work.

———————

"IF YOU DON'T know where you're going, any road will take you there," read the tea bag that drooped against the side of her Styrofoam cup later that same morning on the forty-first floor of a neo-deco office tower on Sixth Avenue. She was filling in for someone named Mary. Someone Named Mary was on vacation at Disneyland. Someone Named Mary wouldn't be back until Monday. A color print of two chimpanzees sharing a banana had been pinned to the corkboard over Someone Named Mary's in box. In a heart-shaped tin frame next to the telephone grinned a generically adorable pig-tailed pipsqueak (no doubt, Someone Named Mary's) posed against a wall of fake clouds.

Phoebe's temporary boss was a cross-looking man named Mr. Habib. A gold watch interrupted the flow of black hair on his wrists. He had rings the size of Saturn's around his olive-shaped eyes. His brows were thick and tangled like grape arbors. When the phone rang, she was to answer it "Mr. Habib's office. How may I direct your call?" It rang only three times the whole morning. The first time it was Mrs. Habib. The second time it was a guy named Stu from the main office.

The third time it was Kevin McFeeley calling to see if Phoebe was still alive.

She somehow hated him for asking—even though she was the one who'd left a distraught-sounding message for him not thirty minutes earlier asking that he call her as soon as possible.

Now she snapped at him, "Would you please stop worrying about me?" Then she hung up, hating him. For knowing too much. For reminding her of the man in the sheepskin coat. In the end, she wondered, was there really any difference between the perpetrator and the pacifier?

She spent the rest of the day destroying her cuticles with the bent tip of a paper clip and wishing that, like Superman, she could turn back the clock. She couldn't imagine ever having sex with Kevin McFeeley again. The very idea repulsed her. She'd never been so exhausted in her entire life. Come one o'clock, she couldn't even rouse herself to go filch lunch.

11. Pablo Miles

OR "The Most Important American Artist of the Post–World War II Period"

SOMETIMES SHE FELT like hot shit, sometimes just like shit. It changed by the hour and sometimes by the minute. City life had that effect on Phoebe—the effect of spontaneous self-aggrandizement that degenerated into self-disgust at the smallest of provocations, the most random of provocations. The insistent bass line of a teenager's boom box, the sickly sweet smell of chicken wings on the subway, the sight of other women taller and thinner and more gorgeous than she would ever be would render the stories she told herself, about herself, pure fiction, and Arnold Allen into the bellwether of her feckless existence. Four months later she could scarcely remember his face. But his hands, his simultaneously chapped and greased hands, she couldn't forget those hands. So it was that while she rode the elevator up to Susan Kenny's Pearl Street apartment, a fleeting glance at her hair (too flat!) and her face (too puffy!) in the polished copper ceiling, the reflective surface of which was as unforgiving as a fluorescent-lit mirror in a public rest room, left Phoebe suddenly dejected and wondering if she ought to turn back.

Oh, but she hated to miss things—hated the idea that there

were men she could have met, men she would have met, had she not passed up the opportunity to meet them. Because men were a living metaphor for her own aspirations, her own quest for approval, since, at the age of twenty-two, sex was all she felt she had to offer. And since she'd come all this way, invested all that time separating her eyelashes, styling her hair, moisturizing her cheeks, lining her lips, trying to be the one you wanted, the one you couldn't live without, the one you found yourself reaching out an arm for her to lean on as she teetered from crisis to crisis to crisis only to collapse in your bed at the end of the night, a tortured sylph in black lace—this was her fantasy of herself when she was feeling like hot shit—she opened the door. Whereupon a barrage of static heat, exaggerated laughter, and stale smells pummeled her senses and left her feeling daunted all over again. She'd never seen so many people packed into such a small space. She didn't recognize a single one of them. She elbowed her way through the crowd in search of the hostess.

She found Susan Kenny sitting cross-legged on the kitchen counter nursing a Corona.

"Susan!" Phoebe squealed in relief. (That she could perform giddy exuberance even at her most defeated—Phoebe had always taken this quality for granted about herself.)

"Phoebe!" chimed Susan, matching Phoebe's exultant tone as she descended from her perch and enveloped Phoebe in an overblown bear hug. As if they were good friends. As if they actually liked each other. As if they hadn't seen each other in ten years when the truth was more like one year (i.e., since graduation from Hoover). "Ohmigod you look SO great!"

"Thanks. So do you," lied Phoebe.

In fact, she'd never seen Susan look worse. Her skin looked blotchy, her legs seemed heavier. It was pretty obvious she'd gained weight. Susan, Phoebe thought to herself with a combination of disdain and jealousy but mostly just disdain, was one of those girls for whom mediocrity was its own reward.

"It's the craziest thing," said Susan, leaning into Phoebe's ear with her hot beer breath. "There are all these totally gorgeous guys here!"

"That's so crazy!" said Phoebe, distracted. She'd already found her gorgeous guy. He was standing over by the potted ficus, a tallish thing with streaks of platinum in his spiky brown hair. He was wearing a brown suede fringed jacket and black leather pants. She had a feeling he was looking at her, too. She wasn't expecting him to admit it. But there he was, not three minutes later—Susan had since disappeared into another overblown bear hug—standing next to her, standing over her, saying, "I've been checking you out," one elbow leaned up against an Ikea bookcase filled with someone's college psychology textbooks—probably Susan's.

"Oh, really?" said Phoebe.

"Yeah, really," said the gorgeous guy. Then he smiled. Then he lifted a plastic cup to his lips. "You're very fuckable," he told her before he bent his head backward and chugged.

Of all the affronts! But Phoebe could play this game, too. Which is why she asked him, "Do you really mean it?" all big eyes and faux grateful.

Except she was. That was the pathetic part. She couldn't help herself. She had a thing for cocky assholes. When they expressed interest in her, it seemed meaningful. When nice guys hit on her, she had trouble caring.

"I really mean it," he said. Then he extended an arm, introduced himself as Pablo Miles.

"Starla Chambers," she returned the favor.

Because she felt like it. And because it sounded like the kind of name that belonged to the kind of girl he'd want to know and she wanted to be—the kind of girl who didn't feel the need to adopt pseudonyms; the kind of girl who took pleasure in impersonating herself; the kind of girl for whom history was less a burden (to be reminded at every turn of how fortunate you were to have been born where and when you were!) than a benign irrelevance. Sometimes she just wanted to be a girl.

Whereupon Pablo Miles got down on one knee, pressed his lips to the back of her hand, then his tongue.

"Ew, gross!" She jerked her hand out of his grasp.

"You know you like it." He smiled mischievously.

"I don't just like it, I need it," Phoebe corrected him.

"Nympho."

"Letch."

"I never said I wasn't."

She lit a cigarette. She wasn't having a bad time.

Later but not that much later, she wrote her phone number on the back of his hand.

THEIR FIRST DATE was more like an appointment. To screw. Pablo Miles called her the very next morning. He arrived at her apartment at noon. They went to bed at one. But first he pushed her up against the door of her closet. "You have a really hot body," he told her.

"So do you," she was going to tell him, then changed her mind, thinking it sounded too aggressive. And because, despite the nympho jokes, he was the conqueror and she was the conquest. That was the arrangement. That was the injustice of it.

"Thank you," she said instead, and smiled demurely.

Whereupon Pablo Miles reached under her skirt. In response, Phoebe made little breathy noises intended to imply her helplessness in the face of such overwhelming desire. She didn't mean most of them. Maybe not any of them. Not because it didn't feel good. It felt plenty good. But it felt insignificant. Something like pissing. She was finding sex could be like that—satisfying but in only the most quotidian of ways. The most idiotic of ways. The most mechanical of ways. In fact, she could come at will. In ten seconds flat. With the right amount of pressure applied to the right number of places. And at the same time, she was never entirely convinced she'd come. Indeed, her orgasms frequently seemed too calculated to be believed.

It was like that with Pablo Miles. After which point he asked her, "Do you want me to fuck you now?"

She told him, "Okay."

Because it seemed like a nice thing to do—to let him fuck her after he'd brought her, if not to orgasm, then to something that loosely approximated one. And then he did. And she enjoyed herself insofar as she enjoyed watching Pablo Miles enjoy himself. So she came again. Or, at least, she made noises to imply that she had. Because Pablo Miles was bound to be both flattered and impressed, which he was. Afterward, he said, "A lot of girls can't come during intercourse."

To which Phoebe replied, "I'm not like other girls. I'm more like a man."

"You're like a man's fantasy," he told her.

She didn't argue with the assessment. She never tired of compliments. They made her feel worthy. She never bought that New Age bullshit about loving yourself. What was there to love? Behind her occasionally witty and apparently sympathetic demeanor, she knew herself to be vain, catty, backstabbing, supercilious—not much of a friend.

———

THEY SHOWERED. THEY dressed. They moseyed on over to some adorable little café with an Italian surname on Mac-Dougal Street, where they sat at a wrought-iron table out front slurping the froth off their cappuccinos. They were both feeling high on themselves—the way people sometimes do after sex that leads to orgasm in a timely fashion—and the conversation reflected it. Pablo told Phoebe he was destined to be recognized as the most important American artist of the post–World War II period. In the meantime, he was getting his M.F.A. at Hunter. Phoebe told Pablo she intended to make groundbreaking documentaries on the "male gaze." In the meantime, she was working as a two-hundred-dollar-a-week production assistant for an all-women documentary collective, currently shooting, *Home Is Where the Husband Is,* a cinema verité exploration of Filipino mail-order brides living in Queens.

Later, the talk turned to all the other guys/girls who were currently hot for the two of them. "There's this total dweeb named Robert who's always calling me, and I feel really bad because he's really nice and he's totally in love with me, but I'm totally not interested," Phoebe told Pablo.

"Believe me, I know what that's like," Pablo told Phoebe. "There's this girl at Hunter who's, like, obsessed with me. Ellen. I think that's her name. She's, like, this big fat girl. Pretty face. Ass like a truck. She's always writing me these love letters. Maybe I should fuck her. You know, just to be nice." (Smile, smile.)

"You're so bad." (Phoebe shaking her head, Pablo loving it, Phoebe loving it, too. What was more ego-enhancing than making dumb jokes at the expense of ugly women? Phoebe couldn't think of anything.)

Phoebe could never decide who she hated more—other people or herself.

———————

THEIR SECOND DATE was more of a date. They met for a late dinner at Rose of India on East Sixth Street, where they split an order of chana saag and talked about the past. "I hated guys like you in high school," Phoebe felt compelled to inform Pablo.

"How do you know what I was like in high school?" he asked.

"I can just tell," she told him. "You probably wouldn't even have talked to me in high school."

"Were you hot?"

"Not particularly," she admitted.

"Then I probably wouldn't have talked to you," he agreed.

"See, I told you," she said, hating him just a little.

"But you're hot now," he said. "So what does it matter?"

She liked him again. She was that easy to appease.

She was even more eager to please.

The only reason she went to the midnight showing of *Wings of Desire* at the Angelika Film Center was because Pablo wanted to. She dozed off halfway through. Pablo nudged her during the credits. "Come on, wake up," he whispered. "Unless you want me to fuck you while you're asleep."

"Rapist," she muttered under her breath.

"Baby, I'm like a rape fantasy," he muttered back.

As they made their way up the aisle, Phoebe thought to herself: we'd have such attractive kids.

———————

"I THOUGHT ALEKAN'S use of chiaroscuro was pure genius," Pablo volunteered in the taxi back to his Brooklyn digs—half a floor of an old turpentine factory he shared with four other guys.

"Alex who?" she asked.

"Forget it," he said, scowling.

"No, why?"

"I thought you said you worked in film."

"I do."

"For future information, Alekan is only, like, the greatest cinematographer who ever lived."

"Well, I didn't know that!"

"Well, now you do."

His canvases hung from the makeshift walls of his room. They were big and loud and crowded, with splattered oil paint half-obscuring cartoon characters from their childhood and free-floating female body parts. There was a familiar quality to all of them. Phoebe was disappointed by the discovery. She'd been thinking Pablo Miles might be a great innovator for our times. In deference to her date, however, she feigned fascination before the largest canvas—Minnie Mouse with a tit job overlaid on a Jackson Pollack. At least, that's what it looked like to her. "I really like this one," she said.

"I like that one, too," said Pablo.

But there was a hint of uncertainty in his voice—a hint of weakness. And Phoebe hated him for it—suddenly hated him for reminding her of herself. He was there to reassure her. Didn't he get it? Didn't he know his job?

Despondent, she stretched out on Pablo's futon and closed her eyes.

"What's the matter?" he said, climbing onto the bed next to her.

"Nothing," she answered.

"Are you horny?"

"Maybe."

"Do you want me to fuck you?"

Was it possible that she didn't know if she did? So often Phoebe found herself unable to differentiate between what she wanted and what *he* wanted, whoever *he* was at the time.

"I'll take that to mean yes," said Pablo, reaching for her zipper.

She let him have it. She found it so much easier letting other people make decisions for her.

She found that the people who made decisions for her were the people she was the most attracted to in life.

She woke the next morning with the distinct impression that something meaningful had taken place. Pablo seemed to feel it, too. "I got to be careful," he said over a half portion of Stouffers' French bread pizza and some strawberry-flavored Carnation Instant Breakfast. "I could get used to this life."

"I know what you mean," said Phoebe, jubilant at the thought that he might be growing attached to her. That she wasn't necessarily growing attached to him was beside the point. He was so handsome, and a painter. He'd even gone to Princeton. It was an impressive résumé, a romantic résumé.

She felt like hot shit just thinking about it.

———

"I WANT TO go away with you," he told her on the phone the following day.

But the idea of going away with Pablo Miles—it worried Phoebe. After all, they'd only met a week ago. And what if they ran out of things to talk about up there in the country with no distractions—no downtown Manhattan or Bohemian Brooklyn to confuse for a context? "You want to go away together?" she said. "I mean, we hardly even know each other."

"So what?"

"It seems kind of soon."

"I want to fuck you in a sleeping bag."

The image excited her. Or maybe it was the sound of the word *fuck* on Pablo Miles's lips. On his lips that word sounded like an imperative. "Where would we go?" she asked him.

"My family has a house up near Killington," he told her. "Nothing fancy. Just an old A-frame at the base of the mountain. Let's go up Friday morning. Just you and me. What do you say?"

"The thing is, I have a shoot on Friday," Phoebe told him. "I mean, it's not my shoot . . ." Because she was just the grunt who unpacked the catered lunch, who separated the clear plastic wrap from the premade sandwich basket. Just the thought of it left her angry and resentful at her Birkenstock-wearing director/boss Dee Dee, who didn't show the slightest interest in Phoebe's creative suggestions and never stopped making loaded comments about her impractical footwear. "Let me see if I can get out of it."

And she did. She told Dee Dee there was a death in the family—a funeral she needed to attend. And who can argue with death?

SHE PACKED THE night before. All her cute clothes. The kind of clothes *Mademoiselle* magazine suggested you pack for a romantic getaway. Puffy socks to pad around the fire in. Oversized chenille sweaters with extra-long sleeves to hide your hands in when you're feeling coy. She was ready to go at ten. At quarter past she looked at her watch. At twenty past the phone rang. It was Pablo calling from the street. "Listen, I broke down on the Brooklyn Bridge," he shouted to be heard over a chorus of honking horns and revving engines and emergency-vehicle sirens.

"That's terrible!" Phoebe shouted back.

"Yeah, the radiator overheated or something. I'm gonna take Betty to the garage. I'll call you when I get home."

But he didn't. He didn't call the next afternoon either. And the next afternoon after that, it was pretty clear he was never going to. You'd think Phoebe would have been upset. She was mostly just relieved.

There was a part of her that had always been happiest alone.

And she didn't know how much longer she could have continued the experiment. In the end, that's all Pablo Miles was to her—another test case to see whom she could fool, and for how long, into thinking she was someone that she wasn't. That he knew her by the wrong name was secondary. She couldn't imagine him understanding why her handwriting changed on a daily basis. Or why her teeth chattered when she thought too hard about yesterday. That was the thing about cocky assholes. In the end, they were only good for sex. In the end, you couldn't wait to get away. To get back to yourself. Even if that self was a fraud, or a freak, or a fool.

At least it was you.

Besides, she suspected that "serious relationships" were antithetical to the biological imperative.

And she was still playing catch-up with Holly Flake, still trying to convince herself that the blah girl running laps behind the gym until she thought her legs would snap, her heart explode, was no longer her.

And she'd let all her other her talents lapse—her tennis and violin strings pop. But she was good at sex. Everybody said so; everybody said she was a great lay. And with every new guy there was new proof—that she was "incredibly gorgeous." Because she was never so gorgeous—not even when she was "incredibly gorgeous"—that she didn't require outside confirmation. Just as it was still some kind of thrill to bear witness to a virtual stranger's face contorted in ecstasy—to feel essential to that contortion, even if it turned out you were only convenient. (Even if turned out he made those same faces when he touched himself.)

And if it ended now as opposed to later, whoever it was would never learn how neurotic and crazy and boring and essentially talentless she really was, and be forced to leave, disappointing them both—especially Phoebe.

———————

SHE RAN INTO Pablo Miles in front of Tower Video a year later—as if it mattered. She was still nowhere, still waiting to be appreciated. "Pablo Miles." She said his name out loud just to be sure it was him.

He didn't respond immediately. Then he turned around with a start and said, "If it isn't Starla Chambers!"

"That's me," she chimed.

"I remember you." He smiled congenially. "You had a really cute ass." He craned his neck around her backside. "You still do."

Phoebe rolled her eyes, shook her head. Of all the offenses! But it was just another performance on her part. In fact, it pleased her to no end that Pablo Miles still thought she had a cute ass. She'd been thinking she was already over the hill. It was the weight she'd gained since she met him—maybe five pounds. It felt like ten. "You always were disgusting," she said, hating herself for her vanity and for her inability to hold grudges.

And for saying the very thing Pablo Miles wanted to hear. That was clear from his answer. "It's true." He grinned lubriciously. "I've always been a sexist pig."

It was only later that Phoebe found out that Pablo Miles's real name was Peter Mandelbaum. (It was only later that she wondered if he'd felt the same things she'd felt.) But by then it was too late. By then he was just another name in her address book whose number she hadn't dialed in a long time—probably never would again.

12. Anonymous 1–4

OR *"Overheard in Bed During Phoebe Fine's Admittedly Short-Lived Experiment with Promiscuity"*

THIS IS WHAT she'd learned about the "male gaze": to walk into a crowded room and have twenty sets of eyes defer to your silver-sequined purse—that was some kind of exquisite power. ("Thank you. . . . Just a lipstick and a twenty and it looks like someone's business card . . . I wonder whose it is . . . I can't imagine how it got there. . . . Debevoise what? . . . I would have made a terrible lawyer. . . . I've always hated conflict. . . . I've never been good at midtown. . . . I need a lot of sleep. . . . I remind you of who? . . . Never heard of her. . . . She's a dancer? A topless dancer or a dancer dancer? . . . Excuse me one second. . . . Sorry about that. . . . You were saying?")

It was the act that followed that finally irked her—the way it always led down the same path, to the same ineluctable conclusion, prompted by the same stiff drinks, the same parted lips, the same loaded glances, the same false promises, the same pornographic drivel, the same leading questions. The same "Do you want me to fuck you?" And "I wanna fuck you so badly right now." And "You know you want me to fuck you." And "Lemme fuck you." And "What are the chances you're gonna let me fuck you tonight?" And "I'm so fucking attracted to you." And "You have such a great body." And "You have such great tits." And "You have such a great ass." And "Did anyone ever tell you that you have a black girl's ass?" And "Did anyone ever tell you that you look like that actress? . . . that model? . . . that pickax murderer on death row?"

And "I really love making love to you." And "I really love making love with you." And "I really love the way your thighs make that triangle shape at the top." And "Lemme pull the shades." And "Lemme lock the door." And "Your hands are so cold." And "Your feet are like ice." And "You're so incredibly hot." And "D'you wanna touch it? . . . lick it? . . . kiss it? . . . suck it?" And "Can I put it in?" And "I promise I'll be careful." And "I promise I'll pull out." And "I'm clean." And "I'm tested." And "I'm sorry." And "It's not you." And "It's me." And "It's nothing." And "It's just that . . ." And "I guess I'm a little nervous." And "Will you kiss it again?" And "Come here." And "Don't move." And "You're so wet . . . so tight . . . so unbelievably beautiful."

And "Can you open your legs a little wider?" And "Will you put your arms around my back?" And "Would you mind squeezing my balls? . . . scratching my back? . . . sticking your finger up my asshole?" And "I can't believe you let me stick my finger up your asshole in the back of the cab on our very first date." And "You're such a little whore." And "You're such a little prude." And "Can you lift up a little?" And "Can you scoot down a bit?" And "Can you move up an inch?" And "Will you say my name?" And "Will you say it again? . . . and again?" And "You can't get enough." And "You're made of sex." And "You fuck like a man." And "You fuck with your whole body." And "Will you sit on my cock?" And "Lemme sit on your face." And "Can we do it doggie?" And "Come to the edge of the bed."

And "Have you ever gotten fucked by two guys at once?" And "Do you think your sister would let me fuck her?" And "Have you and your sister ever gotten fucked by the same guy? . . . on the same night? . . . at the same time?" And "Do you want me to fuck your brains out is that what you want me to do you want me to fuck the shit out of you, you little nigger-loving Jew?" And "Use me." And "Abuse me." And "That's right." And "Wait." And "There's so much air in your pussy." And "There's so much blood in your . . ." And "I thought you said you didn't have your period." And "Can I fuck you up the ass?" And "Lemme fuck you up the ass." And "Are you sure you don't want me to fuck you up the ass?" And "I promise I'll go slow." And "I'll stop if it hurts." And "Forget I ever mentioned it." And "Baby, come here." And "Baby, don't be upset with me." And "I'm such a pig." And "I'm such an asshole." And "I'm such a dick—*aren't I?*"

And "Lemme touch you." And "Does that feel good?" And "Does this feel good?" And "Did you come?" And "Can I come now?" And "I promise I'll be quick." And "Can I come inside you?" And "Can I come on your face?" And "Baby, I'm coming." And "Do you want to come again?" And "That was really amazing." And "That was pretty intense." And "Lemme get a towel." And "Has anyone seen my cigarettes?" And "Where'd you say you were from?" And "Oh yeah?" And "Oh, really?" And "That's cool." And "That's interesting because I grew up in Boston . . . Phoenix . . . Tallahassee . . . Just up the street, on Seventy-ninth and West End." And "My dad moved out when I was six . . . eight . . . ten . . . twelve." And "My mom remarried when I was seven . . . nine . . . eleven . . . thirteen." And "I didn't have a lot of friends." And "I watched a lot of TV." And "I smoked a lot of pot." And "I jerked off, like, eleven times a day." And "Hey." And "Come here." And "Look at me." And "Phoebe." And "Baby." And "Hey, you okay?"

Oh, she was okay, just tired, tired of trying to be the one you wanted, the one you couldn't live without, the one you found yourself reaching out an arm for as she teetered from crisis to crisis to crisis only to collapse in your bed at the end of the day, a tortured sylph in black lace. Except she never really was. And you never really did. Or maybe you did for one night. The next night was another matter. It turned out the world was filled with beautiful girls.

It turned out being beautiful wasn't nearly enough.

13. Nobody 5-8

OR *"Overheard in Phoebe Fine's Head During Her Even Shorter-Lived Experiment with Celibacy"*

THE SPOTS: THEY took Phoebe by surprise—ambushed her one night while she slept. She woke under siege, stippled like an impressionist painting, mottled like a bad apple. The bumps were everywhere, on her nose and her forehead, her cheeks and her chin. And the more she tried to defend herself against their advances, the angrier they became. Until that old joke from junior high school, "Your epidermis is showing," had a certain truth to it. She felt unfit for public viewing. She walked with her eyes on the pavement. She stopped looking at men. Men stopped looking at her. She'd never been so lonely in her entire life. She wondered if she'd ever find love again.

Or were those bumps merely an excuse to be alone—for once?

For as long as Phoebe could remember, she'd had a savior figure hovering in the background—a mommy or a daddy, a boyfriend or a best friend. Now she wondered if the getaway car wasn't better driven by herself. Never mind the fact that she'd never actually learned to drive. Being lonely breeds a certain recalcitrance among its practitioners, a certain indifference to negotiation. Indeed, the lonely tend to revel in their isolation. For Phoebe, even the idea of documentary film had come to seem intrusive. Maybe the camera wasn't turned on herself, but it was still a camera. And she'd grown weary of looking—not just at herself.

And so, with Emily's help, she gained employment at the Third World Knowledge Initiative, a nonprofit research foundation, where she coordinated a fellowship program for African agriculturists. Which is to say, she purchased plane tickets and wired money and sent official-sounding letters to a bunch of guys she never met with funny names like Elvis Ngale Ngale. It wasn't always easy. There was the Sudanese fertilizer expert who was discovered to be spending all his fellowship money on pornography. Even worse, he ran a bath in the historic home in which he was being housed at the University of Virginia, then went out for Chinese food, whereupon the ceiling under the bathroom collapsed. But it was steady work, didn't pay badly, and came with dental insurance. And it gave Phoebe a place to go every morning, a place to lose herself. And she grew to love her little routines—the oat-bran muffin she consumed every morning at her desk. In its own crumby way, that muffin was sublime.

And sometimes it was enough just to be away from Crystal—clueless, incorrigible Crystal Wangert, Phoebe's aspiring-actress apartment mate, who thought she was really gorgeous because all these guys were in love with her at the same time. Phoebe had found her through the classifieds. Objectively speaking, she wasn't a bad apartment mate. She was pretty neat. She cleaned her dishes. She kept her hair off the soap. But she'd waltz into Phoebe's glorified broom closet without knocking and sigh and simper and flip her hair and shake her head and sigh some more before declaring, "I just don't know what to do. I mean, I like both of them. I mean, who do *you* think is cuter—Jeff or Steve?" as if she'd been handed the job of dividing up Europe—when she was really only deciding whom to fuck.

Phoebe would try to be nice. She'd say, "Who cares who I think is cuter, Crystal? Who do *you* think is cuter?"

"I mean, they're both really cute!" Crystal would groan. "That's the problem."

"I'm sure you'll figure it out." Phoebe would smile benevolently even though she was hating her inside—hating Crystal for having referred to her (Phoebe's) body type as "voluptuous" one day when they were trying on each other's clothes. Here Crystal was a gangly five feet ten inches tall—had done some modeling in her hometown in central Florida—and Phoebe had gained a few pounds since college. But she was hardly voluptuous. She still wore a size 6. She couldn't get that comment out of her mind.

She couldn't stop feeling like a tragic figure in her own life.

She listened to Puccini and wrote bad poetry of a self-aggrandizing sort. She ate dry cereal for dinner and read dry magazines on current events. She was back to sleeping with her stuffed basset hound, Walter. She'd had him since she was eight. She'd never cared much for dolls. She'd always preferred scale models.

Walter filled the empty space between her chest and chin.

She tried masturbating. It took too long. Afterward, she always felt desperate.

She tried going to parties; she tried being the belle of the ball. Afterward, she'd stare at her ruined makeup in the mirror over the sink—at the lipstick prints on her cheeks, the eyeliner that no longer lined her eyes, the cover-up that no longer covered much of anything—and wonder if she'd turned a corner that couldn't be turned back.

And she'd think she had.

She went on a few first dates.

There was the dermatologist who offered her dermabrasion free of charge. (She told him, "No thank you.")

There was Jacob the Earnest Young Attorney, who spent all of dinner recounting the "fascinating" stories he'd read in that morning's *New York Times:* "According to an article I read on A13, the Bulgarian Mafia is so powerful they now control the country's waterworks. However, I read another article in last Sunday's 'Week in Review' suggesting that waterworks were just the half of it. It turns out they control the natural gas, as well."

There was Larry the Gourmet Pasta Distributor, who, halfway through his fusilli, laid down his fork, coughed performatively, and inquired, with obvious irritation, "Soooooooo—what's with this, like, ennui thing you're sportin'?"

There was Carlos the Taxi Driver who Really Wanted to Direct. It was true that English was his second language and that he'd only lived in this country for three years. But that he didn't use contractions drove Phoebe insane. He said, "I will come over now," instead of "I'll come over now," and then he did. And it wasn't fun at all.

So when he called a few days later to see about a second date, Phoebe told him, "I am really sorry, Carlos, but I just do not think we are a match."

"I am very disappointed," Carlos replied.

"I do not know what to say . . ."

"Do not say anything," he said. "I will hang up now."

And he did. And that was that.

It wasn't so bad being alone.

It got kind of lonely after a while.

14. Neil Schmertz

OR *"The Great Date"*

SHE FELT LIKE a better version of herself that night, the night of her and Neil Schmertz's first date, her hair swinging, her skin clear, her lips red, her legs long and sheathed in black, her conscience clear, her future, if not bright, then at least unknown. And the way she felt about herself affected the way she looked at Neil Schmertz, who, in all honesty, she'd found only vaguely attractive when she first met him—through a friend of a friend, at a mutual friend's party—but who, it now seemed to her, cut a comely figure in his black three-button suit, his rust-colored open-collared button-down, and his black buckle booties. And he was trim and taller than her. And his sideburns were fashionably long, his fingernails clean, his dark hair, if slightly on the natty side, then neatly cropped, at least.

He smiled when he saw her. And there were dimples in his cheeks. He looked comfortable in his own skin—at thirty, less like a boy than a grown man. Just as there was an ease in the way he kissed her hello on the cheek, helped her with her coat. He smelled clean. He looked competent, too. As if he'd know what to do in a crisis—in a fire, or a robbery, or an elevator that got stuck. Even more impressive, he seemed to know the maître d', who shook his hand before he showed them to their table, pushed it aside so Phoebe could maneuver her way into the banquette, which was upholstered in puckered black vinyl and made squishy noises when she sat down. Neil sat facing her, his back to the room. And the light was soft and flattering. And the buzz of conversation eased the pressures of their own.

"It's nice to see you." That was the first thing out of Neil Schmertz's mouth. And while it wasn't, maybe, the most inspired line ever uttered, the way he uttered it—leaning forward slightly in his chair, his eyes focused, the corners of his mouth lifted in a half smile—made her think he meant it.

"It's nice to see you, too," said Phoebe. At which point a chiseled waiter with a weak chin appeared to take their drink order. "I'll have a glass of white wine," she told the guy.

"By the glass, we have a California Chardonnay, a Pinot Grigio, a Riesling, and a Gewürztraminer from Alsace," the guy told her.

"I'll have the Gewürztraminer," Phoebe giggled at her garbled pronunciation.

"And a glass of Merlot for me," said Neil.

That's how it started.

It continued with a mixed-field-greens salad for her and a Cobb salad for him and thirty-five minutes of benign chitchat regarding the irritations of their respective workdays, the beleaguered state of Phoebe's cuticles, and the intricate web of people and places that had led to their meeting one balmy evening in early July. Then the main course arrived—the Chilean sea bass for her, the filet mignon for him.

Between bites, Neil told Phoebe a little about himself.

About how he'd grown up in a wealthy suburb of Chicago. His schoolteacher mother still lived there. His labor-lawyer father had moved out to Los Angeles after his parents divorced. He had a younger brother who'd graduated from U.C. Santa

Cruz—still lived out there and spent most of his time surfing. Growing up, he was "your basic nerd"—spent most of the time getting high and watching *Saturday Night Live* reruns. He went to Brandeis undergraduate. He moved to San Francisco shortly after graduation. He moved to New York a few years after that. He currently made his home in a rent-stabilized one-bedroom in Chelsea. He currently made his living developing CD-ROMs for a start-up called Atlas Digital (offices on Lafayette and Spring). He had a little black pug named Siegfried and an old Saab he parked near the Holland Tunnel. He was currently unattached. He'd lived with a graphic designer named Diane for almost five years. They'd broken up two years ago. He'd dated a few people since then but no one seriously.

His favorite novelist was Graham Greene. His favorite painter was Edward Hopper, but the abstract expressionists were cool, too. He mostly listened to jazz—Billie Holiday, in particular—but he liked some contemporary stuff, too. Also classical. But he didn't know that much about it. He had a secret-but-not-that-secret thing for Manfred Mann's Earth Band. His two favorite film directors were Martin Scorsese and Stanley Kubrick. He celebrated Chanukah, but he wasn't religious. He used to roll his own cigarettes. Then he quit smoking. On the weekends he played squash, watched movies, and rode his bike. He was on the neat side of the neat-to-messy continuum. Okay, so he was kind of a neat freak. He hated himself for crying at the end of *Forrest Gump*. He preferred foreign to domestic beers. He went to therapy once a week. He was closer to his mother than he was to his father. In fact, his ex-girlfriend, Diane, used to tease him about how often he spoke to his mother on the phone—*just about every day*.

Then their plates were cleared, their drinks replenished. At which point, Neil turned to Phoebe and said, "What about you?"

So she told him her life story, the five-minute version she'd rattled off so many times before it had taken on a life of its own—had begun to sound more like a stand-up routine at a third-rate comedy club than the life she remembered having lived, a life spent semiparalyzed before an unsympathetic mirror. In the five-minute version, on the other hand, she was a happy-go-lucky sexpot/eccentric/drama queen/professional neurotic with a charming fragile streak. She told Neil, "My Marxist phase gave way to my *Barbarella* phase. I thought I was really postmodern and I wore really short skirts made out of fake fur and I was in outer space all the time thanks to this antianxiety medication I was taking so that I wouldn't freak out if my chicken was touching my rice. Plus, I was going out with this married man, and worried his wife would find out . . ." Lies and half-truths, all of it.

What did Neil Schmertz know?

He seemed to find everything that came out of her mouth fascinating, provocative, worrisome, surprising—just this side of insane. And he shook his head at the right moments, expressed concern where concern needed to be expressed. Then dessert arrived—a flourless chocolate-mousse cake to split. Whereupon Phoebe took a final drag on her cigarette and raised her mostly empty glass. She felt suddenly, exuberantly, blitzed. "Bon appétit," she mouthed in the pinched, Anglican clip of Julia Child.

"To our date," smiled Neil, clinking his glass against her own.

"And to our dinner," added Phoebe.

"And to our plates."

"And to our silverware."

"And to our napkins."

It went on like that, with each toast progressively more absurd, until they were toasting the tablecloth, the Dalai Lama, Manfred Mann's Earth Band, the rabbit who had been denied the lettuce that had wound up in Phoebe's field greens. And just then, just as a splash of her drink leapt up and out of its glass and onto the linen tablecloth, where it bled imperceptibly but irrevocably outward, like a dying star consuming its planets, it was, for Phoebe, such joy to be alive. It was the Gewürztraminer. It was also Neil Schmertz, who made her feel special but also normal—wonderfully, tantalizingly normal insofar as she'd always imagined herself sitting across from a guy like him in a place like this.

But her mirth proved fleeting, interrupted as it was by the sight of a famous actress seated just two tables away from their own. She was a woman of Phoebe's approximate age who'd achieved stardom while she was still a teenager. And she was beautiful, but she was also respected, having appeared in several carefully crafted film adapations of nineteenth-century British literary classics, in both cases as a haughty aristocrat in a high-neck dress. It was less jealousy Phoebe felt than a sort of canceling out of her own experience—her own right to find herself glamorous, lovable, poignant. "Isn't that Paige Smithers?" she murmured from inside her glass, unable to halt the forward momentum of her jealousy.

Neil's head cocked left then center. "Yeah, that's her. She comes in here all the time."

"She's really beautiful."

"She's not as beautiful as you."

Phoebe raised a single, dubious eyebrow.

It was all for show; it was exactly what she'd needed to hear.

"You don't have to say that," she told him.

"I know I don't have to say that," he told her.

"Well, thank you for saying it."

"Thank you for having dinner with me."

"Anytime."

"Phoebe."

"What?"

"You're amazing."

It was pretty corny. It was nice to hear. So much so that when Neil Schmertz reached for her hand, Phoebe gave it to him gladly. And while he stroked the back of it, his eyes dissolving inside her own, she wondered if she might spend the rest of her life with this man—not so much because she'd fallen instantly in love but because she was tired of *not* being in love. And he was such a gentleman. He was even Jewish. He was so obviously crazy about her.

He paid the check.

And then he walked her to Canal Street, where he put her in a cab (he didn't want her walking, not at this hour—it wasn't safe), but not before he'd kissed her on the lips in front of a discount electronics emporium all boarded up for the night, Mack trucks roaring by them, mud-flap girls swinging perilously beneath their sixteen wheels. And while it wasn't, maybe, the most inspired kiss Phoebe had ever experienced, it was a good kiss, a solid kiss, a solicitous kiss. And that meant something to her.

It meant he'd want to see her again.

She wanted to see him, too.

In fact, they saw each other the next night—and the next night after that. By then, they were a couple, catching up on each other's days, dropping already familiar names, trading private jokes born of earlier incidents in their short dating career. For Phoebe, the transition was as natural-seeming as it was sudden. Indeed, Neil Schmertz seemed to her like the logical next step—a step in the direction of maturity. It wasn't merely that he always had a chilled bottle of Pinot Grigio waiting in the refrigerator, and showed up at the hour he said he was going to show up, and put to rest any questions in her family regarding her ability to grow up and lead a "normal life." He showed an interest in her future, where others had been oblivious.

Two weeks into their relationship, he bought her a gift that couldn't be equaled by the most expensive perfume—the gift of inspiration: a music stand and sheet music, a turn-of-the-century double-stop extravaganza called "Adoration," by a guy named Felix Borowski, from whom no one ever heard much again. Because she'd told Neil she couldn't think of anything she liked to do better than play yesteryear show tunes on the electric violin. The vibrato! The spiccato! The slides! The schmaltz! What was life without melodies? And what musical genre could claim richer ones? And was there ever a relationship that didn't cry out for its own song—a soundtrack by which love's fleeting impulses might be captured for all time, if only for five minutes, or maybe even three?

Not long after "Adoration" became theirs, Phoebe and Neil began to discuss moving in together. It seemed like the sensible thing to do. They spent all their time at each other's apartments anyway. And it meant a larger apartment for both of them— two rooms instead of one, and possibly even three. And her lease was running out in March, and Crystal was moving back to Florida to work with dolphins. And the idea of merging record collections—it offered up a vision of harmony the likes of which Phoebe hadn't known since she was a child seeking refuge in Leonard and Roberta's bed when the thunder was so loud she feared the house would split in two. But it wasn't just Neil's records she dreamed of appropriating. Almost unconsciously, she began eyeing his Eames chairs—fantasizing about if and how they'd work with her steamer trunk, her standing lamp, her zebra-print rug.

It turned out they worked fine. That April, Phoebe and Neil moved into the second floor of a Victorian brownstone in the Boerum Hill section of Brooklyn. There was hammered tin on the ceiling, wainscoting on the walls. One set of windows looked out onto an overgrown garden, the other onto a historic, tree-lined street. It was pleasant like the suburbs, but it was urban by virtue of the sprawl that surrounded it—the fried-chicken joints and public-housing projects and Islamic education centers. Never mind the Brooklyn House of Detention. It was for this reason that Phoebe could imagine that she and Neil, far from being mimickers of the bourgeois tropisms of their parents' generation, were one of those haute Bohemian couples who lounged around their retro modern flats in androgynous Calvin Klein underwear, snacking on seaweed while debating the relative merits of the latest Don DeLillo novel—when they weren't uninstalling software on their his-and-hers laptops, deconstructing Japanimation, or preparing late-night dinner for their ten best friends, all of them similarly attractive, ironic, and technologically adroit, with a fondness both for "rare groove" and for toasted pine nuts in their warm goat-cheese salads.

Oh, but the reality was something different; the reality was that there were no dinner parties—only dinner, typically taken out from You Bet You Want Szechwan, only to be taken in on Neil's pilled futon couch, the two of them in matching terry-cloth bathrobes, a romantic comedy starring Meg Ryan playing on the tube. Moreover, the less effort they made to connect with the outside world, the more inseparable they became. One pissed while the other one brushed teeth. One opened his mouth to speak and the other one spoke. They confided in each other all their ugliest secrets. Endearing nicknames changed from week to week. ("Coolio" became "Carlos," which became "Julio," which became "Wubble," which became "Booboo," which became "Looboo," which eventually became "Wooboo," for reasons that were never entirely clear.)

During work hours they spoke on the phone up to ten times a day. Phoebe would call Neil to tell him she licked an envelope. Neil would call Phoebe to tell her he moved a paper clip—and that he couldn't live without her; and that he'd never felt this way about anybody before; and that he loved her more than life itself—even while sex was always, somehow, beside the point: the point of Neil's adoration. He acted as if it were a privilege to lie next to her. He acted as if he'd never seen a naked woman before. Or, at least, not one who looked like Phoebe. And the way he held her afterward—no one had ever held her like that before. He held her like he'd never let go.

Is it any wonder she began to let *herself* go?

At least, that's how Phoebe viewed her subsequent, seven-pound weight gain. To hide the ill effects, she dressed in elastic-waist skirts and oversized men's shirts. And she stopped looking in the mirror for days at a time, after which point she'd be unable to do anything *but* look in the mirror—and chastise herself for having been so negligent, so careless, so cavalier with what she still regarded as her greatest asset. It was in those moments that she'd vow to run four miles a day three times a week for the rest of her life and never eat another hot meal. A few days later, however, her resolve would be lost. Because her and Neil's home was built for comfort and satiety, warm blankets and three-cheese ravioli. And because Neil didn't seem to care if she was thin or fat. "I'll love you whatever you look like, Booboo" was among his favorite lines.

You'd think that would have been exactly what Phoebe needed to hear.

In fact, it was part of the problem, her adult identity having been constructed (by and large) on the response she found herself able to elicit in the opposite sex.

Except the opposite sex (minus Neil, whom she came to think of less as a man than as a kind of third-sex family member) was nowhere in sight. Indeed, on Friday nights, while her peers hooked up with strangers at downtown Manhattan martini lounges, Phoebe could be found eating nonfat peanut-butter-cup frozen yogurt in bed. And when the yogurt was all gone, she and Neil (more often than not) eschewed coitus for the far less frenetic and arguably more therapeutic pleasures of cuddling. That sex was far from the centerpiece of their relationship—in practice, it came as something of a relief; in theory, it left Phoebe dissatisfied. It made her think that everyone else was having all the fun, and that the love she and Neil had for each other was somehow insubstantial. She still expected love to be as tirelessly tension-filled as it was in movies and novels.

Is it any wonder she began to resent the very domestic arrangement that, only months before, had filled her with a kind of silly pride?

Where once keeping house had felt like playing house, now Phoebe grew exhausted and listless at the very idea of a supermarket expedition—began to dread the completion of mindless chores like mopping as if she were awaiting surgery on her own heart. And where once she'd dreamed of having a boyfriend who cooked for her, she now recalled eating Lucky Charms for dinner with misty eyes. It wasn't long before she began to blame Neil for having made her fat—as a ploy, she was readily convinced, to keep her away from other men who might otherwise have been attracted to her were it not for *this tumescent tummy, these turgid thighs.* She was mad at Neil for letting himself go, too. For the first six months of their relationship he'd donned crisp shirts and smart suits. Now whole weekends went by during which he wore the same sagging sweatpants and holey Brandeis T-shirt.

Even more offensive, soon after they moved in together, he stopped holding in his farts. At first he'd say, "I'm sorry." Then he stopped saying anything at all. Then he did it willfully. To think that his gaseous emissions had once been a source of amusement, and even hilarity!

Phoebe had stopped laughing.

Seemingly overnight, the smallest things of Neil Schmertz began to vex her beyond reason. There was the way he dispensed with old coffee grinds (directly into the sink) and felt the need to justify his existence ("I'm the kind of guy who works behind the scenes") and walked with his ass sticking out (why couldn't he slouch like everyone else?) and always left the toilet seat up (and sometimes forgot to flush). And he cleared his throat before he made an important phone call. Which is to say, before he made almost any phone call. And he used the word *perspire* instead of *sweat* (Phoebe found it pretentious). And he left her dirty clothes in a pile by the door, as if they needed to be taken out to the trash. And he was always so cleanly shaved—why couldn't he let his beard grow out for even one day?

And he was always nicking himself shaving and glueing little bits of toilet paper to his face to stop the bleeding. And he took even more time in the bathroom than she did (sometimes, just to be annoying, she'd pretend to have a menstrual emergency two minutes after he'd gone in there). And he repeated stories, and hoarded aspirin. And he let his savings fester in the bank when he could have been investing them in high-yield mutual funds. He couldn't get his finances in order, either. In March he'd filed for an extension on his tax return. In June he still hadn't done anything about it. The mole on his back with the three brittle whiskers growing out of it was another matter. Why oh why wouldn't he let her pluck them?

They were minor aggravations—sure.

They began to seem representative of larger deficiencies in Neil Schmertz's character.

A real man, Phoebe thought to herself, wouldn't buy such expensive shampoo and conditioner; he'd wash his hair with whatever he found in the shower. And he'd lose his temper once in a while (just hearing about how Neil let this guy at work, Ernie, "dick" him over filled Phoebe with frustration). And he wouldn't feel the need to talk to his mother every day on the phone (whatever Neil's mother wanted, she got; if she wanted to see Neil tomorrow, he'd get on a plane that night). And he'd wear blue jeans once in a while (Neil only wore suit pants or sweats). And the suit pants he did wear were unfashionably pleated. To think that Phoebe had once considered him a natty dresser!

Increasingly, she was embarrassed to be seen in his company.

And he "made love" to her so carefully, so tactfully, so goddamn generously—always waited until she'd had her orgasm before he had his. Considered himself the reigning King of Cunnilingus. Displayed unrivaled responsibility when it came to birth control. Just as he was only too convinced that Phoebe had been exploited in the past, and only too intent on being the one who really loved her, the one who wasn't just using her. It never occurred to him that she might have had an opportunistic streak herself. He treated her as if she were this tragic slut, this defenseless child. As if she needed protecting. And maybe, in some ways, she did.

She also needed conquering.

She fantasized about being chained to a fence. She wanted to lose herself in someone else's power trip. In the best of moods, she liked to imagine that she needed nothing—nothing but a funny joke and a sweet cocktail and a slow hand sliding up the back of her swan neck, *if you know what I mean.* But in the worst of moods, which was most of the time—that was the problem—she needed a lot more than that. She needed to be worshipped. She needed to be pampered.

She needed to know that someone would be there if she fell apart.

But it began to seem as if Neil might even have preferred it if she did fall apart. Indeed, on those one or two or three occasions when Phoebe had taken steps in that direction—found herself lying on the bathroom floor digging holes in her chest with the sharp ends of her fingernails for no discernible reason, her breath shortening, her pulse quickening, her mind reeling with the possibilities—he'd seemed to love her even more. Or maybe it was just that in those lamentable moments he was the most convinced she'd never leave him. He'd say, "Looboo, I'm here. I'm right here. I'm not going anywhere. I'm never going anywhere." He'd say those things as if he were trying to convince himself of their veracity. Then he'd hold her even tighter than he usually held her. He'd hold her so tight she could hardly breathe.

There came a time when she couldn't—when the safe haven

she and Neil had established began to feel as constraining as the Brooklyn House of Detention.

Because as needy as Phoebe was, Neil was even needier. He wore that on his face—on his prematurely striated forehead and on his perpetually downturned mouth. And thanks to his own shattered family, he was one of those people for whom the prospect of staying together was the most romantic prospect of all. For Phoebe, the same vision of the future had less to do with romanticism than it did with resignation. Because in the back of her mind, she was still waiting to have her "big adventure"; still thinking she owed it to herself; still thinking she "hadn't really lived"; still hating herself for liking the *idea* of adventure better than she liked actual adventure—and for plotting her escape before she'd ever been captured.

It was the image of Emily standing on the back porch, her pale face lit up the color of Wedgwood china, a frenzy of moths circling overhead, that continued to haunt her. And then the *tick-tick-tick* of the gas lighting beneath a pot of stewed chicken; the *krik-krik-krik* of suitcase wheels on wood. "I could really use something to eat . . . Delayed for three hours in London . . . Wow, everything looks the same . . . How are you, Feebs?" Emily's eyes curled with empathy. Or was it pity? And "Maybe at Christmastime," and "Akim and I this," and "Akim and I that." Emily hadn't been home in twelve months. Emily had spent her junior year abroad in Beirut. Emily had done everything first, and better. Phoebe couldn't get over that feeling—that in some fundamental way she'd failed to realize her youth, the lacunae of which seemed ever more notable than the narratives it did contain.

Nor could she fault Neil for the fact that somewhere in the course of life, ambition had trumped Eros. Which is to say that one got to a certain age when one's professional life became the measure of one's self-worth. Which is to say that love was no longer the solution. Now you had to have a title, a tag line, and three phone lines ringing at the same time. And your business card had to reflect that. And you had to know the right people and appear at the right parties. At least, this was the message Phoebe had internalized. Such that her career frustrations— how would she ever make a name for herself playing turn-of-the-century show tunes? How could she ever forgive herself for having a boring desk job at a nonprofit research foundation catering to Ugandan fertilizer experts?—became inseparable from her frustrations with Neil Schmertz himself, as if they were two sides of a coin whose value had plummeted during a time of runaway inflation.

To make things worse, Neil had been hired away by an up-and-coming cable station specializing in pop-culture nostalgia, as a vice president for New Media Development, whatever that meant—Phoebe wasn't entirely sure. But that he had a title at all made her jealous. It made her think Neil got all the breaks. But at whose expense? Phoebe punished him for his success by refusing to partake in it—by moping around their apartment in her terrycloth bathrobe looking miserable and refusing to talk about it. Though if her depression began as a performance, it soon grew into an actuality. Or maybe it never stopped being a performance. Maybe Phoebe's particular brand of depression, like Phoebe's particular brand of sexual fulfillment, required an audience of at least one. (And what closed-door crying jag has ever not benefited from the solicitous knock of a willing listener?)

It was the sounds that got to her the most. The sounds of "domestic bliss." How the toilet went *"prrrushhooooo."* And the coffee grinder went *"ZZZZiinnggg."* And the freezer door went

"*kuplunk.*" And the television went "*kuh-kuh-kuh-kuh-kuh-kuh*"
as Neil rolled it across the parquet floor of their mix-'n'-match
living room so he could watch the evening news while he stir-
fried vegetables in an enormous discolored wok. "Neily's making Wooboo her favewit dinner!" he'd call out over the frizzle of
snow peas, the twaddle of talking heads.

"Oh, yay," Phoebe would mumble disconsolately.

Not that she didn't like stir-fry. But it wasn't enough—to be
cooked for. To be cared for. To be Neil Schmertz's favorite Wooboo. She'd be sitting on their pilled futon couch drinking a glass
of chilled Pinot Grigio, thinking about exactly that. And about
the men she used to know, the other men she had yet to meet.
It wasn't like that in the beginning. In the beginning it was
Phoebe and Neil against the world. In the beginning Neil referred to himself in the first person. It was only later that he
began to refer to himself as Neily. It was around the same time
that he began to speak primarily in baby talk. He'd say, "Neily
doesn't think his favewit bunny wabby wanth to be hith bestest
fwend anymore."

To which Phoebe would reply, "Neily's favorite bunny
wabby needs a little time to think."

Because she thought time would shed light on why those
sounds ("*kuplunk,*" "*prrrushhooooo,*" "*ZZZZiinnggg*") depressed
her as much as they did.

But time only made her sadder—then madder. Though
picking fights with Neil Schmertz was never an easy trick,
since he never actually fought back. He'd just sit there looking like a circus clown—Phoebe kept expecting a red circle
to appear spontaneously on the tip of his nose—and uttering
guilt-inducing inanities like "I've tried to make you a really
nice home."

"But you're already trying to control me!" she'd bark back.

"How has Neily tried to control you?"

"You always want to go to bed early!"

"Has Neily ever told you that you had to go to bed at the same time as him?"

"What am I supposed to do—go out by myself?"

"You could go meet friends. Neily never told you not to see your friends."

"What friends? I don't have any friends! I lost them all when I moved in with Neily!"

So the conversations would go. They'd go on for hours, and they'd end with dire predictions on Phoebe's part: "Maybe it wasn't meant to be"; "Maybe we're just hanging on for the sake of hanging on"; "Maybe we're only together because we're too scared to be apart."

"But I love you!"

That Neil could come up with a line like that in the face of such abuse—to Phoebe, it seemed so terribly weak. She would have had more respect for him if he'd told her to go fuck herself.

"I have to go to sleep," she'd scathe.

Then she'd roll over, and so would Neil. They'd be lying there like two strangers who just happened to be sharing the same bed. It was in those moments that Phoebe would begin to plot her escape. But in the morning she always felt different. The energy to enact change would have dissipated with the previous night's dreams, while her desire for the physical and material comfort Neil was so adept at providing would be all the more overwhelming. It wouldn't help matters that he'd be standing over her with a steaming breakfast tray. The way the butter rode the hills and dales of her English muffin—in those moments, it would be enough.

Except by nightfall, she'd become enraged all over again. The way he never wanted to go out! The way he always tried to control her! By nightfall, she'd pick the same fights all over again. Sex would have been the only thing to put a stop to their miseries. But they no longer had sex. Neil had stopped trying. Phoebe had stopped caring. It wasn't that she lacked an audience. It was that the applause now fell on deaf ears.

Oh, but it wasn't merely that Neil failed to arouse her; it was that Phoebe, being the Overweight, Embittered, Glorified Secretary she imagined herself to be, failed to arouse herself. (For Phoebe, sex had always, primarily been an auto-erotic act.)

Though it was also true that "true love," in so many ways, bored her—the way it always led down the same path, to the same ritualized lassitude, prompted by the same infantilizing gestures, the same debilitating vows, the same saccharine sentiments, the same pop-song platitudes, the same prosaic piffle. The same "I'd be lost without you." And "I'd be devastated if you left me." And "You're the best thing that ever happened to me." And "You're my best friend." And "I want to spend the rest of my life with you." And "I want to be the father of your children." And "I've never been closer to anyone." And "You're the only girl for me." And "I can't imagine life without you." And "I'll always protect you." And "I'll always take care of you." And "I can't breathe without you." And "I want to die in my sleep holding you in my arms when we're both ninety-nine."

And "I thought about what I'd do if you were paralyzed from the neck down . . ." And "I'd be there for you—I really would." And "I'll never ever go." And "Don't ever let me go." And "Let's be good to each other." And "I'm the luckiest man in New York." And "You're my forever girl." And "I'll love you forever." And "I know we just met . . ." And "If you don't want me in your life, I'll walk out that door right now and you'll never see me again—is that what you want?" And "Well, what *are* you saying?" And "Whatever." And "Someday maybe you'll appreciate someone's efforts to be genuinely close to you. Until then, this is good-bye." (She only wished Neil would say so much, but he never did, he never could.)

In the meantime, another year went by. Phoebe couldn't precisely say how. Her few remaining friends had stopped asking. At a certain point Phoebe stopped asking herself. It was easier that way—easier staying put than seeking an apartment she could afford in the current, runaway real estate market. Just as the thought of divvying up her and Neil's record collection was almost too much to bear. (Who would get the James Brown box set they'd purchased in tandem?) And what if he really couldn't live without her? What if he went into a decline and ended up on the street—or worse, floating facedown in the East River? How would she ever forgive herself for that?

And to leave someone for no one—for Phoebe, that was the worst part. All the protecting had made her feel vulnerable. All the babying had made her feel babyish. All the special breakfast trays and "dinner-poos" had made her doubt that she was capable of feeding herself.

Besides, Phoebe sometimes thought to herself, it wasn't a bad life that she led.

It got even better after she put together a band.

From a pecuniary standpoint, it seemed like the sensible thing to do, what with the craze for cruiseship-style fiddling having peaked with the *Titanic*. And given Phoebe's lifelong love of power ballads, the artistic compromise seemed less than egregious. Never mind the psychic compromise. Here, potentially, was a way for Phoebe both to honor Roberta and Leonard's thinly veiled wish for a daughter who fiddled and to fly in the face of the high culture–low culture dichotomy by which they defined themselves. It was Phoebe on the violin, Holly Flake on the drums, Kevin McFeeley on the guitar, and a girl named

Julie (someone's second cousin) on the keyboard. They took turns on vocals. They got along surprisingly well, the origins of their respective grievances having grown fuzzy over time. They called themselves Schmaltz. They practiced two nights a week in a studio on West Twenty-sixth. Their sound was fusion—one part turn-of-the-century show tunes, two parts pop rock. Their songs concerned the naïveté of romanticism and the futility of angst. They dreamt of recording contracts and guest appearances on late-night talk shows. In the meantime, they had jobs.

Holly worked in the marketing division of a cosmetics conglomerate; Kevin shelved books at the Strand; Julie waited tables at a snooty French restaurant in Tribeca. And as of that June, Phoebe found herself gainfully employed as a part-time receptionist at an animal hospital catering to the pets of the superrich. It wasn't much of a job. It paid even less than the Third World Knowledge Initiative did. And it was all the way uptown. But it had a social-service bent that allowed her to imagine that she was contributing to society, not merely consuming its resources. And it was part-time. And Neil paid most of the rent. And thanks to his fancy new job, he was always on the road, traveling to and from L.A.

Except he always came back—that was the problem. Phoebe would walk in on her perfectly nice-looking boyfriend pissing in the bathroom, and the sight of him standing over the pot doing what was, after all, only natural, would disgust her beyond reason. Such that she took to fantasizing that he'd die a painless death, if not in his sleep, then perhaps at sea. She would have felt terrible and all. She could even see herself breaking down mid-eulogy, having just transported the grieving crowd to life-embracing laughter as she recalled Neil's near-religious faith in the value of clean countertops. (In retrospect, his various idiosyncrasies would come to seem charming.) At present, however, his untimely death would have solved a multitude of problems. How important she'd feel to be at the center of such a senseless death! How little choice she'd have but to forge a new life for herself without him!

It was the passion she missed the most—the acting out before an enraptured male gaze. In a weird way, she even missed Pablo Miles. Or Peter Mandelbaum. Or whatever the fuck his name was. It didn't really matter in the end. . . .

15. BO PIERCE

or *"The Boarding School Brando"*

LUST. SHE'D LIVED long enough to know a little about the games it plays with our hearts and with our heads—the way it stamps whimsy with a sense of the inevitable. And proleptically rationalizes the damage it has yet to do. And gloms on to a single name, a single face, a single tableau of our own absurd imaginations, whether it be the slow peel of white tights down taut thighs or the drawbridge-style falling forward of a fully clothed back over a messy desk. (To feel powerless before such pictures!) But then, lust is rarely an uninvited guest. Rather, it tends to limit its visits to those who make themselves open to its demented logic, its rose-tinted guile. It was in this vein that Phoebe first spotted Bo Pierce on the F train to Manhattan, his head bent down over a softback copy of *A Streetcar Named Desire,* the laces untied on his Stan Smith sneakers, the cuffs rolled on his unwashed blue jeans, the seam torn on the neck of his white T-shirt, a coral necklace riding the hump of his protruding Adam's apple, an aura of rage-tinged melancholy hovering in the foreground of his all-American good looks.

As if it had all been downhill since boarding school, since he'd learned to eat mushrooms, and play his Beatles records backward, and get his stomach pumped, and fuck his wispy blond girlfriend, who somehow got pregnant, even though she was anorexic, and had to have an abortion, and everyone cried and blamed each other and listened to Steely Dan's "Aja" alone in their Indian-bedspread-draped bedrooms, because Father was a tyrant and Mother was a wino and the sand in Nantucket was the same godforsaken color of beige every godforsaken summer. Not that Phoebe would have known. She'd never been to Nantucket. She hadn't attended boarding school, either. But she was feeling pretty disappointed herself—what with adult life turning out to be a series of unpaid bills and unwanted hairs.

And Bo Pierce appealed to her sense of endangered youth. She was twenty-four now, and he was the living embodiment of all her teenage fantasies of poetry-reading soccer captains who might have loved her at the age of sixteen, had she been someone else, not herself. And there was something about his eyes— gray-green eyes that invoked images of unmade beds in roadside motels. So it was that she sighed conspicuously before stretching her long legs into the aisle. At various moments he'd shift his not unsubstantial weight from one sneaker foot to the next. But he didn't look up; he wouldn't look up. He kept reading all the way across the East River. It had started to seem hopeless. But at West Fourth Street he let his book fall to his side as he stepped out of the way of a mob of schoolchildren boarding the train.

That's when he saw Phoebe and Phoebe saw him. And they stayed like that—burning cheek to burning cheek, heavy chest to heavy chest—for four whole stops. By Fourteenth Street, she'd already envisioned the two of them Sunday-brunching at Grange Hall. By Twenty-third, they were spread-eagle on a giant pink beach blanket somewhere off the coast of Portugal. By Thirty-fourth, Phoebe was trying to figure out who would bring whom to whose Thanksgiving. But at Forty-second, he turned his back, and she watched him go. She watched him disappear into the throng of commuters pushing toward their offices, toward their microwaved coffee and computer solitaire. And then the window turned to black, and she was hurtling through a tunnel toward Rockefeller Center. She had to assume she'd never see him again.

She looked anyway.

Every morning for a week, Phoebe rode the same car to work—the second car from the front—at the same hour of the morning. But he was never there. Just as it was never his faded khaki windbreaker she'd spot through a crowd and speed-walk to catch up to, only to find it belonged to a grizzled old merchant marine en route to Off Track Betting.

There's a time limit on all fantasies.

Boarding School Brando's eventually expired.

SO IT WAS that when they finally did meet—a little over a year later, in late April, at Grounds for Firing, a Brooklyn coffee bar catering to young mommies, frustrated novelists, and downwardly mobile college graduates pining for the days when reading William Burroughs was an acceptable lifestyle choice— she failed to recognize him. She was transporting a steaming grande cup of French roast to a fake-marble table in back. He was sitting at the next table over. "Excuse me," she found herself inquiring, "Do you think I could borrow your paper for a second?"

"Oh, sure," he said, extending a khaki-clad arm toward her own bare one.

She took the paper out of his hand and pretended to pore over the movie clock. A few minutes later she handed it back to him with a simple "Thanks."

"No problem." He smiled wistfully.

They went back to their respective reading materials.

But now he was the one who found an opening—Phoebe's wandering eyes—several minutes later. "Do you live around here?" he asked her.

"Just around the corner," she told him. "What about you?"

"I moved here a few months ago from Greenpoint."

"I have friends in Greenpoint . . ." she trailed off, hoping to conjure up images of dueling, drug-addled boyfriends—in short, a complicated past. "Why did you move here?"

"The place depressed me." He shrugged. "All those aluminum-sided houses. The only nuclear waste site in New York State."

"Are you an artist?"

"Out-of-work actor slash bartender. By the way, I'm Bo."

"Phoebe," she said, meeting his hand. It was warm and firm. "If it makes you feel any better, I'm an out-of-work electric-violinist slash receptionist."

"I feel better already."

They laughed. They sighed. It was that dumb, it was that easy.

It was something to daydream about between frantic phone calls from beleaguered Upper East Side matrons beset with vomiting Malteses.

———

IT WAS EXACTLY a week later that Phoebe found Bo exactly where she'd left him. She was hoping she'd find him there. Maybe he was hoping the same thing. Now he greeted her as if they were old pals. "Phoebe!" he said, procuring a vacant chair from an empty table to his left. "How have you been?"

"Decent," she said. "What about you?"

"I guess I'm okay."

"You guess or you are?"

"I don't want to burden you . . ."

"You're not burdening me. I love hearing about other peoples' problems. They make my own problems seem more manageable. And besides, as a bartender you probably have to listen to other people's crap all the time."

He smiled appreciatively. "That's actually part of the problem. I work at this little joint down on the corner of Kenmare and Bowery. It doesn't really have a name. Do you know the place?"

"I think I've been there," she said, squinting, as if through the mist of her own misspent youth.

"Anyway, it isn't properly ventilated, and I come home every night feeling like I've swallowed a fucking ashtray."

"Can't you complain to the manager or something?"

"What manager?"

"What about the owner?"

Bo let loose a phlegm-soaked growl. "The owner can eat me!"

"Maybe you could complain to the health department?"

"Yeah, I guess."

Every few minutes, her knee would brush against his knee. Neither of them would mention it. But he asked her, "Are you cold?" halfway through her own life story—the six-sentence version she'd perfected as much out of boredom as anything else. (She was sick of performing at a third-rate comedy club.)

"No, why?" she asked him back.

"You have goose bumps all over your arms," he answered. But it wasn't her arms he was looking at.

Phoebe followed his eyes south. "I guess I am cold," she said, giggling.

Then she looked up. And so did Bo. Then she saw something else, something neither of them was ready to mention. It was that old feeling, that familiar feeling—that all the furniture had risen off the floor.

And that the past only existed in the service of the present.

"Do you want to wear this?" he said, holding out his windbreaker.

"Thank you," she said, fitting her arms into the sleeves. "But I should really be going home."

"Why don't I walk you there?"

She didn't protest, and they left Grounds for Firing together.

They wound up on Phoebe's stoop. She stood on the second step. Bo leaned against the banister. "Maybe we could hang out sometime," he suggested.

"That would be fun," she agreed. "To tell you the truth, I don't have that many friends in the neighborhood."

"Do you live alone?"

"With my boyfriend. But he's away a lot. In fact, he's away on business right now—until next Monday." She said it as if she had nothing to hide. She scribbled her phone number on a piece of notebook paper with the same casual enthusiasm.

She wasn't all that surprised when, a few days later, Bo called to see if she wanted to hang out sometime.

They made plans to meet that Saturday at the Third Street entrance to Prospect Park.

————

THAT SATURDAY TURNED out to be one of those days so heavenly it feels vaguely immoral. (That mere mortals should be allowed to experience cloudless skies the color of periwinkle!) And as she and Bo made their way across the greensward, the smell of barbecue sauce in their noses, and the names of bands they once liked and no longer did on their tongues, Phoebe felt a certain buoyancy of spirit she associated with childhood—even as her own selectively remembered one offered up few examples of such.

It was Bo's suggestion that they go see the bonsai at the Botanical Gardens. Phoebe had never seen anything like them before. And staring into their glass cages, where their limbs seemed to grow inside themselves, she thought of her own limbs, twisted and tangled to meet the expectations of the various men she'd loved, or thought she'd loved, with the possible exception of Neil Schmertz. She'd never really twisted for him. She'd never really tangled for him, either. Come to think of it, she'd never really done much of anything for him.

Now she wondered what kept her from breaking through her own glass cage.

From the bonsai room, she and Bo made their way up a shaded path to a rise overlooking the rose garden. There were no roses blooming that day; it was too early in the season. But there were stems to contemplate—jagged, prickly things as ugly as their blossoms would be beautiful. Bo and Phoebe sat down on a vacant bench. It wasn't clear who fell silent first or why. But they'd been sitting there for almost five minutes without speaking when Phoebe whispered, "Hi."

"Hi," said Bo, pressing his palm against her palm. And then he started to push.

She fought him back but not hard enough. In a matter of seconds her fingers caved in beneath his. "Ow!" she yowled.

"What did they used to call that in school, again?" he asked her.

"No Mercy," she answered.

"No Mercy," he said. "That was it."

"Did you go to school in the city?"

"When I was really young I went to the Montessori school on Ninety-sixth Street. Then I went to Trinity. Then my sister and I got shipped off to boarding school in Massachusetts. My parents were getting divorced. I guess it was easier not having us around."

"Did they break the news to you over Chinese food?"

Bo laughed lightly. "You've seen too many movies!"

"They told you at home?"

"No, they told us at Trader Vic's. It's not around anymore. It was this Hawaiian-themed place in the basement of the Plaza. We were drinking these enormous blue drinks with umbrellas sticking out of them. They'd make them virgin for the kids. My mother waited until the check came. Then she was like, 'Your father and I have something to tell you.' My sister finished the sentence for her. She was like, 'Let me guess—Dad's moving out.' My mother was deeply pissed. I guess she was looking forward to telling us in her *own special way*. . . . So what about you—you gonna marry this mysterious boyfriend of yours, or what?"

"Marry him? Why?" Phoebe smiled to mask her shame. (She must have known that she already knew the answer.)

"Just wondering," said Bo. "I mean, you live together. And what is he—in his early thirties or something? And I mean, why wouldn't he want to marry you?"

She closed her eyes. "Things are really fucked up right now. We hardly see each other anymore. But even when we do, we go to sleep on opposite sides of the bed."

"Is he gay?"

"No."

"Then he's crazy." Now Phoebe was the one who smiled appreciatively. "But do you love him?" he asked her.

This time she didn't answer immediately. She was too busy

marveling at the passage of time, and how the faces change but the questions—it turns out—remain the same.

Except now she was the one with the flimsy answers. Now she understood how love wasn't this absolute thing—more like this shimmering ideal we bleary-eyed mortals grow old stumbling beneath the aspirational banner of. "I guess I love him," she started to say.

But it was no more true than it was false. She had to say it to realize it—that there was no such thing as leaving something for nothing, only something for something else.

"I shouldn't have asked you that," said Bo, backpedaling just as Phoebe had once done on the third floor of the colonial mansion that housed the Center for the Study of the Periphery. "It's none of my business."

But Phoebe told him, "Yes, it is. I mean, everything's everyone's business, or no one's business, depending on how you look at it. I mean, people used to say I asked too many questions. But I never understood that. I mean, what's wrong with being curious?" Then she turned to face him.

"You have beautiful eyes," he said. "Beautiful gray-blue eyes."

"Thank you," she said, smiling. She never grew tired of compliments. But it turned out she liked bestowing them, too. "And you have beautiful gray-green eyes," she told him.

And this time she didn't worry about sounding too aggressive. She felt comfortable around Bo Pierce in ways she didn't always in the company of the opposite sex. Maybe because, for once, he was the actor, and she was the audience.

Maybe because, this time, she'd put her faith in fate.

———

BUT SHE COULDN'T wait to find out what she already must have known was sure to happen. And so, the very next night, she paid Bo a surprise visit at the Bar With No Name. Sure enough, there was no indicating sign on the awning, just a sapphire-blue glow emanating from over the door. She pulled it open. The space itself was long and dark and narrow and not inelegant. Silk paintings of Border collies hung from exposed brick walls. Colored-glass ashtrays complemented Louis XVI–style tables with gilded cabriole legs. All the sofas were upholstered in red velvet. All the girls were upholstered in red vinyl. All the guys had Caesar haircuts and wore black leather car coats. Bo stood at the far end of a copper bar shaking martinis. Phoebe pulled up a stool. That's when he looked up and said, "Phoebe!" And his eyes sparkled like little Christmas lights at the sight of her.

And then he walked over to where she sat. "I'm surprising you," she announced before she kissed him hello on the cheek.

"I'm very surprised," he assured her. "Can I get you something to drink?"

"How about a glass of champagne?"

"Are you celebrating something?"

It hadn't occurred to her before that she was. "Sort of," she hedged.

He didn't ask her what.

She wasn't entirely sure herself.

She wasn't entirely sure until the following afternoon.

———

"ACCORDING TO BUDDHIST theology, this is the difference between heaven and hell," Bo Pierce was saying. "Heaven is this beautiful feast. And hell is the same beautiful feast, only with boards nailed down over our hands."

"Now you're talking about temptation," said Phoebe. "And about how we want the most what we can't have."

"Or shouldn't have, but sometimes have anyway."

Then he turned to look at her, to smile leadingly, to find out what she was thinking and if it was the same thing he was thinking—and what she wanted to do about it. She wanted to ignore it, but she wasn't strong enough. It was nature, it was nurture. It was ten past four in the afternoon, and it was raining lightly, and she and Bo were sitting side by side on his khaki windbreaker spread flat over a patch of grass in the middle of the great lawn. In the distance a black Labrador galloped toward an airborne stick, its master standing in repose nearby. Otherwise, the park was empty. All the responsible people were at work, Phoebe thought to herself as she slid her hand over Bo's.

That's when he turned to her and asked, "Should I kiss you now?"

"There's no script," she told him.

But she was wrong: they were writing it as they went along. Now he leaned toward her, ran a finger down the side of her cheek. "Do you *want* me to kiss you?" he tried again.

"Yes," she said. So he sunk his lips into hers. Then he pulled away. "Yes," she said it again. She said it over and over again until the rhythm traveled, and they came together like two meteors colliding in outer space.

"Someone's coming," she whispered five minutes into their rapture.

But he whispered back, "I don't care."

"I don't care, either," said Phoebe. And in that moment she didn't. She didn't care who she was offending or why. She didn't necessarily even care if she ever saw Bo Pierce again. For all she knew, he was a paranoid delusional whose desiring structure was dependent on triangular situations. She wasn't even convinced he was smart. But even at the tender age of twenty-five, she could see that venery is quickly lost to more noble but arguably less exhilarating pursuits like career and family. "Put your fingers inside me," she told him.

He did as directed. But it only made things worse. She couldn't breathe. She couldn't see straight. They rolled onto the mud. "Where do you live?" she asked him.

"I think your house is closer than mine," he croaked. "And my roommate—"

"Let's go to my house."

———————

THE WALK BACK to Phoebe's apartment was long and wet enough to have a sobering effect on both of them. By the time they got to her door, they were too embarrassed to look each other in the eye. "This is my house," she announced like a perfect idiot.

"I know," he said.

"Oh, yeah," she mumbled.

They climbed the stairs single-file. She led him straight into the bedroom she and Neil had painted a fashionable shade of lime-green. "Cute," said Bo, removing his socks, his shoes, his jeans, and his shirt. So he was naked, and even lovelier than she'd imagined, and shaking ever so slightly.

"Let's get under the covers," said Phoebe, surprised by the show of nerves on display before her. (Here she'd thought Boarding School Brandos' emotional arcs begun and ended with rage-tinged melancholy!)

They climbed under Neil's goose-down comforter and hugged.

Phoebe might have felt guilty.

Instead she felt happy for the first time in a long time—happy and warm and free and stupid and young.

Bo seemed to feel the same way. "Phoebe," he said, pulling her against his boyish chest.

"What?" she said, locking her leg around his own.

"You know the day we met?"

"Yes."

"I didn't tell you this before because I didn't want you to think I was some kind of stalker, but I recognized you the second you walked in."

"From where?!"

"It was about a year ago on the F train. I was on my way to acting class. I don't know where you were going, but you were wearing black tights, and you had your hair pulled back . . ."

Phoebe's memory scrolled backward and landed on a fuzzy frame of a mostly forgotten March morning. "Was that you?" she squealed in disbelief.

"That was me," said Bo.

"But your hair was short!"

"I grew it out."

"You're lying."

"I didn't think I'd ever see you again."

"I didn't think I'd ever see *you* again."

"And look where we are now," said Bo, pushing himself against the inside of her thigh.

"Speak for yourself," said Phoebe, pushing him away.

But she pulled him back in the throes of their laughter. She figured she had the rest of her life to clean up the mess. And she was tired of thinking so much, tired of thinking everything through. And were there really nobler pursuits? Increasingly, it seemed to Phoebe that the rewards on this misery- and humiliation-drenched earth were few and far between.

Later but not that much later in the afternoon, she got out her violin and played Bo Pierce a nude rendition of one of Stinky Mancuso's old anthems, "The Devil Went Down to Georgia." Somewhere along the way to hell—or was it heaven that awaited her? Who was she to say?—she'd learned the notes by heart.

Acknowledgments

Special thanks to: Dan Menaker and Jeanne Tift, for giving me a chance; Maria Massie, for never losing faith; my loving parents, Peter Rosenfeld and Lucy Davidson Rosenfeld; my inspiring sisters, Sophie and Marina Rosenfeld; and also Christen Kidd, Carri Brown, and Dennis Ambrose; and the many friends who saw me through this book, editorially, existentially, and otherwise—especially Ariel Kaminer, Meredith Kahn, Malcolm Gladwell, Larissa MacFarquhuar, John Cassidy, Virginia Heffernan, Nina Siegal, David Kirkpatrick, Elyse Cheney, Matthew Affron, and (above all) Greg Pond.